Blo

M. L. RAYNER

JIM ODY

M. L. Rayner

Jim Ody

Bloodline

Question Mark Horror

First published in 2023 by Question Mark Horror

Copyright © 2023 by Question Mark Horror / M. L. Rayner

Bloodline/ M. L. Rayner. Jim Ody – 1st edition
ISBN: 9798358740471

Cover Design by: Emmy Ellis @ Studioenp
Edited by: Sue Scott
Promo: Question Mark Horror

Foreword

When the ancestors conspire to bring together two authors of horror, each successful in his own right, who are mere mortals to refuse? M. L. Rayner and Jim Ody have merged their talents to create a tale of a family tree whose roots run deep and entangle mysteries in the town of Burntwood. Missing girls and a grandfather who just disappears one day are linked by branches and stories of a family in crisis. As various forces converge and merge to reveal the interdependency of the friends and strangers, it's difficult to deny the existence of help from the old ones, ones that have left this plane. After all, they are the ones that watch and warn those of us who are still in this realm of the living. With a bit of help from genealogy research, the clues in Burntwood, after years of being buried, will be uprooted and finally see the daylight.

The two authors have created a tale of secrets; of friends and family and a town struggling for answers.

Sue Scott

Every Root Holds A Secret

Prologue

The poorly trained dog yanked so hard at the leash that it almost pulled poor Layla over. She caught herself just in time before she fell. Her mum would be spitting feathers if she ruined her new school trousers again. This would be the third pair she'd got through in a month.

"Shakespeare! Calm down!" She commanded the excited Dobermann in as tough a voice as any twelve-year-old could muster. "Hold on and I'll let you off the stupid leash." The dog glanced back with hopeful eyes and whimpered, desperate to run wild and free in the open fields of the common.

Bending down, Layla grabbed his silver studded collar, playfully rubbing Shakespeare behind one ear which distracted the dog for the time it took to unclip him. Then like an athlete hearing the starter pistol, the black and tan pinscher turned and jolted, darting off into the long, swaying grass.

Layla loved that stupid dog. More than she thought she could ever love any animal. She'd had him for only a few months now, and the dopey mutt appeared to love her right back. They were an inseparable pair. As thick as thieves, you might say. And without a doubt, she had come to learn that he couldn't live without her either.

It was a pleasantly bright day on the common as the sun blossomed into a steady, comforting glow. In the distance, a few pregnant clouds peaked high over the golden hillside. Their colour, dark and gloomy as the grass around her hissed and waved like a stormy sea. Layla tilted her head like a question mark, sure on today of all days the clouds would glide on by without rain.

The walk back to the house was only a couple of roads and a dark, narrow alleyway behind her. A short stroll really. They never went too far on their walks. She owed her mum that much. *"No wandering off,"* she'd tell Layla whilst unhooking the dog lead from a coat hook kept hidden behind the pantry door. *"Stick to the trail."* And for a time, Layla would. But Shakespeare, on the other hand, loved the freedom of the open fields, and Layla didn't have to pick up his turds, instead admitting she never saw him do it. She smiled to herself and looked out to where she'd often see large, brown hares darting into a row of stubby bushes. Needless to say, it didn't take long before her faithful hound followed in pursuit. To his credit though, Shakespeare never really caught anything. Well, not to Layla's knowledge. He was good like that. For Shakespeare, it was never so much about blood and gore but more about the thrill of the chase.

"Well... Hello, there, love." A soft voice called from over her shoulder. Layla spun on her heels and gazed up at a tall, smartly dressed man gripping a fancy wooden stick in his hand. He didn't look that old, she thought curiously. At least, not old enough to warrant a walking aid.

"Oh, I'm sorry to startle you, my dear. But you haven't seen a beautiful golden retriever, have you?"

Layla smiled a nervous smile, noticing the empty lead that dangled from the poor man's wrist. She shook her head cluelessly. It would be sad if he'd lost his dog, she thought. She didn't know what she'd do if that should happen to her. She couldn't even sleep in her own bed anymore without Shakespeare huddled at her feet, ruffling up the covers and snoring through the night like a pig.

"Ah, pity that," replied the man as his eyes drifted down to his dark green wellingtons. They were caked in dry, flaky mud. "It's been a little over two days now," he said quietly. A look of devastation draped across his pale, slim face. "Poor old girl must be starving."

Layla cleared her throat to speak, only to be interrupted by Shakespeare barking like mad at the branches of a nearby oak tree. *Probably just another squirrel*, she thought.

"Shakespeare, shut your cakehole!" her little voice travelled sternly.

"Yours, is he?" laughed the man, his eyes scouting yonder for the mischievous dog.

"Uh-huh." Layla nodded, twisting the ball of her foot to the earth.

"Shakespeare, was it?" he asked inquisitively. "What an unusual name for a pooch. That is... If you don't mind me sayin'?"

She looked at him blankly, watching as the sun peeked out from behind a cloud and cast a fiery halo on his head.

"Don't speak much, do you, lass?" said the man, rubbing the ridge of his chalky stubbled chin.

"I'm not..." Layla hesitated, clapping one hand to her mouth. "I'm not supposed to talk to strangers,"

"Oh, is that right?" the man snorted. He seemed somewhat amused by it. "Who says?"

"My mum." Layla crossed her arms stubbornly. "She told me that stranger equals danger."

"I see." He nodded approvingly, bearing both hands to his stick. "Then your mother sounds like a very intelligent woman, young lady. Best to take note."

The man turned slowly without so much as another word. The end of his walking stick sunk into the dirt as he limped across the uneven ground. Layla stood by and watched. She couldn't help but feel a little sorry for him. After all, what if it were Shakespeare that had vanished? What if it was in fact she who needed help?

"We called him Shakespeare because at the dog shelter Dad said it was to be or not to be," Layla shouted after him.

The man looked back with a charming smirk. "I see." He winked. "How very clever of your father."

"What's your dog's name then?" asked Layla curiously.

"My dog?" The man cocked his brow.

"Yes... She's lost... Isn't she?" Layla pointed to the lead that swung loose at his side, skimming the blades of grass as it dangled.

"Oh, yes," the man replied, tripping over his words as he spoke. "Millie... Her name's Millie. However, the wife and I are quite taken to calling her Moop."

Layla smiled, tucking a loose strand of hair behind her ear. "That's a very pretty name."

"Well... she's a very pretty creature," he replied proudly. "The most beautiful beagle there is."

The girl's frown narrowed. "But... I thought you said she was a golden retriever?"

The man raised his hand, slapping it harshly to his forehead in embarrassment. "But of course, of course. How foolish of me," he said whilst beginning to chuckle at his own expense. "My other dog's asleep. Curled up on the front seat waiting for me, so she is." He gave her a sideways nod. "That's quite some memory you have there," he said, watching as Layla's cheeks glowed red from the compliment. "Very impressive indeed. Say, I have a photo in my pocket. Would you like to see?"

"Yes, please," grinned Layla, leaning herself forward for a closer look. It would be good to see what Millie actually looked like just in case she happened to spot her playing about the field with Shakespeare.

He patted his chest in a hurry, before searching one pocket to the next. "Oh, where is it," he grumbled, losing his balance and stumbling. Layla jumped to his aid, catching the man's elbow for support.

"Oh, thank you kindly, my dear." He smiled gratefully. "Quite the little helper, aren't we?" He had kind eyes. Fatherly and wise.

"You're very welcome," she replied, remembering just how important her manners were. Her mother had always said so. And if life had taught Layla anything, it was that her mother was always right.

"Ah, here it is," the man said pleasantly, pulling his hand from his inner pocket. Layla smiled; her eyes as large as saucers. Right up until the handkerchief smothered her nose and mouth and the man's hand pressed fiercely against her cheeks. She felt lightheaded. And soon the world around grew blurred before hazing into an empty darkness.

The sunlight had been chased from the sky by the time Shakespeare eventually found his way home. He had a rabbit hanging from his jaws but no girl following in his footsteps. Layla Jones didn't come home that night. Nor the next.

Nor the next.

For weeks on end, locals searched the common fields in panic. Cameras flashed at press conferences where the parents of poor Layla Jones could barely summon the words to speak. When Billie-Jo Hooper, a young girl from Rugeley Rd, became the next victim, the locals couldn't help but look upon their neighbours with a little more suspicion. Panic had struck the town of Burntwood.

Months later, the thumbtacks that had valiantly tried to secure the missing person's poster to the telephone pole gave up their hold. The posters floated away in the autumnal winds as leaves were whisked away in the breezes. The pictures of Layla spun to the ground and were relegated to the memories of Burntwood.

Bloodline

Some Years Later.

Andrew Hall, or Drew to his friends, cut a lonely figure trudging back from the far end of the school playing field. Football practice was finally over, and after a tough school day of mock exams and an oral French assessment, he was mentally and physically beaten. He wasn't even a big football fan. To be truthful, he bloody hated it. Nevertheless, the new headmaster was desperately keen to have a team representing the school this year, even if they were struggling to field a starting line-up which included talentless subs. It was simple. If you turned up then you got in. His nan had pushed him to join, and since she was his only family, he couldn't admit to her that he would rather shit in his hands and clap than run around a field chasing a ball of air.

Drew's nan had been his legal guardian since his parents had pissed off on a business venture five years earlier. The initial reconnaissance mission to Europe had been a success, and within a blink of an eye they'd packed up their stuff and gone. It was meant to be for a month or so. Only a handful of after-thought emails had found their way back to Drew, and these grew shorter in length and lighter in content by the month; each one warranting only a short reply. His nan pressed the point that they were hard at work and busy setting up a life for him. And in the end, their huge sacrifice would ultimately be his gain - once he'd finished his education, of course. On some level he was proud of their dedication and in some way a little excited at the prospect of joining them in the future. On the other hand, Drew just couldn't help but feel a pang of rejection. But the very fact his nan still backed them suggested theirs was a venture worth pursuing.

He continued the forever walk back towards the changing rooms; the rest of the team had long since disappeared. During the game, Drew had sliced the ball with the outside of his boot and watched birds scatter from a nearby tree as the sphere startled them from their rest. Such was the lack of school funds these days that he was sent on a quest to retrieve it like he was some knock off Indiana Jones or Lara Croft without the tits. A treasure hunter traipsing through stinging nettles and brambles to heft the object he'd sooner have left there. But his nan had raised him to be diligent and he was successful in his mission.

He glanced around. Nobody wanted to walk alone, not since those girls had been snatched a few years previously. It had truly shaken the community of Burntwood. Even now, with no new disappearances, the fear from parents was still prevalent and hung over all activities.

All three girls would've been the same age as Drew was now. That was the truly sad thing about it. They might've been his friends, and now they were merely a warning and an example of the dangers of strangers.

He held tightly to the ball and silently cursed his team-mates for buggering off. They were probably half-changed and goofing around the way teenage boys did. The teacher, Mr Rogers, would make himself scarce, of course, busying himself with unnecessary paperwork in his office before returning later to lock up and confirm there was no one still left under his supervision. The way things are in current society, no teacher wanted to be seen around the students' changing rooms. Not without the fear of paedo accusations, job losses, and lawsuits, and Mr Rogers had his own enemies as it was. He also had a way of looking at you with a penetrating stare that seemed to reach deep into your soul. He never had to utter a word. The silence was intimidating and quite intrusive. But the main reason the kids grew wary of Mr Rogers was that, for a brief period, he was what the police called a person-of-interest. Which as everyone with a television knows was an unofficial way of saying - suspect. Admittedly, much of the talk was built on the unreliable foundations of hearsay. Apparently, he was released when he produced an alibi: his mother. Probably the same way Norman Bates worked his magic in those movies a lifetime ago. Or the books before them.

That said it all. Some said a huge question mark has followed him ever since, and it was another reason why the football team was so poorly represented. The rumour mill worked overtime making accusations that nobody wanted to believe, but that was school life, and it added some much needed excitement to a lesson a lot of kids hated. PE was great for those that loved sport, but by Drew's age, most had given up physical exertion for fast-food, games consoles, and vaping out of sight.

On reaching the sports hall, Drew saw a couple of lads leaving. They were his mates - well, sort of. The kind of kids who barely got wet in the showers as they jumped in and out for fear of ridicule. They nodded their heads Drew's way but refused to hang around, instead glancing back to the sports hall.

He pushed open the door, suddenly feeling anxious, as waves of laughter came from within. With it came the waft of Lynx body spray, sweat, and testosterone.

"Mountain!" shouted Jon, a large lad with perfectly styled hair. He'd given Drew this nickname after some American fizzy drink. He was tall and filling out with muscle as his body embraced manhood. "Got your ball?" The hangers all around him giggled like schoolgirls as if he were the world's funniest fuckin' comedian. He wasn't. He was a grade-A dickhead.

"I kicked it over, so it was my fault," Drew replied matter-of-factly, walking to the bag that held the rest of the footballs and dropping it inside. He hated these arseholes. They were all strength, no brains, and being left alone with them was all Drew bloody needed. That said, most of the time they left him be, unsure of what to make of him. Some people actually thought him to be a little weird. There were a lot worse things to be in high school.

"You can't kick for shit, you know that?" a rat-faced little twerp called Stevie grinned. He was the type that gained power only from association, although Drew had seen him in a fight once or twice after school. And he could be a nasty little shit once he got going. He fought like a psychotic girl. All scratching and no punches. Not to mention the hair-pulling, biting, and peevish pinching. He acted as feral as he looked. He should come with a warning – or a tetanus jab at least.

"I sliced it, alright!" Drew shrugged. "It happens. Get over it." He tried not to make eye contact, wanting nothing more than to grab his stuff and leave.

"You slice it more than bread," Jon laughed, which to Drew didn't really make sense.

"Who gives a shit, honestly?" Drew shrugged. The other lad sitting across from him remained mute. His name was Rob Sherrin. Or to his mates, Jugs. He was as husky as he was ugly. A defender in his own right, built like a brick shit house with little skill to show for it. However, the guy was imposing enough. And the last thing you'd want out on the pitch was him breathing down your neck. He was the muscle that needed direction. But with much strength came little I.Q. And it came as no surprise that the lad was unable to think for himself. Instead, he did pretty much whatever Jon instructed him to do.

"Who cares," Stevie mimicked, which included childishly turning his fists against his eyes in a mock crying gesture. Drew rolled his eyes and walked towards his folded clothes. He wanted to punch him square in his pointed little face, but he'd probably get bitten and need rabies shots. Plus Rob would be activated to kill by the slightest nod.

"I saw that look," Jon said accusingly. The guy seemed to be itching for a scrap. "We thought Rogers was helping you find it in the bushes. He likes balls–"

"–*and* little girls!" Rat-faced chimed in.

"Yeah! You're lucky you've got a cock-"

"Sort of!" Stevie grinned.

"-you might've been on a poster tomorrow!"

"Whatever." Drew began to strip off awkwardly for a shower. He was trying his best to show he didn't care about them watching him.

"I heard that, too," remarked Stevie.

"Well, I said it loud," replied Drew. They were beginning to really test his nerves now.

"You want us to leave?" Jon said loudly and added with a menacing grin. "Like your parents did?"

"Oooh!" Rat-face Stevie goaded. "Nice one."

Drew ignored them. He took off his socks, then his shirt and shorts. He felt the walls closing in on him as he tried to swallow back the urge to explode into a whirlwind of fists.

"You ever wonder why everyone around you leaves you?" Jon continued playfully, slapping Rob on the arm and forcing his breasts to jiggle. Again, Drew did his best to ignore him.

"Your grandad left, too, didn't he?"

Suddenly, Drew felt his heartbeat thud in his chest. He knew they weren't finished there. Not by a long shot.

"And your girlfriend…" Jon continued in almost a sing-song fashion.

"She's...." Drew took a long deep breath. "She's not my bloody girlfriend!" replied Drew through gritted teeth.

"'Cause she's gone, right?" Stevie was now giggling like a schoolgirl with a crush and looking at the others for approval. Jon turned to Rob and nodded. Wearing only his underwear, Drew had his hand on his towel as the three lads, now fully dressed, stepped forward.

Drew swallowed. He wasn't small, but he was certainly no match for these three. As they jumped at him the door of the dressing room burst open and a broad, bearded figure stepped inside.

"Hey!" Mr Rogers shouted, but not before Drew saw his clothes flung into the cascading spray of the showers. "Knock it off! What are you lot playing at?"

"Nothing, sir!" Jon said, his bag now hanging off his shoulder.

"Just leaving now, sir," Stevie added.

"Everything alright, Drew?" Mr Rogers boomed but in a way that suggested he didn't really wish to know about it and in actual fact just wanted to lock up for the day and piss off down to the Nags Head pub. It was always two for one on a Thursday afternoon. No right-minded teacher would dare snub their nose at such a deal.

"Peachy," Drew said under his breath, and after retrieving his clothes from the shower floor, redressed back into his football kit.

"Come on, lads. Come on!" Mr Rogers shouted, not once asking why Drew's clothes were drenched right through nor why he was putting his dirty kit back on. "I want you all out in..." Rogers glanced at his stopwatch fixed around his neck. "60 seconds," he said. "If you're still here by the time I get back, it'll be three laps around the bottom field for all of you. You too, Jon." He pressed the button on the stopwatch, encouraging the group of boys to scarper. Stevie was slammed into the door when they exited. That sight alone was enough to cast a smirk on Drew's face.

"Thanks, sir," remarked Drew as he pulled the knot of his laces.

"Don't mention it, lad." Mr Rogers winked, and stepped closer, clearly invading his space. He placed a hand on his shoulder. "Now, Drew, if you want to build up a bit more muscle, why not let me help you reach your full potential."

Drew stepped past him feeling awkward. His teacher may well have had good intentions by offering to help a student who seemed an outcast. But on the other hand, the rumours, the look in his eyes, and the subtle touching... It was all too much.

"That's fine, sir. But really. I need to go."

"Yes, of course, son," said Rogers, allowing Drew the space to pass. "Your nan."

"Yes, sir. Bye, sir." Drew walked quickly away from the situation, exiting the sports hall as fast as his legs would allow. A small part of him wondered whether keeping his nan happy by going to football practise was even worth it anymore.

He never wanted to be alone with Mr Rogers again, and with each step Drew took, he thought back to little Layla, the first missing child. Blonde hair pulled back with a warm yet cheeky smile. Dressed in her school clothes, the picture, deemed to be her best by her parents, still remained tattooed on the mind of every man, woman, and child in Burntwood.

As he crossed the road, the nettle stings on his legs began to burn and itch. And once again, Drew's mind drifted, considering all the things that might've befallen that small, innocent girl.

The bedroom fan *hummed* loudly as it rotated in the corner. Uncomfortable and frustrated, Drew leaned back from his desk. A pile of papers lay scattered across the surface in front of him as the warm summer's air gently forced the pages to flutter in a wave-like motion. He was denying the digital revolution as long as he could, preferring the tactile feel of papers through his fingers over switching tabs on a computer screen.

The summer's day was hot. The hottest it had been in some years. Drew slouched forward to study his ink-scrawled notes, peeling his sweat-soaked shirt from the back of his chair as he smeared the glaze from his forehead. It was always the same this time of year. Heat enveloped the old house like an oven on full. There was never a way of escaping the seething temperature; by midday, even the thriving swarms of outdoor insects wouldn't dare flutter inside the house.

A bead of sweat dropped from Drew's temple, splashing on the jotted notes and causing his scruffy handwriting to blur. If the strange acts of Mr Rogers the day before hadn't been bad enough, he now had a homework deadline looming over him, and the conditions were only making things worse!

"Toss!" he cursed, smudging the letters further when he tried to wipe it away with his clammy palm. "Why is it so damn hot!"

Drew pushed away from the desk, the legs of the chair grinding back and projecting a hollow scream that winded its way through the upper floor of the house. For a moment, all he could do was rest, the heat overwhelming him as he studied the endless cracks on the ceiling. There was nothing good to be said about such an old house, especially one as drenched in history as this.

Regardless of everything, Drew knew he could fight the heat. He'd managed it year in and year out, and this year was no different than any other. He could take the sweating, the stickiness, and the hot sleepless nights. But the smell was something else. The smell he could barely tolerate.

Every year like clockwork the same odour lurked its way through the house like an unwelcome guest, the rising sun brewing the stench even more. It had been like this as long as Drew could remember. And the heat of the summer months made matters much worse.

Drew removed his shirt, wafting it in front of him, allowing the humid air to circulate around his body before he let the shirt drop to the floor. Finally, his skin could breathe a little.

This was the problem with his nan's old house. Theirs, like a handful of others, sat slightly back from the uniform line of the newer houses heading off down the street toward the main road. Of course, the sprinkling of houses, with the woods behind, was the original part of the street. New money had flowed into the estate years later and new cookie-cutter houses popped up around them. However, his nan's house had seen many better days, and now summers were too hot and winters too cold.

The rumpled pages of his research refused to help him out. His keen interest in genealogy was no easy task these days, and hitting a research wall presented itself far more often than he'd liked.

Drew sat back and stared out his bedroom window, wondering what his friends were up to. His mate, Paul, refused to come around anymore, claiming that the old place prompted headaches and nausea, but Drew thought that not to be a valid excuse. The truth of the matter was a few weeks back, Paul had snogged a girl called Sally Cawood. Not one of the popular girls but one of the outside-circle types. A hanger-on. Not hugely pretty either, but she was a dab hand with her make-up which made her seem mildly attractive, and her sturdy and chubby physique blessed her with rockin' tits. It had impressed them all nevertheless. He claimed to have slipped his hand under her bra and later on even sucked on her nipple. Drew wasn't the only one to doubt the last bit, but Paul hoped to exploit his stated conquest for the rest of the summer, making the rest of the boys feel like losers. Now, Paul was out chasing that same high, deluded that he was some super-stud or something. He honestly believed one of the other girls would be compelled to invite his sweaty little digits underneath her underwear, too. Drew was happy for him, but personally he couldn't be bothered with all that. He was infatuated with another girl, and when he looked out of his window he saw her house opposite, sitting back on an old plot surrounded by birch trees. Becca.

The pair had a close relationship, and as if by some strange telepathy and Drew's need for a break, she appeared with a rap on his bedroom door.

The door swung open before Drew had the chance to answer or make a grab for his shirt.

"Hiya!" greeted Becca Bradshaw, instantly grimacing and holding both hands to her nose. "God, it stinks in here!" She glanced at him sitting there topless and grinned. "I'm not interrupting you, am I?"

"No," he answered with an eye roll. "And, nice to see you, too!"

"Well, that should be obvious!"

"You know the smell is not me, right?" Drew quickly added in his defence, attempting to lift himself off the chair and cover his naked flesh. Despite having known Becca since they were small, he'd become embarrassed around her of late. He got it. He'd discovered girls, too. His eyes had been opened to this one in particular, and he was suddenly conscious of showing off any part of his body.

"It's not?" questioned Becca, her eyes wide open. "Who is it then? Phantoms with flatulence!"

"That, by the way, sounds like a great movie. But no, it's just the drains."

"Again with the drains," she muttered. "You're always harping on about that."

"Well, that's because it's true. It's the same every year, you must've noticed?"

"To be honest, I just assumed it to be you."

Becca walked gracefully across the room. In spectacular fashion she'd blossomed from a stumbling tom-boy into an elegant young woman. At first, she'd worn baggy tops to hide her new womanly curves, but now she appeared to embrace them. Her once dark blonde hair that she used to brush idly out of her eyes or absentmindedly forgot to comb was now carefully maintained. Professional hands regularly highlighted it and she seemed unable to leave her house without it looking photoshoot-perfect. He wondered when she'd suddenly started caring. And for who? It was his first adventure into a brand-new emotion called jealousy.

Until about a year ago, Becca attended the same school as Drew, but like many teenage girls, she had a wild side that authority found hard to tame. Her overprotective parents restricted her life with so many rules she naturally rebelled. At first, it was her tardiness, then her backchat, sneaky vaping, and eventually missing classes. Once her parents were called into the school, the proverbial writing was there on the walls for all to see. Within the same week, strings had been pulled, cash had been exchanged, and Becca was shipped off to an all-girls' boarding school in the next county. Drew lost his best friend, although when she came back at the end of each term, he was the one she always sought out first.

Within the last twelve-months, his best friend had changed remarkably. She'd found make-up and moved from being unfalteringly androgynist to become unquestionably feminine, and with that change Drew knew he harboured deep feelings for her.

She sat close, landing softly on Drew's bed and began to make herself comfortable. A whiff of sweet perfume fought through the sour stench of the house. She was a mysterious kind of girl to Drew, was Becca. The perfect attributes of a best friend were now packaged into a woman he'd admit only to himself he now desired. It pushed their friendship onto a new level, one neither was willing to admit was happening. He could be promoted up a league or two, and he would still consider the person staring back at him in the mirror to be average at best. He felt stuck in some kind of purgatory, and if he dared make a move then there would be no middle ground. He'd float up to heaven or be banished to the bowels of hell. By his nature, he wasn't a huge risk taker.

Becca smiled that familiar infectious smile. Her laugh alone warmed Drew to the point his stomach would spin and provided him with an overwhelming sense of giddiness. He just didn't know how to tell her.

Today she wore a white vest and thigh-hugging jeans, complimented by a cheap plastic necklace with a black heart that swung low. He tried to focus on that rather than her breasts. It was hard work. She was such a petite little thing that even a subtle change to her body was obvious, and further to that, another example of how the dynamics of their relationship was evolving.

Becca rolled over to her stomach and moved the strands of hair from her eyes. "So, what causes it?" she persisted, not letting the matter drop.

"Wah?" mumbled Drew, his mind had slightly wandered. He'd become distracted, not because of her but from something he'd just found in his bag when searching through his books.

It looked like a letter. A letter he'd never seen before.

Her voice snapped him back. "The drains, you plank. What causes the stench?"

"Shit smells, Becca."

"Oh, come on!"

"I dunno!" Drew shrugged, his back now facing towards her.

"Haven't you ever called anyone about it? No disrespect, Andrew, but it reeks in here." He was sixteen and living with his nan, he hardly thought it was his place to do such things.

Drew paused, pointing his nose to the air and sniffed. "Yeah, my nan has. Many times."

28

"And?"

"And… There isn't much to tell. The main sewage line clips the side of the house apparently. It really isn't that bad… Is it?" He already knew the answer.

Becca bit her tongue and sat up pretending to strangle her throat. "No, only if I try to breathe." She laughed aloud as Drew started to collect his papers.

"That's another thing," Becca continued. "You know your grandmother answered the door?"

"Well, it's her house."

"Let me finish, you tart! She opened the door draped in blankets again."

"Oh that… yeah, she does that," said Drew, this time with little interest as he compiled the clump of papers into an organised stack.

"But… But why?" asked Becca.

"She thinks there's a draft."

"In the house?"

"No, *outside.* Of course, in the house!"

"Drew, it's like one hundred degrees in the shade!"

"I know! But try telling her that. She's had me up and down ladders searching the house for months."

Drew stacked the documents as one, securing them tightly with the use of a single elastic band. He'd had enough of his homework for the day.

"Is she alright, Drew?"

"Nan? How'd you mean?"

"I mean… Alright upstairs?" replied Becca, giving several light taps to the crown of her head.

"Oh," said Drew, scratching the back of his neck. "Well, the wheel's still spinning, but I'm pretty sure the hamster's on its way out."

"Drew!" said Becca as a fit of giggles took hold.

"She still insists on going out to her monthly bridge club, or whatever the hell it is, so she can't be that bad."

"It's good for her to get out," Becca stated.

"I agree. In fact, I wish she'd go more often."

"So you could be alone?" She made a rude noise with her mouth before laughing.

There it was again. That same delightful laugh. If he had the chance, Drew could listen to it all day, even though she'd made him slightly embarrassed.

His attention fell to the blank envelope that he was holding in his hands. Flipping it over and over.

"What you got there?" said Becca, breaking Drew's curious stare.

He gulped and quickly replied, "Oh, I dunno. It's… I found it stuffed in here."

From down stairs the sound of his grandmother's music drifted to the floor above. "Oh, not again!" moaned Drew as the intro jumped into *Unforgettable* by *Nat King Cole.* Her father's favourite song. She always delighted in reminding him. Through the walls it had a slightly muffled and haunting sound to it.

"Open it up," Becca said grinning. "It might be from an admirer."

Drew slipped a finger underneath the flap and slid it along the side to open it up. "If that was the case then there'd be hearts and shit, plus…" he stuck it under his nose and inhaled deeply. "It would smell of… Oh, it actually does-"

"Perfume?" queried Becca.

Drew nodded and quickly looked inside. There was a single piece of wafer- thin paper. And as he removed it between finger and thumb, he saw the message was only a few lines long:

Your grandfather. The missing girls. You must uncover the truth.

Go to the library on Sankeys Corner. Seek these three books:

Hamlet

Twelfth Night

As You Like It

"Anything else?" encouraged Becca patiently.

Drew shrugged before turning over the paper and reading the single line out loud. His voice filled with confusion.

"It says… *Page 21 holds the answer…*"

Bloodline

Becca snatched the note from Drew's fingers. "You got this from your bag, you say?"

He nodded reassuringly. "Yep. I didn't even know it was in there." He sighed heavily, leaning his chair back on two legs and inquisitively shook his head. There was nothing else to do; he had to follow the instructions. He'd take any chance to find out what happened to his grandfather. Even if it were nothing more than a wild goose chase. If nothing came from it, at least there might be a chance he'd find out what had become of those poor girls.

"We're going, aren't we?" urged Becca. She had always been one who craved adventure. When sleeping outside in his tent as kids she'd been the one to suggest walking around the woods after midnight in nothing more than pyjamas. She was obsessed with mystery books for a time, too, and eagerly longed to be part of

33

one. The idea of smugglers, haunted houses, catching criminals excited her. "Hey, anyone home?"

"Uh?"

"I said, this might actually be fun!"

Hastily grabbing a fresh shirt, Drew stretched out the creases before rolling it over his head.

"Ready?" he asked, gazing at the captivating girl whose sparkling smile now shined only for him.

"Ready, willing, and able," she retorted.

"You seem incredibly happy for someone who might find out sad and macabre details."

She shrugged and replied, "Well, there's no air con here for starters. It's as hot as a hooker's doorknob on payday, that's why!"

"You took the words right out of my mouth," replied Drew as he packed the rest of the papers and zipped up his bag.

"Why are you bringing your homework, too?" She pointed at his backpack.

"Research."

"Research?" She looked even more curious. "Research for what?"

"My family tree, that's all. It's what my school project is on."

Becca's face dropped as she swung her long legs from the bed and sprung to her feet.

"Really? You're such a dork," she moaned. "Can't we forget about that? Let's solve this riddle instead."

"We will, it's just…"

Becca folded her arms, childishly. "Can't we just get the books, find whatever is inside, and then do something else?" she asked with a stubborn tone. "In fact, I can save you the time looking up your relatives. Let's see, you come from a long-line of circus performers known to frequent the sideshow attractions and have mental issues!"

"You're a bloody clown, if I ever saw one!"

Drew threw the bag around his shoulder, switched off the fan, and quickly headed to the door, listening to Becca's petite footsteps follow as he made his way to the staircase. He was happy to leave the stench of the house but also more than happy to be seen with her in public. He hoped to God that Paul would see him. Or maybe he didn't. The last thing he needed was Paul drooling and speaking to her tits.

"It's because of what they said, isn't it?" The humidity hit them head on when they stepped outside. She was serious now.

"What?" Drew pretended like he didn't have a clue what she meant. He'd told her about the incident in the changing rooms. The voice of Jon echoed in his head daily: *"Why does everyone leave you, Mountain?"* It got him thinking about his granddad. Everything he knew about him said that he was a strong, good, and caring family man, and yet one day he'd just walked out the door and never returned. He'd always found it to be so hard to understand. Especially after his parents left, too.

"You know, Jon and his little gang-"

"They're not a gang. A gaggle of dickheads at best. Jon barks out orders and the others fall in line like his bitches." He tried to make light of it.

"Well, whatever," she sighed. "Don't listen to them."

"I'm not. I don't." He lied, but they both knew the truth.

"Have you honestly no idea who sent you the letter?"

"Note."

"Letter. Don't be a smart alec. It was in an envelope, wasn't it?"

He puffed out his cheeks. "Note or letter, I have no idea. I mean, why choose me to tell about those missing girls? Why not go to the police?"

"Maybe they're scared? Maybe they know you're looking for…" she spun around and clicked her fingers. "They must be connected!"

Drew didn't hold the same enthusiasm for that hypothesis. They walked on, periodically glancing around almost expecting to see strangers in the shadows or suspicious folk sitting on benches with a broadsheet newspaper opened and eye-holes cut out. A cartoonish expectation that told him they were still kids at heart.

"My granddad was not a twelve-year-old girl. If he had been then my family would've been even more fucked up."

He felt her hand reach out to his shoulder. "You're not fucked up, Drew. Your family is unconventional, but you've turned out just great."

"You reckon so?"

"I know so."

As they walked on, they stuck to the shade. Drew's mind was spinning with so much emotion. It was more than teenage angst, he was sure; the pressures of school work; the social struggle with the popular kids; the strong attraction to his childhood best-friend; his research of his family tree that included the events surrounding the disappearance of his granddad; and now somebody was watching him and wanted him to find out exactly what had been going on with the town's most notorious crimes. If he stopped to think about it for even a moment then it would all be too much, the pressure of it all swirled around his head like birds threatening to peck him to death.

They walked in silence as they approached the library. He wanted to reach out and grab her hand. To just graze it at first and hope her hand would search for his. Accept it. But of course, he didn't.

"It must be someone you know," Becca said, as they turned into the recently pedestrianised street. A host of pigeons gathered in front of them, their small heads bobbing up and down at what appeared to be nothing in particular. They were so used to humans they were in danger of being trampled.

"I've been racking my brain. I don't know who it would be or even how they managed to get near me or my bag."

"What about that weird PE teacher?"

"Rogers?" He sighed. It was almost too obvious, but he wanted to forget about the man altogether.

"Yeah. He was interviewed by the police, wasn't he?"

"He had an alibi. He was at home."

"He lived with his mum! Seriously, how much more serial killer can you get than that?" Then she jumped on her toes and swung her arms. "He drives a Beetle, too!"

"So what?"

"It's a serial killer's car of choice! Well, Bundy had one. Everyone knows that."

Drew smirked. "You can't convict someone for living with their mother or driving an old car! No matter how poncey it is."

"Anyone else had the opportunity to slip a letter into your bag?"

Drew thought back to that day. PE was the only time his bag had been left out of his sight. His teacher was the last person to leave the changing rooms, but then any of his classmates had the opportunity to do it.

"Shit! You won't believe this," whispered Becca "Don't look now but guess who is sitting outside of The Nags Head pub?"

Drew huffed. "I can't look, can I? So how can I tell you?"

She leant in. "Rogers."

Drew's eyes widened. "You're shitting me!" He turned and flashed a glance.

"Don't look!" she hissed, elbowing Drew firmly by the arm. But it was too late. It was definitely his teacher alright, and now Rogers had turned and locked eyes with Drew.

"It can't be," he said, pretending to look away. He sneakily snuck a second glance, but this time all he saw was an empty space with a lonely coffee mug and in the distance the back of his teacher's head as he walked quickly away, soon to be swallowed up by the local crowd.

"He knows," Becca said quietly. "He can see the library clear as day from here, and when we appeared, he left."

"But-"

"Sometimes the obvious is the right answer. You know who said that?"

"You."

"No, dickhead. Sherlock Holmes." She clicked her fingers with a wink.

"Did he?"

She half shrugged. "I dunno, if I'm honest, but it sounds like something he'd say."

"Of course it does." Drew muttered, but his mind was drifting elsewhere. A mother would do anything for her son. Were all the rumours actually true about Rogers? There's no smoke without fire, his nan was often heard to say.

Could Mr Rogers really know what happened to those girls? His grandfather?

Could his teacher really be the sinister Child-Snatcher that drowned all of Burntwood in fear?

As the library's dominating structure loomed in front of them, neither of them truly knew the answer. But a nagging little voice at the back of Drew's head persuaded him that he couldn't dismiss him either.

The library's revolving doors spun with a disagreeable whine as Drew and Becca made their way through to the main hall. The building was ancient, dark, and unkept. The funding for upkeep on such a place just wasn't there anymore. The sound of their footsteps echoed off the murky glass ceiling and back down to the solid wooden floor making the entire room aware of their presence. Drew didn't know what it was, but there was something he quite liked about the old building; his love of history perhaps? He allowed his hand to touch the standing pillars as he passed. The aged-smell of the books' varnish permeated the air around him and added a touch of magic to everything he saw.

The library was usually quiet, especially around this time of year. Nobody wanted to read in such weather, and it pleased Drew to think he had the building all to himself.

Becca followed behind Drew, dutifully indulging him in his strange obsessive ways, as she so often did.

Behind the counter, the librarian sat on a tall metal stool. She was an elderly woman wearing thin framed glasses, her hair pulled fiercely back into a bun as she sorted books into piles for stamping.

The librarian raised her eyes and watched them closely as they slowly approached the desk.

"Yes?" she grumbled. "May I help you?" The old woman spoke in a snobby, impatient manner. She moved her wire-rimmed glasses down the ridge of her nose, squinting over the counter as her stamp hammered down to the page of a book. "If you've come for that Question Mark Horror series, you've wasted your time, I'm afraid. It's nothing but gory gibberish. And further to that, none of you youngsters have the respect and decency to return books in the same condition they were in when you borrowed them. So, if that's what you're after, be gone with you! You'll have to try again another day." She spoke with a flick of her wrist dismissively, lowering her head back to the task at hand.

Becca gave Drew a nudge, forcing him forward a step.

"I just wanna access the archive section," he said discreetly, making sure his voice was lowered to the acceptable level.

The old woman leaned farther forward. "Which archive section?" she asked, scowling all the while and making him feel it was some dodgy under-the-counter dirty secret.

"Burials... More so, local burials." His tone went up slightly at the end making it sound like a question. Or like some sort of bad Aussie impression.

"Hmmm." The librarian sat back tapping her nails on the cover of dusty hardback. "What Parish?" she demanded, squinting her eyes as though she were testing him. She seemed to quite enjoy it.

Drew scuffed his foot on the floor, producing an unexpectedly loud *screech*. "I'm not entirely sure. I thought..."

"Yes...?" she was certainly enjoying it now.

"I thought I could just have a mooch."

"A what?"

"A browse, that's all."

The old woman stared back at him with hard eyes. "Hmmm, very well. But no funny business. Trust is king, young man. Do not disappoint me." She pointed down the hall with a trembling hand. "Study Room Two is free, I believe. Here," she grumbled whilst straining to hand him a key card. Her fingers were riddled with arthritis and had obvious difficulty clutching the card.

"Thanks," said Drew, studying the hall signs on the wall. "Which way is it?"

"I ain't no tour guide, you know?"

"No, Ma'am, I know. That's why I'm asking for directions."

The old woman grunted, motioning her hand to direct him. "Down there, third right and second door on the left. If you find yourselves next to the water dispenser you've gone too far.... Or is it not far enough?" she asked herself.

"OK. Thanks for that..." Drew took the card. An unsure smile shadowed his face as he gave Becca a nod indicating she should follow. They both looked back as they walked. The librarian's head peered over her desk, watching until they walked out of sight.

"What the hell's her problem?" whispered Becca.

"Oh, she's always like that," Drew shrugged, followed by a momentary pause. "What the hell is Question Mark Horror, anyway?"

Becca returned the glance and rolled her eyes. "God knows! But it sounds like utter shite."

The hanging batten bulbs flickered sharply as the key card was swiped at the door, the lock coming free with a swift, violent *click.*

Both entered Study Room Two. From one end to the other were displayed rows and rows of tall metal shelves, all cluttered with a jumble of seemingly endless boxes that appeared to be covered with years of settled dust. There was also a single, lonely microfiche machine that appeared to be zapped straight from the 90s.

"Are we not going straight for the books?" Becca queried as she pointed out of the room in the direction of the general stacks.

"All in good time, my dear Watson. I need to check something first."

"And that's more important than solving the town's only mystery which would make us heroes, is it?" The humour had slipped.

"Since when have you ever wanted to be a hero, Becs?"

Her smile was forced and masked a pain she tried so hard to hide. "Yeah, true."

Drew breathed in the musty air and browsed the lower shelves. "Where to start?" he asked himself whilst rubbing his palms. "Fancy giving me a hand then?"

"No thanks," said Becca, slumping down on the first available seat. "Old Stuffy-Knickers said no funny business remember. I don't want her shouting at me whilst you shoot your man-stuff over old archives!"

"Huh?" Drew was mildly shocked.

Unfazed, Becca shrugged. "I'm just here for moral support, Drew. Besides –" The words were lost as she looked around.

"Besides what?"

"Well, those boxes are bloody filthy!"

"Fine! I'll do it myself," groaned Drew, shaking his head in disappointment as he studied the faded labels. This was the girl who'd happily jumped in muddy puddles with him and splashed dirty water so high it muddied their grinning faces. He guessed it was the trade off now because these days she always looked perfect. Sometimes he wished he could just take a picture of her.

"What are you grinning at?" asked Becca, watching as Drew's blank expression broke out into a smile.

He looked up at her. "Man-stuff! I've never heard you say that before."

She tried to keep a straight face but lost it to a giggle instead. "I'm older now, Drew. As are you," she said. "We're no longer kids. You'd be surprised at what else I can say!" He looked at her sitting idly under the dim light, indulging in his little fantasy. Everything about that was a good sign, and yet because he was a pubescent male and still overly shy, he broke eye contact to chase shadows along a paper-trail that seemed to go on forever.

One by one a box was pulled from its resting place, the dust smothering the room with a damp and musty scent that encouraged Becca to purposefully cough. It wasn't long before the boxes' contents were spread wide across the tired old carpet, and Drew became engrossed, almost forgetting the girl he'd dragged along.

"You know, this is exactly what they created the internet for?" said Becca, flicking the desk lamp on and off.

"I know," replied Drew. "But it's just not the same."

"What isn't?"

"Researching. There's just something far more personal and organic about it this way."

"Yeah, and it takes so much longer. Not to mention the filth!"

Drew looked back, giving a motion of his chin for Becca to join him. "You know, if you help me, I'll be done quicker," he said, throwing a playful wink.

Sitting up, Becca sighed loudly. "Fine!" she said, slouching down to her knees beside him. "Go on then, what are you looking for?"

Drew didn't respond. For a second, he was again far too enchanted by the girl who knelt beside him. The skin of her arm was almost touching his, and the smell of her perfume paraded into the air and disguised the stink of the uncleanliness. He loved being this close to her. Adored it. He wished it would last a lifetime. Hairs stood on the nape of his neck as he watched her out of the corner of his eye. He breathed in deeply, savouring the moment. He wanted to cross the line. To reach out and place a hand on her cheek, maybe guide his lips towards hers... but he knew he didn't have the guts. She still saw him as the goofball friend. The kind of friend who splashed in puddles and danced in a silly manner to the strains of *Cotton-Eyed Joe* in an attempt to make her laugh.

"Well?" questioned Becca, catching where Drew's sight lay. She smiled confidently. "Hey, my boobs don't have all the answers."

"I wasn't..." he began, but she only grinned more.

"You were, and it doesn't matter." She was enjoying watching him squirm. She put on an old lady accent and stated: "*Because funny stuff is strictly prohibited, whether it's consensual or not.*"

Drew couldn't help but feel a tad embarrassed. His eyes jumped back to the spread-out papers, silently changing the subject whilst also thinking about the word *consensual.*

"What exactly are we looking for?" She tried again.

Drew thought for a second, his tongue unwilling to cooperate. He tried again.

"My grandfather, Arthur Hall."

"What? What do you mean?"

"Exactly that."

"You don't know who your grandfather was?" asked Becca whilst gently touching his shoulder and giving it a comforting squeeze. "I remember him. Well, sort of."

"Of course, I do," he replied, unzipping the documents from his bag and persuading Becca to take them. "I remember him fine. I just don't know what happened to him, that's all. My parents had already left the country…" He shrugged. It seemed silly when he tried to verbalise his feelings, especially in front of Becca.

"You want answers," she said, sitting back. In hands that showcased perfect nails, she clutched some of the pages. Once her nails had been bitten like his, but now they were long and feminine and painted a bright colour. She browsed the endless list of family names scribbled in black biro ink, fanning from one page to the next.

Drew had been looking long and hard down a log of data indexed for the microfiche machine. A half-smile twitched at the corner of his mouth as he stood. "I think I might have something."

"Something?" Becca looked unconvinced.

"Yeah, just let me get this box of microfiche film and we'll take a gander."

She looked blankly at him like he'd just declared to her that he was off to milk a leprechaun.

He left the study room and walked across the floor towards the large bank of drawers that stored the boxes of microfiche film. He glanced down at the slightly discoloured labels, following them in numerical order to find the one he needed most. He was about to grab the next drawer down, too, when out of nowhere he caught the slightest movement in his peripheral vision.

He glanced up, snapping his head to the right. *Odd* he thought. He was certain he'd seen a figure darting out of sight. Small in stature and, although he couldn't be entirely sure, long blonde hair. Quick footsteps and a small childish giggle echoed through the silence of the library. They were quiet at first but then grew louder and louder by the step.

The lights flickered.

Drew scanned the area expecting to find an adult at the ready to scold the child. He leaned slightly over the cabinet to see the old librarian, but the woman was in a world of her own, a frown permanently etched on her face as she raised her stamp like a gavel.

In the corner of his eye, Drew witnessed movement from the highest shelf. A book. At first, he convinced himself it was shadows. A simple mind trick. Nothing more. But lo and behold, the book moved again. And again. His eyes opened wide, catching a small silhouette of a dainty figure reaching up high for the shelf.

A flash of blonde hair waved through the dimly lit aisle, seeming to dance with the flicker of light above.

The book continued to move, protruding out until it reached the shelf's edge. It wobbled, then fell to the wooden floorboards with a *thud*!

Again, Drew whipped his head back at the librarian, but she had no reaction at all. Not even a twitch. Instead, she continued to groan and grumble whilst stocking the shelves from her over spilling cart.

Then suddenly before Drew's eyes, the childlike figure began hovering, now shifting farther back, gliding between the gaps of the bookshelves. It was like she was playing some sort of childish game with him.

Drew couldn't help it. He jogged around the final bookcase, carefully peeking his head around the edge.

"No running, you!" the harsh and authoritarian voice of the old woman shouted.

"Sorry," Drew apologised with a raised hand. So much for stealth.

"And no shouting," she demanded while pointing to a sign which read *Quiet*. "Hush." Another crooked finger pressed firm against her thin parted lips.

Again, Drew complied and walked slowly back down the centre of the aisle. With each few steps a new row appeared at either side, stretching longer and longer. He turned his head swiftly, half expecting someone, or something, to be lurking nearby. He could feel it. As though it were watching his every move, preying on him through the spaces between the shelves and catalogued books. He scanned the cluttered shelves beyond, waiting for any disruption. But there was nothing.

The figure had vanished.

Bloodline

Drew knew what he'd seen. There was no denying it. There had definitely been a child, or something that looked like one. But as the seconds ticked by, he started to second guess himself. The more he played it over in his mind, the more bizarre it sounded. Downright ludicrous, in fact. He decided then and there that he'd keep it to himself. It was for the best. His chances with Becca would take a serious beating if she began to think him even the slightest bit crazy. A real nut job at best. It just wasn't worth jeopardising his chances.

"Hey," Becca screeched discreetly. "I thought you'd ditched me!"

"Huh? Oh, yeah... sorry. I couldn't find the box." He almost let slip the real reason, but couldn't bring himself to say the words out loud. I mean, what would she think of him, really?

"We should find those books, Drew." Her tone was now showing signs of frustration. "They'll be locking up soon. I didn't come here just to spend my afternoon in some dusty old room."

"We will... I just want to check these records first." He pointed to the machine in the corner. "It's from when my granddad went missing." With his thumb and forefinger, he carefully pulled out the flimsy plastic and slipped it underneath the piece of glass. He pressed the large orange button, illuminating the monitor before using the one working knob to focus the detail on the slide.

"But... This is ridiculous, Drew." Becca spoke with an air of annoyance, glancing at the dusty clock on the wall. It displayed the wrong time. "Can't you just ask your nan about all this? I mean, who would know better than her, right?"

"You'd think, wouldn't you," muttered Drew, lifting his head from the screen. "But it's hopeless," he groaned.

"But... But why?"

"*Because.*"

Black and white newspaper stories whizzed by as he quickly scrolled the titles.

"That's helpful..." Becca tutted.

Drew was hunched over in front of the screen, now fully engrossed. "She just won't talk about it, OK?" he snapped, casting his eyes over the blurry text; his attention panning over every detail he could.

"How come?" Becca persisted. She knew this was touchy ground, but it was fair to say they knew each other well enough to know how far to push.

Drew would break eventually.

"It just causes her too much heartache. I mean, would you wanna talk about losing someone you spent your whole life with? Somebody you loved?" He turned around to face her, and for the longest moment their eyes locked. And despite Becca's ever-growing confusion, she decided not to press. An awkward silence filled the room as Drew's attention diverted back to the screen, moving the knob more slowly now as the date he was searching for came into view.

"You never cared about this stuff before," Becca said suddenly, and Drew looked up like he'd been scolded. "I mean. I know you've sorta wondered, but it was only when those fuckin' idiots said what they said… *you know?*"

He did, and nodded. "I just got to thinking. Part of what they said was right. Everybody *has* left me. My grandfather, my parents…" he stopped the screen, his fingers hovering over the knobs now. "You."

Becca reached out towards him.

"I've not left you, Drew. I'm here, aren't I? I was sent to that bitchfest of a boarding school. I didn't want to go! And when the term ends, where do I spend it? With you, you daft twonk!"

She was right as always. Of course, she was. She didn't have to be here but still she always stood by him.

"I guess... Thank you," he muttered softly. "What I mean to say is… I appreciate you being here."

"Even without the funny business?"

That was enough to have them both laughing. "Shoosh!" hushed Becca, quickly lifting a finger to her lips. "We'll be kicked out!"

"That's as rock'n'roll as we get! You can tell your chums at your posh school that you were chucked out of the library, they'll shun you for being such a working-class numbskull!" Becca smiled but for a moment it slipped. There was something else behind it.

"Look," Drew said, pointing at the screen with excitement. Becca leaned in closer behind him. Her smell engulfed him as her breath tickled his cheek, and she looked at the illuminated page in front of them. It was a newspaper article.

Local Man Nominated for Prestigious International Photography Award

"Wow," Becca said, impressed. "I didn't know that!"

"Neither did I," replied Drew as he tapped his finger to the date. How did he not know? "I knew he had a photography business, but I never knew he entered contests. He must have been really talented. Why didn't my nan tell me?"

"Wait… isn't that?"

"The day before he went missing." They turned to each other. Their noses merely inches away from one another. Drew's pulse increased. He tried not to gulp.

Bang! Bang! There was a pounding on the door.

Drew and Becca parted quickly as the door creaked open. The distinctly unhappy face of the librarian appeared and accusingly asked the pair, "How much longer are you going to be?"

"Um, I'm just going to print this out and then I think I'm done."

"Good." She nodded sharply. "I'm no babysitter, you know!" She stepped back on her heels and without another word she was gone, letting the door swing closed behind her.

Drew and Becca couldn't help but smirk. Becca grinned into his shoulder, but of course the moment was gone.

Drew clicked the button to print and grabbed the newspaper article from the tray, stuffing it into his bag alongside his other notes before quickly preparing to leave.

The switch was flicked off on exit, sending the room into instant darkness, the door behind them slamming closed.

The halls (unsurprisingly) were as peaceful as earlier that day. They turned towards the hallway that would lead them back to the front desk, preparing themselves for whatever lecture the librarian had in store for them. Luck would have it, the desk was vacant.

"Right, then..." huffed Becca, brushing off the dust from her trousers. "Let's get what we actually came for, shall we?" She untied the bobble from the side of her head, allowing her hair to fall free. "Three books, right?"

"Right," replied Drew as he watched her wavy curls playfully bounce off her shoulders. It was like one of those slow-motion scenes from that beach show his nan watched sometimes. "Yeah," he agreed again. "Three books."

"So... which one first, numpty?"

Within seconds, Drew uncrumpled the note from his pocket before studying the genre of the nearest bookcase. "Hamlet. By Shakespeare," he whispered, trying his best to keep quiet.

Becca frowned. "Who?"

"Shakespeare... You know... William? *'Now is the winter of our discontent.'*"

Becca shrugged cluelessly.

"You can't be serious?" hushed Drew. "How have you not heard of William Shakespeare?"

"Space and planets just don't interest me, Drew."

"Space?"

"He's the guy out of all those Star Trek shows, right? I can't stand him."

Drew cocked his brow. "That's bloody William Shatner, you 'tard!"

"It is?"

"Yeah... It is." Drew sighed deeply, pinching the ridge of his nose. "What the hell do they teach you at that private school?"

"Not much." She bit her lip. "We just hang around in the shower together. Rubbing each other and stuff."

"Really?" Drew's eyes sprang open. "You're joking." It was Becca's turn to make fun.

"Yes, Drew, I am."

Behind them, a door creaked on its hinges announcing the arrival of the librarian who was pushing her cart into reception.

"Let's get moving," instructed Drew, grabbing Becca firmly by the hand as they wormed their way through the narrow passages of ceiling high bookcases that seemed to stretch forever.

"What about here, Drew?" asked Becca, pointing to a tall corner bookcase, each shelf colourfully labelled with the letters A to Z.

"Sure, if you're interested in taking up cross stitch or stamp collecting..."

"Are you trying to be funny again or something?" asked Becca, losing Drew's grip and slapping both hands to her waist. "If you are, it's not sexy."

"What? No," insisted Drew. "This is the Hobby and Lifestyle section." He reached out his hand once more, waiting for her to take it. She did. "We need to head to the back of the library."

"How the hell do you know where to look?" asked Becca. Her arm was being tugged as she followed closely at the rear. "All these books look the soddin' same to me!"

"Classics," Drew answered without glancing back. "They keep them cluttered away at the back.

Shakespeare, Wilde, Hugo. They're all there, huddled away, collecting dust."

"That's kinda sad, isn't it?"

"No one around here reads classics anymore, Bec," Drew exhaled with disappointment. He felt old doing so. "Especially not from a library. I borrowed *Great Expectations* by Dickens just last month." He paused. "You do know Charles Dickens, right?"

"I know who Charles Dickens is!" snapped Becca.

Drew gulped slowly and wondered whether or not she'd actually been taking the piss earlier about not knowing Shakespeare. "Well, as you know they stamp the title page of a book when anyone borrows them."

"So?" Becca quizzed.

"So... Turned out the last person who borrowed that book before me was in December 1978."

"Wow," said Becca, her head lurched back with surprise. "That's crazy! You mean it just sat on a shelf all that time, just... just..."

"Just waiting for someone to read it," Drew confirmed.

They turned a sharp corner, followed by another and then another. The passageway was so tight in places that the light from the hanging bulbs barely reached the floor. Tired books lay scattered in their path, some stacked up in piles. The overflowing bookshelves were cluttered, bowing from the strain of leather-bound editions and giving the impression they could collapse at any moment.

"Keep your eyes peeled," said Drew as he scanned a collection of well-worn novels which all stood slanted on their sides. "It should be around here somewhere... I think."

"You think?" spouted Becca. "There are literally thousands upon thousands of books here..." She glanced up to the highest shelf. "It'll take us hours to search through this lot! Days even."

"Have a look down there," Drew pointed. Another line of bookcases loomed ahead. Becca nodded and walked tentatively towards them as Drew walked on towards the next row. He stopped suddenly and listened. He wasn't entirely sure, but he swore he'd heard something. A voice. It was soft and trembling. And what started as nothing more than a muffled sound grew clearer and clearer by the second.

Shakespeare! Shakespeare!

"Did you hear that?" he whispered, watching Becca reach up to a shelf.

"Uh? Hear what?"

"That. Just then. The voice?"

"I can't hear anything. There is literally no sound in this damn-"

Shakespeare…

"Shh!" commanded Drew. "There it is again."

The voice grew closer. So close it felt like a whisper tunnelling down his ear. Drew spun on his heels. The hairs on his arms stood up on end, prickling with electricity.

"Drew?" called Becca from the other side. "You alright?" She glanced between the tarnished spines, oblivious to what Drew had heard or felt.

That's when he saw it. Shakespeare's *Hamlet*. A blue weathered hardback with worn down gilt. With greedy hands he snatched it. The coldness now escaped him in an instant.

"Ooh," Becca responded, grabbing it from his grasp with a grin. "Well done, Watson. Well done."

"You know that was Doyle, right?" remarked Drew, breathing out slowly through his nose.

"Sorry?"

"Doyle. He wrote Sherlock Holmes, not Shakespeare."

"Whether he did or he didn't, it's all elementary, my dear Andrew."

Drew shrugged off the statement and turned back to the section filled with adaptations of long forgotten plays. The various volumes were a mix of sizes, with some looking like antiques whilst others were new imprints fashioning piss poor versions of vintage covers.

"Got you," he muttered beneath his breath as he stood on his toes reaching for the sixth shelf. "Here's the second one. *Twelfth Night*." He handed it straight to Becca who secured it under her arm.

"And the last one?" she moaned.

Drew scanned over the final bookcase, second guessing if he'd somehow missed it. "It's not here."

"What do you mean it's not here?"

Drew shrugged. "Someone must have borrowed it."

"Selfish gits!" mumbled Becca, double checking the pile of books near her feet.

"Anything?"

She scuffled further on the floor "No, Drew. Nothing. Just a few books that have seen better days, that's all."

Again, Drew quickly unfolded the note. "Yup. It's right here in black and white. "*As You Like It*. By W. Shakespeare. Read it if you don't believe me."

"I didn't say I didn't believe you, *did I?*"

They both stood in silence, eyes scanning over the spines that now grew more familiar over time, but no matter how many times they read and re-read the same old titles, *As You Like It* was not amongst them.

"You know what we're going to have to do, don't you?" Becca said with a nudge. "Ask the old trout at the front."

Drew sighed heavily. And as much as the old gal set him on edge, he knew it was the only way. "Oh, come on then," he conceded whilst brushing the hair off his forehead. "Let's get this bloody over with before she locks up and we get stuck in here all night!"

They carefully retraced their steps through the winding, dark corridors and back to where the daylight was once again their friend.

Shakespeare... A voice spoke slowly and with a haunting whisper.

He turned to the bookcase near the edge of the lobby, noticing that the book which had fallen was still there, flat on the floor. Curiously, he couldn't help but find himself walking towards it. Drawn to it like a magnet. It was as though the book itself was calling him. Enticing him.

It couldn't be, could it?

"Drew?" asked Becca as she stopped. Confusion clouded her face. "What... What is it?"

He held up his hand, slowly stepping under the faint glow of a lamp. On the cover, a faded illustration of an injured deer stood marked in matted blood. Beneath it, in bold striking letters, read the words: *As You Like It*

"How did...?" Becca said, as Drew held it up high like a trophy.

Together they scurried away into a corner, placing the books on their laps. Drew's fingers pulled out the first note. And as he did, the hanging lights overhead began to flicker – just like they had done before. Becca inhaled deeply as she pressed herself closer, grabbing Drew's arm in alarm. Even the slivers of daylight from the far-off windows had suddenly faded to a heavy dusk.

Shakespeare...

"What the fuck was that?" Becca said as she pushed up tight against the bookshelves. Drew could feel her shaking.

"You heard it?"

"Of course I heard it," she snapped while trying to climb up to her feet. "What the hell was it?"

"I... I don't know," he stuttered. "Let's get the notes and get the hell out of here!"

As predicted each book held the notes on page twenty-one. Without so much as looking at them, Drew and Becca snatched them up, leaving the books where they fell. The library had become a spooky asylum and Drew detested the uneasy feeling that came with it.

"Hey!" shouted the librarian making her way around her desk. She placed her hands on her hips, blowing out her chest like she was going to shout even louder.

"We're leaving!" Drew yelled as he and Becca, hand-in-hand, ran past the grumpy old woman and out into the dazzling sunlight, leaving the dusk light of the library behind them.

Outside, clasping the notes in their hands and finally feeling a sense of safety, they stood and embraced. This wasn't about teenage attraction, nor sexual tension, this was pure relief to be out in the hot sun and surrounded by hundreds of people who had no idea of the horror they'd just experienced. They needed a moment. Or two.

Behind them the clunking sound of the library doors being locked from the inside could be heard.

Wasting no more time, Drew unscrewed the rumpled notes, sharing them with Becca as she eagerly read out loud.

Midday Saturday Church
Me Meet
Mary's St At

"What the fuck is that suppose mean?" Drew grumbled as both sat down on the curb.

"Where's Mary's Street? There's a St Mary's Church but it doesn't make sense?" Drew was mumbling nonsensically under his breath. He stopped and looked at Becca.

"The words... they're not in order," pointed out Drew.

"Uh?"

"They're backwards. Look." He moved the notes around before standing back, allowing Becca to read them.

"Meet Me At St Mary's Church Saturday Midday."

"But who?" Drew asked.

"That is the question, isn't it."

"You think it's Rogers?"

"If it is, we aren't hangin' about. There's something really dodgy about that bloke."

"Wait..." Becca looked puzzled. "How did they know we'd find the notes today? Or tomorrow?"

"Oh, you're right," Drew said, and that only caused him more anxiety.

They began to walk away from the library and away from the hustle of the High Street.

Eventually they came to a familiar line of houses, and Drew was overcome by a scenario of how they would likely part. He wanted more than a dismissive bunch of words, but how would he ever instigate anything more?

"Let's meet tomorrow after you've finished school, yeah?" asked Becca. "Meet me at Devil's Ditch?"

"OK. And maybe we could check out St Mary's before Saturday, too."

"Yeah, maybe," she uttered, which in actual fact meant they probably wouldn't.

Bloodline

The noise of the television escaped through the crack of the door as Drew removed his key from the stiffened lock. He stepped inside, listening to the canned sounds of yelling and gunfire. The living room was shrouded in darkness. The blackout curtains had seen to that, blocking any glare that might seep through the window and settle on the surface of the old glass screen. Drew stepped inside. The 22" screen projected bursts of light on all four walls, each burst casting shadows that appeared suddenly then vanished in the blink of an eye.

The sound of heavy breathing emanated from the room's corner, each breath transforming into a rattling snore. Drew's grandmother sat slumped; her waist sunken into the cushion of the armchair in which she now spent most of her days.

Another flash of light struck the room from the television set, followed by a distorted *boom*! blasting through the television speakers. Though it made no odds, of course. His grandmother remained undisturbed, almost sedated; her mouth fully agape as snores continued to escape her.

He made his way to the TV, switching it off with the flick of a button and sending the room into a thick darkness.

"Oi! I was watching that!"

Drew jolted as he turned to face the corner.

"You trying to give me a heart attack or something?" Drew panted heavily. He sensed his eyes bulging from their sockets.

The lamp next to his grandmother flickered, spilling a dim light into the room. She sat up in her chair and groaned from the stiffness caused by age and lack of movement. She could really relate to the old saying that getting old ain't for sissies!

"Now I'm not going to know who did it," she moaned, covering her mouth to hide a sneaky yawn.

"Who did what?"

"Who poisoned the landlord," she continued. "Somebody rudely turned off the television, didn't they? And just as it was getting to the juicy bit, too!"

Drew raised his eyebrows. It was hard to believe she had a clue what had been going on at all. "You wouldn't have found out anyway. Away with the fairies, weren't you?"

Drew's grandmother repositioned herself, firmly rubbing at her thighs that had lost all sense of feeling. "I most certainly was not," she grumbled.

"Yes, you were, Nan. Your eyes were closed and everything."

"I… I was just resting them."

Drew frowned.

"What?" she questioned, staring back at him, the bags under both eyes appearing dark and heavy as though she had not slept well in some time. "An old woman can't so much as rest her eyes now?"

"But… You were snoring, Nan."

She gave a short huff in return. "What can I say? I'm a heavy breather." She leaned forward, reaching out her hands. "Now then, help this old girl up. I can't feel my legs."

Drew aided his grandmother, hooking his hands carefully under each arm before beginning to gently lift. She found her feet soon enough, her ankles shaking beneath her frail body as she started to gain her balance.

"Want me to help you upstairs, Nan?" asked Drew, his grip never loosening until he was sure that she was safely standing.

"No, no," she replied with a quick wave of her wrist. "It's much too early. Guide me to the kitchen, if you would be so kind."

They sat at the kitchen table and listened as the sound of the kettle coming to a boil filled the room. Drew kept a mindful watch on his grandmother. She looked frail, much more than usual. And these days it seemed that even so much as a sneeze could knock her flat. Drew thought highly of the woman - that was without doubt - and regardless of her sometimes irritating habits, he could never forget all she had done for him, all she had sacrificed by taking him in and providing a stable home when his folks had given up on him and left. It couldn't have been easy for her. Not for a woman of her age. And throughout the years Drew accepted that. He'd even go as far as to say he respected her all the more for it.

The kettle *clicked* in sequence with the old woman's infectious yawn.

"Tired, Nan?"

"Always," she yawned while tensing her bony frame. "Good sleep just doesn't seem to come easy to me anymore." She yawned again, showing a number of missing teeth – she'd had a nice bridge of white dentures fitted, but at some point they'd been misplaced, and now her smile was a sorry reminder of her mortality.

"You going to be alright for your bridge game on Saturday night?" he asked her.

"Of course, I will," she scoffed. "It takes more than a bout of old-age to bring this old woman down!"

Drew was amused by her dogged determination as he drained the teabag from the cup then added a single dash of honey before stirring slowly. He placed the tea on the table in front of her, watching the stream rise from its surface. Then, knowing she'd not eaten, he made them both sandwiches. It wasn't much, but it was food, and he worried that she was beginning to forget the simple things like feeding herself.

His parents disappearing from his life had made him grow up quickly. The role of carer that used to be provided by his nan had been reversed over the past twelve months. He stepped up to being a man as she visibly deteriorated.

"Ah, lovely," she whispered as her arthritis riddled fingers awkwardly roped around the cup's handle. She blew gently before sipping. Then she set about a cheese sandwich in a way that made Drew wonder whether she'd missed lunch too. He sighed to himself and made a mental note to keep an eye on her dietary consumption.

"Nan?" asked Drew.

"Andrew?" She returned his inquisitive glare and took a healthy bite.

"Are you OK?"

Placing the sandwich down onto the plate, she nodded wearily. "Of course. I'm fine," she shuddered. "But this pesky draft will see the end of me."

Drew stood up, placing another blanket more securely around the old woman's shoulders. The night was setting in, but it was in no way cold, certainly not to him.

"There must be a way to stop it," she continued, making a play for her sandwich again.

"Stop what?"

"The draft!" she snapped disappointedly. "You were never one for paying attention, Andrew. Your father was very much the same. Always having to repeat myself. I said, the draft will see the death of me."

Drew reached across the table, grabbing her thin, stiffened hands. They were warm and clammy to the touch. Certainly not cold. "Stop it, Nan. Don't even joke about that. What would I do without you, hmm?"

She squeezed his hand gently in return and took another large bite of her sandwich. She really was making short work of it. "You're a sweet boy, Andrew. But don't you worry, dear. I'm not popping my clogs just yet."

A silence surrounded them as Drew thought about how to broach a subject he'd wanted to discuss for a while.

"Nan? Why did my parents leave? Was it really for a business?"

A hesitant smile played upon her lips, and with her sandwich now devoured, he lovingly wrapped the blanket tighter before she buried both hands beneath.

"Your dad was a busy man. His mind was permanently feeding him ideas that his body struggled to keep up with!" She glanced at her tea and chuckled into the steam. "He couldn't sit still and life never satisfied him. He was focused on his work – *not that it was a bad thing* – but he didn't have much time for a family. He spent days away… actually weeks sometimes, and I wonder, as I know your mother did, whether he began to enjoy being absent more than he did being home. When he returned, he seemed lost; his mind still away as if it hadn't come home with him. Your mother always sided with him the way a devoted wife should-" She paused as she began to cough. A deep, and rattly hack. Her face turned red as her fist balled up against her chest.

"It's nothing to do with you, Drew," she said when she'd regained her breath. "Your father was called away to work and your mother chose to go with him. It was an opportunity I guess they couldn't turn down."

"Without me?" Drew swallowed the lump that had grown in his throat. "Where'd they go?"

His nan waved a frail hand dismissively in the air. "Europe, mostly. France, Italy, Germany. Then Spain," she frowned. "But you know all this. They sent you emails-"

"The emails say a lot without saying anything at all, Nan. They're vague… And I haven't heard from them in months." He swallowed back another lump that had appeared from nowhere in his throat. He hadn't realised just how much his parents' absence hurt him until he spoke about it out loud. He knew what it was like to be busy, but to him family life was everything. It was what Becca had, and he wanted that, too.

His nan jumped in. "They're trying to build a better life for you. A business; something for you to take on."

"But what if I don't want that?" he said a little too forcefully and took a pause to calm himself before continuing. "What if all I want is to have my parents here with me? To ask for advice? To see on Christmas morning… to… to be around on birthdays. To be a family…" He looked away as his eyes filled up. A teenage boy hates to show weakness even to his nan. He was aware he sounded a little like a petulant child, but he was just being honest. And raw.

"Am I not enough?" the frail old lady offered. He turned to her and threw his arms around the bag of bones that she'd become.

"More than enough. But it's not fair to you, either." She hugged him back as tightly as her arms could manage. She took a deep breath as they pulled apart, holding onto the blankets for warmth.

He wanted to bring up how the local girls had gone missing and how their parents were left in pieces and almost unable to carry on with life, then in complete contrast his parents upped and left without a care. It just didn't seem fair. He couldn't understand their reasoning.

"You've grown into a man I know they'd be proud of."

This was the first time she'd spoken so candidly about his parents. Previously, they'd tip-toed around the subject, both guilty of forming excuses as to their absence. They were painted as good people who had no choice, but now Drew knew this was just his nan being the kind woman he knew her to be. Always looking for the best in people. Her Christian attitude towards others shining bright for all to see.

"Thank you for everything you've done for me. You've been both my nan and my parents. I know it's not always been easy."

It was his nan's turn to gulp back the emotion as a tear escaped and left a line down her heavily powered cheek.

"I'm sorry," she said in a small, croaky voice. "So sorry." They sat back at the table and listened to the ticking of the old cuckoo clock.

"One other thing," he ventured, feeling brave. "Was Granddad really that great at photography?"

His nan took a pause. Her eyes narrowed briefly, and then unconsciously she glanced towards the door in the corner of the kitchen.

The door that was always kept under lock and key. The entrance to the cellar that was once his granddad's darkroom.

"Your grandfather was incredibly talented in a number of things," she said, almost dodging the question. "Yes, he had the ability to catch on film the unspoken truths of the world. It was his world."

Drew had many questions but knew he had only a small window of opportunity to ask them. His nan was already closing up and shutting down this line of questioning.

"I heard he'd been nominated for a huge award but went missing before the winner was announced."

She cleared her throat, making zero effort to smile. She found it a painful subject to breach. "He walked away from me. From you, too. We don't know the reasons why. Remember this though, Andrew, a picture can be interpreted in many ways. All your grandfather did was point the camera and press the button; it's the viewer who interprets the magic." Drew thought it to be a strange response. She was dismissive and almost belittling of his talents, and Drew wondered, not for the first time, whether being caught up in work and neglecting the family was a trait held by him, too.

"Do you think he's still alive?"

She nodded and reached for her tea. "And living it up with some fancy woman no doubt."

"Really?"

"Andrew, I care not to think about that man any further."

She physically slumped back and closed down. Drew looked towards the locked door. Some years back, his nan had closed up the room and forbidden him to go down there. It was filled with his granddad's things, and his nan had mentioned on many occasions that she'd pile it all up in the garden one day, and after throwing a human-sized effigy on top, she'd light it up like Guy Fawkes.

Did the answer to everything lie in a single photograph? He wondered.

Bloodline

Drew was tired, and despite how much water he drank, the muggy summer's air always seemed to cause his mind to blur. He stood sluggishly, scraping the chair beneath the table.

"Stay for a moment longer," requested his grandmother. And with that, Drew found himself settling back onto his hard wooden seat.

"Who's the girl?" his grandmother continued. "You never mentioned her, though she seems to wander this house just as much as you these days."

Drew blushed. He didn't quite understand why. "It's Becca, Nan. You know Becca, she's lived in the house opposite since she was born."

The old woman paused for a second almost as if she were racking her brain for a memory. Then she smiled suspiciously in recognition, tapped her head, and nodded. "Ah, Rebecca! My, is it really?" Her frown deepened as she scratched the side of her noggin. "Why, I've known the girl since she was a babe in arms. Lovely lass, too. And growing into quite a young lady so it seems." She slurped the last of her tea. "You should invite her round more, Drew. She is always welcome here."

"I would..." replied Drew.

"But?"

Drew chose his words carefully. "But... it doesn't exactly smell like a rose garden in here."

His grandmother bit the top of her lip. "Oh. I see." She looked somewhat disappointed.

"When will you call someone out to sort it?"

A hand protruded from the blankets and tapped weakly on the table. "Funny you should mention it. Someone paid a visit today!"

"They did? Really?" replied Drew in surprise. "And? What did they force feed us this time?" He was always cynical and suspicious of anyone who had any opportunity to take advantage of his nan. Sure, she could be feisty at times and, should the moon's cycle be such, she was also a little cantankerous, but she was still a slight old lady that looked like her best days were long gone.

She looked back at him with a raised brow. "They didn't bring food, Andrew. No, they came to find a solution to the drain problem."

Drew placed his head into his palm. "So... what did they say exactly?" He was getting a little impatient. It was always the way when he became overly tired.

"Who? The man?" asked his grandmother.

"YES, the man!"

The elderly lady hunched her shoulders and pulled her lips tight as though she was about to attempt an impression. "He said 'Mornin', me love. Blistering weather, ain't it?' Stocky fella he was too, no hair. I couldn't quite pinpoint the accent."

Drew sat, elbows resting on the table, his fingertips pulling at the skin beneath his eyes as he listened to the woman waffle on. They were now back in the swing of normality, the awkward talk about his parents buried once again.

"No, Nan. What did they say about the drains? Have they sorted it?"

"Hold your horses! I'm getting to that part." She rested back, clearing the dryness of her throat. "He told me everything was fine."

"WHAT?" Both Drew's hands slapped the table, his mouth fully agape.

"The man said that the drain lines are shared by most of the homes on the street, and if there was so much as a dead rodent blocking it, he'd be able to find it."

"And he found nothing?" questioned Drew.

"Well, he did find some things down there but I wouldn't like to repeat what. Not after the cheese sandwiches."

Gross thought Drew, scrunching his face up at the thought.

"Yes, quite," she said, limping her way to the kitchen counter.

"So… what do we do now?" asked Drew.

The old woman made her way back to her seat, bearing down on the edge of the table to support herself. She sat down with a moan, a light sweat glistening on her forehead. "Here," she said, extending her arm and dropping a small card on the table.

Drew studied it. "What's this?"

"The company's business card. He told me, should the problem get any worse, to give them a tinkle. He thinks something was probably stuck but has now dislodged itself naturally. The guy seemed to think we should have fresh air in no time!"

"Well, at least that's something," replied Drew as he twirled the laminated card between his thumb and forefinger, although the truth of the matter was it wasn't any better yet.

The stupid cuckoo clock struck the hour with the sounds of pullies, clicks, and chimes as the conversation fell into a peaceful silence. Drew's head nodded wearily, the thought of sleep beginning to take hold of his body.

"So, what have you been up to? You and Becca?" his nan asked. There was something of a twinkle in her eyes now.

Drew's neck sprang back, unsure if he hadn't actually drifted off for just a brief moment.

"Uh?" he replied. He could think of nothing else to say.

His grandmother paused before sounding out an unimpressed *tut*. "You and Becca. Is there something I should know?"

"No," he replied, willing his eyes from closing. "We just... you know?"

"No, Andrew. Unfortunately, I don't."

"We just hang out, that's all," he replied, staring back at her gaunt expression.

"Why?" Drew asked as he finally understood what his nan was suggesting.

'I just like to know a little about what you get up to. With school and all, you're barely in the house these days. Sometimes I forget you live here at all."

Drew shook his head like a tired, old man and forced himself from the chair. When Becca was away at school, home was the only place he seemed to be. "It's late, Nan. Can't we talk about this some other time?"

His grandmother gave a look of sympathy in return. It was clear she wanted to talk. After all, except the bridge club, who else did she have to speak to recently? Drew forgot that it wasn't just him his parents abandoned, they had left her, too.

"Just a few more minutes? Please, Andrew. I miss our little chit chats. I may not be your number one anymore, but you are most certainly still mine."

Guilt swirled inside Drew as he stood by her and planted a kiss on her head. "I'm sorry, Nan. I do have school tomorrow." She had him, of course. The years she'd looked after him, clothed him, and put food on the table. Even buying him the bike he wanted when he knew she was struggling for cash. Despite his tiredness, he knew deep down he could spare this old woman a minute or two.

Her wrinkled face glowed back in return, expressing a look that only a parent would show for their child. "That's quite alright, love," she said, "I know you're busy." She softly grasped the hand that rested on her shoulder. "But I really would like to know."

This was not a discussion that Drew was prepared to get into. Not at this hour. He considered a lie, but only a little white lie. Yet it was not within him to do it. He knew first hand that once a lie began it never stopped. It would grow and grow until eventually there would be no way of stopping it, not until it all came crashing down and leaving him to face the consequences.

"I've been going to the library," he gulped.

"That's wonderful," the old woman said with a smile, giving his hand another frail squeeze. "I love to see you reading. It warms the soul. There's nothing quite like getting lost in a good book, is there? It can take your mind off all the problems in the world. Wouldn't you agree?"

For reasons unknown, Drew nodded. He didn't know why. But he suddenly felt his hands begin to sweat. He hesitated. "I've been visiting for research."

"Research?" the old woman's frown deepened. "Whatever for?"

Drew swallowed dry air, the lump in his throat seeming to have doubled in size. "To find out about Granddad," he mumbled. "And the rest of the family. I'm researching our family tree for my school project."

The grip of her hand became slack, and for the briefest of moments the air could be cut with a knife. The frown was transformed into a scowl as her eyes lifted to meet his.

"Why? We've spoken of such things." Her voice was stern with hints of anger.

"But we haven't, Nan," replied Drew. "We've never spoken about it. Not properly."

The old woman stood unaided and slammed her hand to the table, causing the empty cup to shake. "Because there is nothing to tell!" Her voice raised higher as she spat out the words. It was a disturbing tone that didn't sit well with Drew. Not one bit. Especially when it came from such a frail and vulnerable figure.

"People don't just vanish, Nan," countered Drew.

"How many times must I go through this?" She cupped her head into both hands, pushing the thin grey curls from her face. "He didn't vanish! He just simply walked away." A tremor in her tone began to take shape, intermittently breaking into spurts of emotional sobs. She then added, "As you know it runs in the family! I married into a bunch of nomads. Stones forever rolling!"

A wave of regret crashed down on Drew. He had never seen his grandmother act like this. Such loathing, such emotion. And regardless of what he thought, it was all because of him. *Why couldn't he just let it be.* If it was good enough for her, why wasn't it good enough for him?

"It happened when you were young. Well, barely ten or eleven, Andrew," she muttered as she wet her lips to speak.

Drew remained quiet, waiting for her to finally enlighten him with the truth he had waited so long to hear. The passing years had blurred his memories of that time, and he was told half-truths and fibs to appease her rather than him. He swallowed up the lies with his juvenile naivete.

"It was just a day like any other," she continued. "Your grandfather hadn't been himself. Not for a long time. Call it a trifle of depression, perhaps. I recall on that morning I decided to make his favourite breakfast. A simple gesture, just to cheer him up a little. I put out a full spread; he was always one for food, was your grandfather. Sometimes I wondered where on earth he managed to put it." She paused and collected her thoughts before moving on. "Anyway, on that morning he came downstairs much happier than usual. For the first time in months a smile lit up his face. He had a wonderful smile, so he did. A grin that could light up a room and turn every head in it. I remember asking, *'What's got a spring in your step?'* He pushed away his plate, telling me he had something important to share. I was intrigued, truly. But as I sat beside him, he stood without explanation. '*I'll be right back*,' he said. And walked through that door."

She sat for a moment staring at the kitchen door, reminiscing, while sitting on the very same chair as the day it happened. "He never came back," she muttered. "That was the last time I ever saw him."

"I'm so sorry, Nan," said Drew walking around to her side. It seemed such a sad tale. The person she loved dearly disappeared just like that, never to return.

"Do you know the cruellest thing about it all, Andrew?"

"What, Nan? What is it?"

"Why is it that out of all our happiest memories, all the times I shared with your grandfather, that one day, those few seconds, are now the most vivid memories I have left?"

Drew knelt beside her, offering a scrunched up tissue he had found in his pocket. "Forgive me," he whispered while leaning his head on her shoulder.

The sobs soon diminished, leading only to recurrent sighs. She patted Drew's head.

"Don't you worry, my love. I'm getting to be an emotional old biddy with age, your grandfather always said so. I just... I just miss him dearly, you know?"

Drew gave a loving squeeze. "I know, Nan. I know."

She wiped the dark patches under her eyes. Though smudged slightly, her thick makeup remained intact, and she looked at the clock as it chimed again. "It's late. Best get yourself some sleep."

Drew nodded, making his way to the door before glancing back at the lonely figure. "What about you?"

"I'll stay put. My room's as chilly as an ice box recently. I'd much rather stay down here."

Drew nodded again, presenting a humourless smile. Despite the day now being over and the moon at its highest, the humid air still filled the house. The thought occurred to him that he'd give his left arm to sleep in an ice box if he had the chance.

"One more thing, Drew."

He turned back, and a bead of sweat fell from his temple.

"Do the rounds for me. Make sure all the windows are closed, please," she insisted. "We don't want to catch our deaths."

Drew sighed, nodded, and whilst he walked away he wondered why his grandfather's disappearance affected him more than his parents' did.

Life constantly threw up questions that were hard to answer.

Bloodline

The sound of scratching interrupted the quietness of the night. Drew awoke with a fright as an uncontrollable shudder shook throughout his body. With the squint of a single eye, he gazed tiredly about the room, half questioning if what he'd heard was nothing more than a very lucid dream. He'd often get them, waking to sounds in the middle of the night that were never truly there.

He sat up, watchful of the darkness that climbed up all four walls, and leaned forward on his bed, grabbing the covers which at some point in the night had fallen to the floor. It was then he stopped and gazed at the sight in front of him. Drew slowly exhaled, hypnotized by the breath that escaped him as it visibly formed into a thick, frosty cloud. His mind playing tricks perhaps? But as Drew waved his hand, the vapour shifted, dancing about his fingers before fading to nothingness.

Clenching both arms, Drew rubbed them roughly, longing for the warmth that friction would surely create. It didn't help at all. The room was deathly cold. And no matter how hard he pinched himself to waken, the cold night air bit at his skin, persuading Drew that this was no dream.

His old spring mattresses creaked as he lifted himself up from the bed, the soles of his feet pressing hard onto the floor and he flinched. "Jesus!" he shrieked through tightly clenched teeth. The floor was crisp, freezing under his toes. So cold, he felt he was walking on ice. He rubbed the tired ache from his eyes and made his way over to the window.

The blackness of the night masked the outside world. Not so much as a street lamp lit the long, narrow street. It was as though the world had been swallowed up, dissolving any hint of moonlight and taking him with it. With the palm of one hand, Drew smeared the condensation settled on his window, brought on by his own steaming breath. There was nothing out there. Nothing but emptiness. And staring out onto the soulless street made him feel that much colder. His teeth began to chatter as he cloaked the duvet tightly over his head. But no matter how he tried, he could not shake away the insidious chill. He could feel it preying on him, climbing up his spine and stretching out over his limbs, causing his flesh to tingle.

Something felt wrong. It was then he sensed his throat contract. The sudden shortness of breath pressing on his lungs. Drew grabbed at his windpipe, as though the single action would somehow relieve the pressure. It didn't. And to his dismay, the invisible rope around his neck grew tighter and tighter as he struggled. A sick feeling swirled in the pit of his stomach as panic swarmed around his insides.

The faces of the missing girls flashed before him like fireworks. Silent screams, wide eyes, and grasping hands reaching out towards him from a darkened space.

And then as quickly as it had started, it stopped. Completely.

Everything was so quiet. Too quiet. The shifting and placement of Drew's feet forced the floorboards to cry out as if in pain, the sound amplified in the silence as sweat poured down his brow.

As Drew stood motionless in the dark, a greedy sense of fear grabbed at him from every angle. The haunting sensation that he was not alone soaked into his bones. Drew panned over to the darkest corners of the room, half expecting someone, or something, to be lurking there. He saw nothing, of course. Still, the sense of being watched continued to linger over him.

Over Drew's shoulder the door to his room remained fully open. On the other side of that door lurked a space as empty as the outside world. It was then that something commanded his attention and forced his heart to skip a beat. There was movement. Although it was very slight, it was movement nonetheless. Drew was frozen to the spot, the sound of his pulse shooting up into his ears as he strained to see through the doorway. There it was again! But what? It was impossible to determine, as darkness against more darkness merged together as one.

Fixed to where he stood, Drew dared not move. Only the length of his neck stretched out as his eyes remained wide and unblinking. He waited, and again his fear increased. There was no doubt something was out there. The movement was now so much clearer than before. Whatever it was seemed to draw nearer. And before he had time to think, Drew realized it was not a 'something' that stood beyond his door, but a 'someone'.

A shadow of a person.

"Na... Nan?" His tone softened, uncertain. "Nan, is that you?" He felt about eight-years-old again.

There was no answer, only movement: the rise and fall of shadowed shoulders as half *its* body peeked past the door frame in an almost playful manner. It was watching him. Watching and waiting. For what? Drew couldn't hazard a guess. He hadn't the nerve to ask as the covers wrapped around him came loose and fell to the floor about his feet.

Drew stepped backwards, clumsily tripping on the ruffled duvet and hitting the floor with a *thud*. The room swirled around him as he vainly attempted to recover. There was no stopping it. He felt shackled to the spot where he lay, a weight pushing down on top of him, accompanied by the sight of the looming shadow as *it* hazed in and out of existence. Drew's eyes rolled as his head again swiftly hit the floor.

His door slammed shut.

Everything went black.

Drew rolled to his side and groaned. Beams from the blazing sun shone down through the window and directly on where he lay. He groaned wearily as cold drool glazed his chin. At first, he couldn't remember how he got there. In fact, he couldn't remember anything. All that mattered was his aching back as he pulled himself off the floor. Sharp pains shot up his ribs, sending a jolt throughout his body. It was then he remembered. The covers around his ankles, the knock on his head. And as he looked around the room a sinister memory returned to him of the shadow that lurked at his door.

As disturbing as it was, Drew tried to push the thought aside. It was something he often did, attempting to convince himself that the whole ordeal was nothing more than the effects of an overactive imagination; a perfect example of how the human mind can create its own reality. He had been pushing himself hard lately. The endless school work, the in-depth study of his family tree, not to mention his growing, uncontrollable feelings towards Becca. There was certainly no doubt any one of these could create a mountain of stress. Maybe it was all too much for him?

Drew still felt strange. Like something was happening around him and he had no control over it. He sighed heavily, parting the hair off his forehead as he listened to the chime of the kitchen clock.

"Shit!" he cursed as the final *ding* struck nine. He pictured his teacher looking over at his empty chair, making snarky comments to the class.

Drew clambered about the room in a panic, gathering the scattered clothing he had worn and discarded only the day before. He sniffed them briefly, but threw them on regardless, followed by his unlaced shoes as he hurried to the stairs.

Downstairs in the living room, his grandmother slept soundly in the comfort of her chair. It was as though she hadn't moved from the previous night. This was happening more and more often these days, and Drew wondered whether one morning he'd come down to find her lifeless in the exact same position.

Drew crept past the living room, quickly grabbing an apple from the kitchen table and wedging it firmly between his teeth as he began to button up his shirt.

"Little late this morning, aren't we, Andrew?"

Drew spun around, attempting to speak with the apple still lodged in his mouth. He took a chunk, allowing the citrus taste to overwhelm his taste buds. "I... I overslept."

The old woman hobbled closer. Her walking stick buckled under her wrist. "Not slept well, my heart?"

Drew stopped chewing, his determination to dash off somewhat less urgent as he studied the apple's core. "Actually... No, I didn't."

His grandmother nodded in return, displaying a sympathetic smile. "Best get yourself to school, love. Don't want to be late now, do we?"

Drew nodded, securing his bag strap over his shoulder, and stepped out into the melting sun. He turned back.

"Nan?"

"Yes, love?"

"You didn't happen to be wandering around the house last night, did you?"

She glared back at him; her head tilted to the side as though she were in some way satisfied that he'd taken the time to ask.

"Me? No, dear. I settled back into my chair for the night as soon as you ventured upstairs." She half turned away before asking. "Why do you ask?"

"Oh, it's nothing," Drew shrugged.

"Then get yourself off to school!" she urged with a half arsed shake of her stick. "Learn something. And please, make sure to shut the door, will you? I'm freezing my bloomin' tail feathers off in here."

The door slammed behind him and Drew looked up at a bright blue sky, the morning heat enveloping him as he ran. Not a single cloud was in sight, and yet he felt something invisible looming over him.

Bloodline

The sound of the school bell drilled sharply into Drew's ears. Lifting his head from the fold of his arms, Drew sluggishly looked about the classroom, wiping the sleep from his eyes. The desks around him were deserted. His classmates, who only a moment ago sat impatiently waiting for the class to be over, were gone. Drew began to sit up, yawning aloud as his mind felt distant and foggy.

"A-hem."

Drew raised his chin. His maths teacher, Mr Drake, towered above him. An elderly man on the brink of retirement. Needless to say, the old man's patience with teaching and his students had reached its limit over the recent years, and he wasn't bashful to show it. He was a tallish man, his neck thin and long, balancing an almost perfectly round head that grew out tufts of iron-grey hair around his dry, flaky ears. Most days he barely had the motivation or the time to acknowledge his class. He simply sat on guard behind his cheap wooden desk, watching his students like a hawk. Mr Drake may have been called many things as a teacher during his time, but a kind man was certainly never one of them.

"I'm ecstatic to see that you find my lessons so invigorating, Andrew," groaned Drake as he flicked the pages of a textbook.

"I... I just," hesitated Drew, rubbing the glaze from his eyes.

"Yes, spit it out, boy," demanded the elderly disciplinarian. "You... just what?"

"I just..."

"If you have something to say then you better say it!"

Drew jumped at the outburst. In truth, he didn't know what to say.

"Let me save you the trouble," remarked Drake as the textbook slammed closed in his hands. "Come to my class late one more time, and you'll be doing detention for a week –"

"Yes, sir."

"I'm not finished!" barked Drake, dropping the textbook to the desk and missing Drew's fingers by an inch. He leaned himself down, extending his neck to Drew's level. "Come to my class late and decide it's the opportune time to doze off? Well... it'll be detention for a month. Do I make myself clear, boy?"

Drew forced back a gulp. His throat all of sudden felt exceedingly dry, and his palms were sweating like crazy.

"Well...?" continued Drake. "Do. I. Make. Myself. Clear?"

"Crystal, sir," said Drew with a fearful nod.

Mr Drake stretched himself back to full height. The ceiling light illuminated the top of his smooth bald head.

"You're a waste of space," he muttered, watching Drew with great displeasure. "Now, don't just sit there. Get out of my sight."

"Yes, sir!" Drew answered sharply as he shot up from his seat like a rocket. He hurried to the door, knocking against tables and chairs as he stumbled out of the room.

Outside stood a gaggle of kids laughing and joking by the school gate.

"Hey, here he is!" A lad with a mop of scraggly blond hair grinned, walking towards Drew and dragging his bag behind him like a silent statement of rebellion.

"What is it, Max?" Drew said, nodding the way lads do.

"Old man Drake was ripping you a new one, wasn't he? You can hear the old git's voice travel from here! What d'you do? Ask him his age?"

"Fell asleep in class."

Max threw up his hand for a high-five. "Legend!" Drew cringingly obliged. It was hardly an accolade derived from a daring act of anarchy. It was an unconscious and uncontrollable protest from his body. "Serves him bloody right, I say. If he put half as much effort into actually teaching as he does shouting his mouth off, he'd pass as an alright teacher."

Another lad came over with a fierce haircut, some false swagger, with his tie half undone.

"Paul, this absolute legend just fell asleep in Old Man Drake's class! Drake was spittin' feathers!" He flicked his fingers together as a sign of appreciation.

"Mate, you're brave! Drake's gonna have it in for you now until the end of the year!"

"I mean, I fell asleep," Drew shrugged, not getting why they were so excited about it. He never meant to.

"What you up to now?" Paul asked, pulling out his older brother's disposable vape. The battery had long since died, but that didn't stop him. To Paul, it made him look sexy. Not only that, the sixth-form girls loved it and was one of the reasons he ended up getting his fingers inside Katie Brayford's bra, or so he said!

Drew looked at them both. There was no way they were tagging along. If he was struggling to speak to Becca whilst the two of them were alone then these two reprobates were only going to make things a million times worse.

"I have to help my nan with something."

The two lads shared a glance, but it was Max who spoke up. "Mate, your house is right weird, you know? Don't take this the wrong way or anything. But last week when I was there my head was pounding. Literally, the minute I was out of there it stopped. What the hell is that all about?"

Paul was in agreement. "Yeah, to be fair, I was feeling really sick, and my throat..." he stopped the flow and quickly finished with, "I just felt rough, and like Max said, as soon as I hit fresh air, it went."

"Fresh air," Max grinned. "Your house honks, mate!"

"It's the drains. We've got someone coming out to look at it," Drew said defensively.

"Good thing!"

"Anyway, I gotta go," Drew said. He was a little hurt even though he knew it was true, but the last thing he needed was for it to get around that his house reeked.

"Yeah, me, too," Paul said. "The sixth-form girls will be out any minute." They fist-bumped. "There's this one girl that's totally pining for it. Keeps giving me the eye." He glanced at Max, winked, and made a move with his hands like he was grabbing a pair of heaving tits. Max was grinning, and all of them knew despite the bravado, not a single one of them would be caressing any breasts today.

Or tomorrow.

Drew set off at a quicker pace than normal. It seemed everywhere he went was at super-fast speed nowadays.

"Drew!" a voice called as he got to the gates. His stomach sank. He wanted the world to swallow him up, or at least hide him for a while.

Mr Rogers.

"Have you thought anymore about what I said?" Rogers walked towards him, his left hand fiddling with the whistle around his neck, a polite and innocent look on his face.

"Sir?"

"Bulking you up, son. Some after school training?"

Drew glanced around. Part of him wanted his mates to witness this conversation, and another part of him was embarrassed by it. Was he sending out some sort of pedo signal or something?

"I can't," said Drew, still looking for someone else. Anyone. "I have to look after my nan."

"I see. You up to much at the weekend?" said Rogers, trying to be all buddy-buddy, which was even worse.

"My girlfriend," Drew spat out. "I'll be with her."

"A girlfriend? Well, well. That is… nice." He looked somewhat disappointed.

"I really have to go, sir" lied Drew, glancing at his wrist.

"Enjoy your… er, girlfriend," Rogers yelled. Somehow Drew knew he could tell he was lying.

His footfalls smacked heavily along the footpath, accompanied by the sound of Drew's breathless gasps. It was far too hot to be running like this. And although Drew's waning energy and pain-filled legs tried to persuade him to stop, the idea of keeping his date with Becca was much too hard to resist.

Becca was a free-spirit, and part of the allure that surrounded her was the way she did what she wanted, and breaking rules was something she excelled at. She wasn't a criminal, nor particularly anti-social, she just hated to be restrained by authority. She, like Drew, had regrets that her actions at his school had meant she was quickly shipped out, and their time together was so much shorter than it could've been. But to change that about her would be to change too much.

They went weeks without seeing each other, but conversely when Becca was home, they always hung out. It had been within the last couple of terms that she had left as his best friend and returned as a potential girlfriend.

Sweat poured from his head, sparkling his face as he ran. He turned onto a long and narrow path that fed back onto the rear of terrace houses. It was a tight squeeze but without doubt the fastest route out of the estate. The alley soon ended, opening up into a country trail, the grass so high it grabbed at his shoes and ankles as he ran. It wasn't too far now; through a small patch of woodland that would shelter him from the blazing sun and then out into the open fields. Drew paused, catching his breath as he leaned against a fallen tree. Across from him, the vibrant green field inclined, stretching up into a steep and tricky hillside. At the very top, he could see Becca sitting crossed legged on the ground, waiting. An angel glowing in the sunlight. Drew moaned, pushing himself from his resting spot to jog across the open field. The uphill trek was tortuous, and the burning in his legs grew more intense with every step.

There was certainly nothing sinister about Devil's Ditch, except its name, of course. At the top of the hill a wall of birch trees covered its centre. Hidden away behind them was a steep canyon-like ditch, dug out from the middle of the hilltop. Nothing interesting ever happened there. It was a place for one thing and one thing only: for teens to get wasted. That and the rumoured doggers that attended every fortnight – not that Drew knew very much about that sort of thing.

Drew looked up from his stride, the shape of Becca getting closer and closer by the second.

"Hey!" shouted Drew, waving his hand ecstatically, though he barely had the energy to speak.

Becca remained seated, waving her fingers as though she were playing an invisible piano. She smiled pleasantly; the grass was so high it covered the tops of her knees. From afar she almost appeared to be sinking. "Where have you been? I was beginning to think you wouldn't show," she asked impatiently. "I thought I'd been stood up!"

Drew's pace fell flat as he reached the hill's peak, his shadow casting down over Becca. He let himself go, allowing his knees to buckle and his stomach to fall flat on the ground. He rolled over, his eyes firmly shut. The grass around his face tickled his skin, and the sun blazed down like a heat lamp, baking the ground where he lay. Drew gasped heavily.

"What the hell is the matter with you?" questioned Becca. "Are you going into cardiac arrest or something?" she smirked. "Am I going to have to pound *Staying Alive* on your chest until you recover?"

"Funny," he managed, still trying to regain his breath. "You threaten to sing *any* Bee Gees and I'm going home right now!" They laughed together.

Becca shuffled over to Drew, her head blocking out the giant ball of sunlight.

"Thanks," said Drew. He smiled, placed his hand on hers, then squeezed.

"Jesus, you're sweating like a pig!" moaned Becca, throwing his hand away.

"No, I'm not."

"You totally are!"

"I don't sweat..." he hesitated. "That's just my fat crying."

"Whatever! You look like a complete wreck."

"I know. Sexy right?"

"No!"

A mild breeze swept over them, though it was short lived. Becca pulled a cigarette from behind her ear and popped it between her lips.

Drew sat up. "I thought you packed that shit in? '*No more smoking*,' that's what you said. *On your family's life!*"

Becca grunted, her lips imitating Drew's, making her cigarette start bobbing. "Yeah, yeah, yeah. I know, I know. Don't you fuckin' start," she mumbled, but slipped the cigarette from her mouth and placed it behind her ear again.

For a time, Drew forgot why they were here, instead simply enjoying being outside with one of the most important people in the world to him. He was content just lying here with Becca. More content than he had ever felt with anyone. He couldn't explain why exactly, she just made him feel, well… happy. And as he watched her blue eyes shimmer in the evening sun, the thought finally dawned on him.

"So…" he began as more of a hint to say something. "What d'you make of it all?"

"What? Life?" She gave a cheesy grin, but then replied. "I don't know, Drew. I guess neither of us will know until tomorrow. What do you think?"

Drew pushed himself up onto his elbows. He squinted slightly at the sun and noticed the kink in Becca's blonde, flowing hair. So much was now spinning around Drew's head. His mind was a huge jumble of questions and possibilities. How could his granddad's disappearance be connected to those girls?

And then a thought popped into his mind and his stomach reacted instantly.

"You don't think my granddad had anything to do with those girls going missing, do you?"

Becca was already shaking her head vigorously. "No, no. Do you?"

"No… I can't see it. He was a gentleman. He was…" Words now escaped him, stolen from his mouth by circumstance and a diet of true crime documentaries. "My grandfather."

Becca said nothing, absentmindedly stroking the grass by his side. She looked at him. *Really* looked at him. "You're a good person, Drew," she said.

"I fell asleep in class today." He didn't know why he'd suddenly said it. Was he trying to impress her? Perhaps make her laugh? Thankfully she did the latter.

"Careful! You little rebel, you. You'll be shipped off to an all-girls' school, too!"

Drew grinned at the thought. "That sounds amazing! I could do with a shower!"

97

Becca rolled her eyes and playfully punched his arm. "Not really. In fact, it sucks."

Drew wasn't sure but it felt like they were sharing a moment. He wondered whether he should try and push things further, but as usual he was over-thinking things and it was Becca in fact who spoke first.

"It's important to you to know the truth, isn't it?" she asked.

"I reckon it's because my parents left,"he admitted. "Nan says they were working hard and at some point forgot about us." He put it bluntly.

"She said that?" Becca looked surprised.

"Well, not exactly that, but pretty much..." he sighed and looked off over the town. The place appeared peaceful from up there, a mass of trees that eventually broke out into houses and an industrialised town. It was like a model of a village.

"I used to be jealous of your family," he continued, smiling back at her. "You are all there for each other. You-" A tear was making a lonely descent down her cheek.

"You're crying. What's wrong?" he asked worriedly. He never wanted to upset her.

She wiped the tear away and threw her arms around him. He felt her slender body pressing against his, and her familiar smell engulfed him. He drank her in.

"It's nothing," she sniffed. "I'm just being... *a girl.*"

"That's one of the things I love about you," he said, realising too late that the 'L' word had slipped out from his mouth.

"What's another? That I have boobs now?" She went for humour, too, still clutching him tightly. "I just get sad sometimes," she admitted. "And you're searching for your grandfather, and your parents aren't around... Look, Drew, whatever happens in this world you're a good person, you know that, right?" She placed a cool hand on his warm chest.

"I guess I just feel lost," he said. "I feel like I don't know who I am. And now the pressure of someone asking me to find out about the missing girls. It's such a... you know?"

"Huge responsibility?"

"Yes! Exactly!"

"Then make your own mark in this world. Embrace your own identity. You're sixteen, Drew. Everything that you will ever achieve is way ahead of you. Don't let what has happened to your family define you... You're much too good for that." Her hand grazed up to his cheek. "Be careful when you search. You might not always like what you find."

"I'm prepared," he said.

"I hope you are," she replied, once again looking forlorn.

They locked eyes and Drew was sure they were about to kiss. It was just like when they'd been in the library the day before. He'd seen it in the movies. That magnetism forcing them closer together. But at the last minute, Becca moved, and her soft lips pecked him on the cheek instead.

"Come on!" she said, and held out her arms for his. "Be free!"

Becca was such a free-spirit. He shook away the negativity before it had a chance to manifest itself and joined her. They swung their arms and shouted out into the sky, scaring birds out of the trees and sending wildlife scurrying into bushes and undergrowth. But Becca was right. This was what being young was all about. He just couldn't understand why it didn't seem to be enough.

After a while they stopped. Large grins painted on their fresh faces. A jolt of serotonin blasting around their bodies. A recharge of positivity.

"Just live your life, Drew. Be something, yeah?"

"Agreed."

"Come on," she giggled, squeezing his hand. He squeezed back greedily. It felt good. Her hand was perfect in his, just like it belonged. He didn't know where they were going and he didn't care just as long as they were together.

The violet sunset softly faded away, blurring along the distant horizon and dissolving into an endless haze of blue.

Their pace slowed as they walked up the street.

Drew glanced over at Becca as their eyes mistakenly met. They exchanged a brief smile; an innocent expression of their nervousness towards one another.

"You wanna come in for a bit. My parents would love to see you," asked Becca, her hands tucked shyly behind her back as she twisted on the ball of her foot.

Drew peered up at her house. Each and every window spilled with a domestic glow as silhouettes rushed about the rooms inside. It was what he missed. Not that his memories were recent enough to recall.

"You sure your parents won't mind?" he asked, turning back to look across the street. His own home sat back from the road, slightly at an angle and with trees on either side. The building itself was shadowed in the dusk light. The single lamp which glowed weakly behind a curtain in a downstairs window was slightly brighter because of it. He felt a little guilty, but he wouldn't stay long. He was sure his nan would be okay for a little while longer.

"Of course not," replied Becca, tugging at Drew's wrist. She pulled him close and linked him by the arm, smiling as she did so, giving Drew the impression he had very little choice in the matter. And it felt good. Really good.

"Okay," said Drew as he hurried alongside her. "But only for a spell. I should be getting back."

The house inside was lively. Music played through the living room speakers, blasting out a mixture of oldish tunes and setting a calming mood throughout the home. Becca's mother was in her element as she busied herself in the kitchen, lovingly preparing the family meal. The mouth-watering fragrances of her dishes drifted slowly from one room to the next. She hummed pleasantly through full red lips, collecting plates from the dishrack before placing them neatly onto the table. She was a nice enough lady, was Becca's mother. That had always been said. Some would say a real looker, too, even if she was pushing her mid-forties. She had a pretty face and stunning blonde hair that shimmered off her shoulders, reminding Drew of those terrible shampoo commercials. Paul had seen her the week before and whistled under his breath whilst uttering the word, "MILF." He was right. Drew had struggled not to agree with the derogatory acronym, though he'd never admit it. Drew couldn't help but see a striking resemblance to Becca in her mother's good looks. It was a flash of what she'd look like in the years to come, and that was nothing if not exciting to think about.

As they walked down the bright open hall, Becca's father remained settled in his favourite chair. An old leather bound book in one hand, a large glass of brandy swirling in the other. He wore a thin pair of glasses as he read, the spectacle grips pinching firmly on the end of his nose as he lurched his neck forward to the open pages. He laughed aloud from his belly, his eyes never straying from his book, as he indulged himself further with another generous swig. Skilfully, he turned the page with a single thumb, giving his lasting chuckle the chance to run its course, still making himself absent to the family as he read.

The sound of stomping feet trampled overhead causing the ceiling to shake. Becca's father begrudgingly looked up from his book, rolling his eyes at the disturbance. The careless thumping continued as heavy thuds of a child's steps came speeding down the staircase and whirling around the hallway. Becca's brother, Spence, shouted playfully at the top of his lungs, wafting about one of his father's priceless golf clubs as though it were some sort of spear. The small boy had evidently just showered. His dripping wet hair hung flat on his face, dotting the wooden floor with droplets as he ran. He had changed into his pyjamas, with no help from his parents. That was particularly obvious. From the head down his shirt was buttoned in a lopsided manner. His trouser bottoms were inside out, and on this very occasion he seemed to be missing a single Mickey Mouse slipper.

"Christ!" said Becca in amusement as she placed one hand to her head. "Who the hell's dressed you?"

Spence momentarily came to a halt, looking up at his big sister and the visitor she stood beside before looking back down at his own handy work. "Me!" the young boy snarled before yelling excitedly, "I did it. All. By. My. Self!" and showing off a rather mischievous shark toothed grin.

"I wouldn't have guessed," replied Becca as she inclined a humorous nod towards her father. "Just don't let Dad see you playing with his signature golf clubs, will you?" she whispered out loud, though purely intentionally.

Spence's eyes widened excitedly, followed by an outburst of laughter as he scurried back down the hall and disappeared into the kitchen. Of course, Becca's father wasn't far behind. Abandoning his book, he lunged down the hallway with a heavy foot in an attempt to rescue beloved golf club, his brandy sloshing down his shirt.

Her family obviously had much love for each other, and the family unit was held together by organised chaos. At times Drew found himself looking through a window towards his own dark house, seeing nothing but the lonely, single dull light in the downstairs window. A pang of uncontrollable regret washed over him even though there was absolutely nothing he could do to change the situation.

Becca caught him looking. She smiled, brushed his hand with hers but remained silent.

From there, they both crept upstairs without so much as a whisper. On either wall, photos hung in their numbers, proudly presented in gold plated frames. There were so many that Drew couldn't help but study them, his pace gradually slowing as he followed after Becca. They were all treasured moments of the Bradshaw family. Each and every one was a priceless image frozen in time, and Drew couldn't help but wish he could have been a part of it. With each step farther, the figures in the images matured, moving through the precious years they shared together. Birthdays.

Holidays. Christmases. The list went on. In the briefest of moments, Drew had observed the frozen memories that were Becca's life. He had seen her as a child, standing beside her grandparents whom to this day she spoke about so highly. He has seen her ride her first bike on a cold morning of a winter's frost. And as another step was climbed, Drew studied a past image of Becca, sitting on a hospital chair, holding her brother, Spence, for the very first time. Yes, it was certainly something special. And as they reached the well-lit landing and turned to walk down the hall, Drew couldn't help but think he had watched the motions of a new born baby, quickly growing into the young woman he felt so strongly for today.

Becca guided Drew into her darkened bedroom, hastily slamming the door as he entered. The room felt cooler.

He waited anxiously, his eyes squinting as Becca scouted the wall for the light switch.

Light flooded the room in an instant, highlighting the calmness and comfort of neutral painted walls. Above Becca's bed, her favourite movie posters smothered the ceiling. He recognised many of them as being from classic horror flicks. A maroon shaggy rug filled the room's centre, and a pile of tattered books were spread out across the floor. Some stacked up high against the wall like an unfinished game of Jenga.

"Make yourself comfy, then," Becca insisted, brushing past his shoulder.

Drew sat down on the bed the way he had many times before, except everything was different now. Previously, they had been children, she'd talked about crushes she'd had on movie stars and musicians. She'd even admitted to liking a guy from Drew's school who was a few years older. But times had changed. She was different. She was no longer an adolescent with a poor fashion sense and a short-boyish hairstyle. He'd never felt threatened, or even thought about them as a couple. But now? She couldn't be further from what she was back then. She realised herself that she was cute. Growing her hair out and accentuating her new body shape only showed the world what he already knew. Becca was beautiful on the inside and the outside. She was a slightly troubled girl wrestling to be seen in a world where women had to fight harder. At school she was surrounded by influences from other girls, and she plagiarised little things and made them her own, but her peers came from wealth and there was a lot of model potential that made Becca wrongly feel inadequate. It didn't matter that they were shallow, and as much as she hated to admit it, she didn't like always being on the outside. Refusing to be part of the cliques was her natural reaction, but as it was a boarding school she was left lonely and lost. She wasn't bullied, just ignored, and to a teenage girl that could be so much worse.

Despite this, she cared about Drew and what he was feeling. "Are you okay, Drew? *Really*, okay?"

He nodded as a standard reaction. He was with her and to feel sad was nigh on impossible.

"For the most part."

"Speak to your nan, Drew," she said, picking up a notebook and slipping it into a drawer. A journal of her darkest secrets.

"I have."

She turned back to him. "No, *really* speak to her. She knows so much more."

Drew considered asking her exactly what she meant but felt like he'd only be repeating himself.

"I've got something to tell you," whispered Becca.

Drew felt his heart skip a beat, then pump hard. Was it nervousness? Anxiety? Fear? Did she have a secret boyfriend? A girlfriend? Did she want to reiterate that they were just friends?

"Well... this sounds super serious," he said looking deep into her eyes.

"It is, Drew," she said. "It really is." Becca paused for a moment, allowing her some time to think. "I just really wish I had told you sooner."

Bloodline

Time almost stood still. Drew knew this was the start of a new chapter. Closing one marked *before she told me* and starting a new one *after she told me*. He just didn't know which would make him feel better, and in some ways not knowing was often more preferable.

"I can see things," said Becca.

"See things?"

"Colours and shapes... I get feelings..." She was struggling to explain herself.

"Hold on a sec. Take a breath and rewind a little. What exactly do you mean?"

"I think... I think I'm psychic."

Drew grinned. "Shut up, Becca! Don't take the piss!"

She looked hurt. Drew instantly knew he'd gone too far. "Oh." He was quick to add, "You're serious?"

She nodded. "Just forget about it." She tried to wave it off. "I knew you wouldn't understand."

"No, no," he said, desperate to get things back on track. "I'm not saying that. It's just... you know we've laughed at people, haven't we? I didn't think you believed in that stuff?"

She nibbled her lower-lip, nervous and slightly vulnerable. "I know. I didn't... until...until I did."

"Sorry, I don't mean to laugh, it's just..." words failed him.

"I know. I know," she said, but she was disappointed. And that was worse than anything.

"How long have you known?" He was desperate to show her in some way he cared, even if he was a little sceptical.

"A few years, I guess." She thought for a moment. "I saw something when I was talking to a friend at school. It was faint. An outline around her: an aura. I can't explain it. Then she became ill."

"You see *ill* people," Drew grinned. "*Walking around like normal people?*" he tried to inject some humour but instantly felt stupid for doing so. This wasn't an M Night Shyamalan movie, this was her real life.

"Not just that," she said sadly. "I saw dark shapes all around. Sometimes moving and sometimes still. They were like shadows but without anything attached to cause them."

"Oh, wow." Drew's mind flew back to the night before.

"It was scary, Drew... it still is, but I guess I accept it a bit more now."

"What does it mean?" He realised that his question was huge. On par with asking the meaning of life. She would never have an answer.

"Who knows," she said with a voice that lacked conviction. It had been a long day and she was clearly tired. She wasn't comfortable talking about it and needed time to think.

He closed the gap between them and pulled her close. "Listen… Thanks for telling me." He almost whispered.

"You're my best friend, you plank. Why wouldn't I tell you?" He grimaced into her shoulder.

"Well, Bestie," he said, pulling away. "I'd better get going. You got any plans tomorrow, or d'you fancy hanging out with me again? We've got that little thing at St Mary's church, if you're still up for it. Could be interesting."

"Could be shit more like," she joked. " But yes, definitely. As long as you don't mind being with a weirdo like me?"

Drew got up. "I think I can manage it!" he smiled.

As he crept down the hall, the house appeared quiet and settled. Becca's younger brother, Spence, had been tucked in for the night. His childlike mumbling leaked out through the crack of his door where the nightlight shone across the landing. Downstairs, Becca's father had returned to his chair, sitting peacefully with his book on the armrest. He wasn't moving a limb, and his eyes frequently fluttered with the rise and fall of his gut. The reading glasses that before were so perfectly perched upon his nose now climbed across his face in a drunken mess. The glass of brandy had been knocked. Its contents spilt across the lower part of his shirt and onto his flashy trousers.

"Goodnight, Mr Bradshaw," said Drew as he leaned over the stair rail.

The tired man gave an unconscious grunt. His lips slapping together like a dog who'd drunk his fill of water. He turned in his chair, sinking himself farther into the comfort of padded cushions. His movements caused the book to fall from the armrest to the floor.

"See you tomorrow, then?" Drew said, looking back at the sad silhouette of the beautiful young woman.

She nodded pleasingly. "You bet," and blew him a kiss.

Outside, darkness had started to blanket the sky. Though Drew didn't care. The same rush of excitement still circulated around his body, replaying the look on her face when he left. He felt content. *So, this is what it feels like,* he thought. It was a feeling like no other, a feeling he wished to savour.

With almost a new vigour for life, Drew walked down the garden path and sat on the curb of the quiet street. He breathed slowly and deeply.

Overhead a single bat flew out from a tree, flapping its wings with a high-pitched squeal as it circled the nearby houses, searching for his nightly meal of insects. It was still warm outside, but Drew didn't care. For once the world was perfect. Both hands spread to the slabbed pavement behind him while he leaned back, bending his neck back to the sky. The ground was still warm to the touch. And despite the sky above being clear, not a single star yet sparkled. None of that mattered, not right now, as he let out a steady yawn, watching the moon as it peeked from behind a distant rooftop.

Bloodline

The front door closed behind Drew with a rush of air. The house was silent. It was nothing unusual.

His bag was carelessly thrown on the bottom step, and his still-tied shoes kicked off and neatly tucked beside the coat rack. Drew realised that not even the familiar sounds of the television rumbled through the house. He made his way to the kitchen, searched the cupboards in hope of finding at least one clean cup, and filled the kettle to boil. He realised then that he'd not eaten since lunch. His stomach complained with an unexplainable noise.

Drew pulled out the teabag, leaving it on the basin to slowly drain. With one hand he grabbed the beverage, calling out to his grandmother, who without doubt probably sat stiff in her chair.

"Here we are, Nan," said Drew as he trod the gloomy hall which led into the cramped living space. "Got you a nice cuppa t –"

He flicked the light switch. The blaze of light revealed an untidy room and, in the corner, an empty chair, its sponge cushions dented from recent use. Drew quickly turned to look back down the hall causing the hot tea to spill and run down the cracked handle, burning his finger. He gritted his teeth in shock. The hall was bare.

Where was she? Panic was quick to take hold of him as he chastised himself for not coming home sooner.

Setting the mug down, Drew brought his hand to his lips and blew gently to dull the burn. A *thud* came from the upper floor, startling him, followed by an immediate scraping noise as an object slid across the floorboards stopping with an abrupt rattle. At the base of the staircase, Drew stood discreetly, following the steps that gradually faded, turning into a dismal black hole.

"Nan? You awake?"

There was no reply. Only the faint sound of a crying cat that sulked beyond the window. He was beginning to worry. What if she'd had a funny turn? One of her dizzy spells leaving her in an incapacitated state.

"You up there, Nan?"

He reached his hand out to the stair rail, tightening his grip to guide him. Moving slowly, Drew's feet trod the worn, grey carpet, his other hand sliding the surface of the bare wall. In a single flash, Drew's mind cast back to the house across the street and the dozens of pictures hanging proudly on the staircase wall for all to see. He frowned hard, noticing a dim glow escaping beneath the bottom of his grandmother's bedroom door. As he always did, Drew gave a gentle knock and quickly twisted the handle as he stole a look inside.

On the far side of the room his grandmother stood upright, staring at the door intently.

"Oh," said Drew, surprised, losing his crouched posture and allowing the door to naturally swing fully. "There you are."

His grandmother huffed, turning her back towards him as she shuffled about in her belongings.

"Yes, here I am." She spoke agitatedly. "And where have you been?" She looked back over her shoulder, her favourite burgundy dressing gown swaying above her thin, naked ankles.

"I've just been across the street is all," replied Drew, staying in the doorway.

"School work I assume?" she enquired with an undertone of sarcasm while she opened up a tall wardrobe, burying both hands inside.

"No, not exactly."

"And you didn't think to call? Or pop your head in to save my worry?"

Drew curled his tongue within his mouth. He felt more than guilt. He felt ashamed.

"Indeed," she nodded, her hands still scouting through the wardrobe's clutter. "Your silence speaks volumes. How very unthoughtful of you, Andrew." She hobbled to finally face him. "You know how much I worry."

"I'm sorry, but when Becca is back..."

He saw the shake of her head and could just make out the mumbled words of, "That girl..." He ignored her. Yesterday she'd sung the girl's praises, and now her opinion had done a full one-eighty.

In her hands she held an old shoe box, its fragile lid sealed shut with dark brown tape on every side. She held it close to her chest and staggered over to the bed, lowering herself down to the old, spring mattress with a tiresome grunt and rested the box freely on her lap.

"Don't just stand there," she encouraged with the curl of her finger. "You're letting all the heat out."

Drew leaned back on the door, forcing it closed as he watched his grandmother lovingly stroke the box lid as though it were a faithful pet. She seemed more out of sorts than usual as she closed her eyes and motioned for Drew to sit beside her.

"Are you alright, Nan?" asked Drew, by now feeling quite concerned. "I heard a thud just now, when I was downstairs."

His grandmother raised her head, her eyes parting slowly. Still, her grip remained clenched around the small, narrow box. "A thud?" she repeated, her face serious. There was no urgency in her response. Nor did she wish there to be.

"Yes, just now when I was downstairs," Drew repeated. "You didn't fall, did you? I need you to tell me if you did."

"No," she insisted defiantly with a shake of her head. "No, I didn't fall. Lost my stick, though."

"Your stick?" questioned Drew.

"Dropped the stupid thing, didn't I. Rebounded off my foot like a rocket, too. Bloody thing's gone and slid under the bed somewhere. I'll find it, don't you worry," she said, returning her attention to the object on her lap.

"You sure?"

"Quite sure," said his grandmother impatiently. "Now, please, stop fussing. Come, sit with me," she instructed, placing her palm on the sheets and circling her hand in an inviting motion.

Drew walked towards her, his eyes drifting from one side of the room to the other. The space was hardly used these days, and by the looks of it was no longer fit for purpose. Piles of papers and boxes lay heaped across the floor, and furniture was scattered in a haphazard manner. Belongings that once held so much meaning were strewn about, but she couldn't bring herself to part with them. Old clothes draped on hangers hung on every cupboard door, dresser drawer, and picture frame. In some places, they were piled up like bundles of dirty laundry, carrying with them the stench of time. There were the occasional dresses that sparkled and held fond memories of a time when she went out and danced the night away. Now they were nostalgic empty vessels that when touched replayed happier times like a movie in her mind.

"Sit," she insisted.

Drew did as he was told and perched on the end of the rickety bed. It wobbled under his weight.

With no further delay she picked up the shoebox, placing it between them, her one hand never leaving its lid.

"Open it," she whispered unpleasantly.

Drew looked down at the small, rectangular object, having no clue as to what it could possibly hold.

"What's inside?" he asked inquisitively as he snooped around all corners. It held no label nor a hole to peek through.

She let go, staring hard at her aged reflection displayed in a narrow mirror. "Just open it." She spoke quietly, trying to fight back her emotion.

Drew very carefully picked up the box. It was light in weight, its contents rattling freely inside with the slightest shuffle. Peeling the tape, he heard his grandmother groan long and hard. The lid, as flimsy as it was, shortly began to loosen. Drew removed it, leaning it against his lap. Inside, thinly cut strips of newspaper covered the top layer. One particular strip, Drew happened to notice, was dated the year he was born. He removed the cuttings delicately as if the paper itself was valuable and liable to break. At first, he

117

sensed there to be nothing in the box at all but for the newspaper. He gave a curious look to his grandmother.

"Look deeper," she insisted.

Drew scraped his nails below the last layer of packaging, his fingers touching several objects lying flat on the bottom of the container. He grabbed them, lifting them out into the room's dim light. It was a bundle of photographs. There were not many from what Drew could assume, perhaps four. Maybe five or six at a push. Each photo was layered on top of another, tied securely with the use of a frail, pink ribbon. He flipped the stack over to untie it.

"Here," uttered his grandmother. Like magic she produced a pair of scissors and offered them to Drew.

The ribbon came loose with a single snip, softly falling to the ground about his feet. Drew spread the images in his hand, fanning them out like a deck of playing cards. The first showed a black and white image of a young man and woman. It was a wedding photo of a couple standing on the grass verge of a small country church yard. The woman, beautiful and proper, wore a white full-length dress with frills of fabric covering both arms all the way down to her wrists. The young lady's eyes appeared filled with happiness and wonder. Her hair was tied up, partly concealed by a flowing veil. Though not even a veil could hide such beauty. The man, whose hand the woman held tightly, was a tall, lean character. And even from Drew's opinion, he was a well-presented figure at that. His hair was dark, slicked back, and his perfectly straight teeth sparkled as much as the wedding dress he stood by. He looked happy. They both looked happy.

"Who is this?" asked Drew. He concentrated on inspecting the happy couple. "It's not…?"

"Why, come now, Andrew."

Drew lowered the photograph, turning to listen to his grandmother.

"I may be old," she continued, "but I'm not that old. Do you honestly mean to tell me you see no resemblance at all?"

He smiled, looked at her and then down at the photo again.

"You both look so good," he spoke with amazement.

"Quite," she mumbled softly. "Happy times from a long time ago." She took the photograph from him, gazing at the image through tired eyes. "You see, I was a pretty girl once, wouldn't you agree?"

Drew nodded his head. There was a captivating beauty to her, his granddad stood so proud and filled with joy.

"What I wouldn't give to turn back the clock, Andrew," she said with an air of sadness. "Yes, I'm afraid that once pretty girl has all but gone. Her memory remains, of course. Well, just about. But this shell of an old woman is all that's left." She handed the photo back to Drew, accompanied by a humourless smile.

It was a strange thing. Drew had never thought of his grandmother being young before. Never considered she had been vibrant with a look of welcoming anticipation for her life to follow. Of course, he felt stupid for thinking such a thing as he stared down at the young lady's radiant youth. The figures' eyes looked out past the print and into Drew's. "This is my grandfather?"

"Yes." A slight crackle projected in her voice. "That man in the picture is Arthur Hall."

The wardrobe door slammed shut with a BANG, forcing them both to jump.

"Whoa!" Drew said as his nan shot a hand to her chest.

"It happens sometimes. The hinge has a mind of its own! These old pieces of furniture are spring-loaded but quite durable, don't you know."

For a moment, Drew held his breath, his attention now back to the picture he'd not borne witness to before. He sat there stunned as a slight sense of excitement overcame him.

"Arthur Hall," Drew whispered aloud.

"It is the Arthur Hall I fell in love with, yes," she responded bluntly, alongside a simple gesture of her fingers as they stroked across the man's face.

Drew searched through the remaining pictures, all of which showed the same man throughout the years.

"I don't believe it," he spoke, if only to himself. "I didn't think there were any pictures of him."

"Well, now you know. And I'm sure you can appreciate why I don't make a habit of breaking out these old photos. My happiest times were in my past, Andrew. I like to keep them there." A shiver took hold of the old woman as she leaned to the end of the bed. "I'm tired, Andrew. I must sleep."

Drew nodded and tucked her into the bed, making sure the cover was wrapped tight and the pillow sat right beneath her head. He collected the photographs, taking one final look before packing them away in the box. A hand urgently grasped his wrist.

"No, you keep them," his grandmother mouthed, her voice barely audible. "Your need for them is much greater than mine. Pictures don't always tell the truth, Andrew. Please remember that."

He looked again at the newlywed couple in the print. "Are you sure, Nan?"

"Course," she mumbled in agreement. "They have been hidden for far too long. It would be unfair to return them to the dark."

Drew placed her hand back under the covers. Her skin felt warm, yet she continued to tremble uncontrollably.

"Look after them for me," she spoke, her eyes tightly shut.

"I will, Nan. I will," answered Drew, rising to his feet. He turned off the lamp, then closed the door softly behind him.

"Andrew?" the frail voice called.

"Yes, Nan?"

"Perhaps now you can stop this nonsense of digging up the past, yes? Leave it alone and just get on with your life. You have everything ahead of you." She echoed Becca's exact words from earlier.

"OK, Nan," he replied, knowing all too well he was lying.

Maybe that's where it all began to go wrong. If only he'd been more accepting and left it there.

If only.

Bloodline

fter grabbing a quick bite to eat, Drew quietly crept back up to his bedroom. The old photos were placed with care on the edge of his desk as he quickly changed, pulling out a Garfield t-shirt which faintly displayed the words *I Hate Mondays* and a pair of God-awful tartan pyjama bottoms that he had received as a Christmas gift from his grandmother several years earlier. '*Do you like them?*' he recalled her asking. Her strong smile stretching from ear to ear as she anxiously knitted her hands together. '*The store manager said all the popular kids are wearing them.*' He placed one leg into the bottoms followed by the other and tied the cord into a much-needed knot. He blew out through his nose at the sight of them. *The store manager wouldn't know fashion if it drop kicked him in the face!* he thought.

Out through his window, Drew stared across the street and over to the Bradshaw's residence. The night was crystal clear as he watched their front lawn gently wave in the shallow breeze. The inside rooms of Becca's house were shrouded in darkness. All except one. A figure was silhouetted alone by the window.

Drew waved like a fool, hopeful to catch Becca's attention before resting his forehead to the pane. The glass felt cool and refreshing. He sighed aloud, watching as the night claimed the street. A loud clatter struck behind him. Drew spun around on his feet uneasy, only to find the small shoebox his nan had given him had fallen from his desk, the photographs spread across the floor.

A cold breeze danced around the room as the temperature quickly dropped, bringing back fearsome memories of the night prior.

Drew picked up scattered photos, stuffing them back in the box and placing it with care on his bed.

The pictures of his grandfather were now mixed up. The unfamiliar handsome man wasn't always smiling, but he looked far from unhappy. A much taller man stood with him. He was half of a couple that included a woman dripping in sparkling diamonds. Drew flipped through the pictures and once again found the wedding photograph, and there standing chest-out proud and next to his grandfather was the very same guy.

"Who are you?" Drew whispered as goosebumps spread up his arms. A gust of wind appeared from nowhere and lifted up some of the old wafer-thin pages that still lay spread across the floor. And there, smiling with arms around each other and dressed in running gear, was the man and Drew's grandfather. The small story was carefully snipped out from a newspaper and told of how the two men were about to run a gruelling race for charity.

Benjamin O'Reilly was the man's name, and something deep inside Drew pushed him to remember it.

In an exceedingly dark corner of the room, he swore he could see movement. Gentle at first, then it appeared to climb the wall. He felt numb. Not exactly scared, but hardly calm and at ease. He quivered as a tingly sensation crept up his spine.

And then it stopped.

So much was whirling around Drew's head that it was an age before he was able to accede to sleep. The disappearance of his grandfather only produced more questions, his nan was physically and mentally going downhill, and now with Becca back for summer she provided him some excitement that he wasn't sure he could handle. The pressure of being a teen, and of his life in general, was evident.

He forced his eyes closed, thinking fondly of Becca; the same girl who was practically his best (if only) friend and the one person he could truly depend on. He thought of their younger days. The days when their friendship was nothing more than innocence. A time where their summer months consisted of childish games of riding horses that in reality were nothing more than bicycles. He thought of them trudging through the local park's streams in their Wellingtons, re-enacting scenes from a monster movie. To this day he could never remember which movie it was, though the memory stayed warmly with him. The winter months were usually a quieter time on the estate. There was never much to do in winter, especially the rainy season. They would spend days by the window with mugs of steaming hot chocolate, watching as rain turned into icy sleet, pelting down from the heavens. The weather, no matter how aggressive, seemed harmless back then. Everything seemed harmless back then.

The sound of persistent coughing travelled down the lightless hall as Drew listened to his grandmother retch violently. There was no doubt his nan was getting worse. She had not been the same in some time. Again, Drew recalled his early years with her. The years after his parents left for Europe. Back then it was enough. He held no strong memories, except the feeling of love. He recalled the sweet smell of baking from the kitchen as she stood over the oven, her red and green oven mitts and her apron displaying a tranquil winter scene of children playing in the snow. He remembered her looking down at him, rolling pin in hand, and stretching out the dough as she sprinkled flour on the worktop. Her eyes were kind and full of life. The eyes of a saint. Not that he had ever met a saint. Nor did he know what a saint should look like. Yet he felt the statement was a fair one. A saint was kind and good-spirited. And that was exactly how his grandmother had been to him, though all of this was a long time ago. The fire of life she once had had now vanished, gradually deteriorating as the weeks, months, and years passed by. There were days she appeared to have very little life left in her at all. Drew had watched as the guardian he loved and admired slowly shrunk in stature, her neck bending forward, the hump on her back becoming more prominent. And soon, even the fullness of her shape seemed to be devoured, leaving only the frailness of skin and bone.

He tossed and turned on his bed, his thoughts slowly slipping away. He wished he were old enough to fully look after her. He was still considered a child, and should anything happen to her he really didn't know what that would mean for him. And that truly scared him. More than he ever thought possible.

Eventually, despite everything in his mind, his body gave into sleep.

Bloodline

Drew awoke suddenly struggling to catch his breath. It felt as though his lungs had ceased to function, causing the oxygen in his throat to clot and stick. He inhaled with determination, forcing the air into his chest. The feeling persisted as his mind became giddy and sick. Drew cautiously turned on his back, making a grab for his phone. The beam from the small screen sent a path of hazy light across the bedroom walls, soon finding a shadow looming at his window, the defined shape of its head turned from the glass, tilting downward to the bed where he lay. It watched him intensely. Its stillness like an ornament on a shelf, waiting for him to flee.

Drew made no movement. He didn't have the nerve to move. Instead, he remained plastered to his bed, the covers half burying his face like an old lady who'd spotted a mouse in one of those old Tom & Jerry cartoons. A noise escaped his lips, shaking and weak, soon interrupted by a dreadful smell permeating the room. It was a smell he knew, though now the stench was intensified beyond belief. Drew coughed violently, the scent so thick it caused an overpowering need to gag and forced his eyes to water. The odour twisted and twined up his nose and to the back of his throat. He breathed in deeply, taking in the taste of what he could only describe as vulgar and foul.

Suddenly, Drew's mind snapped back into reality, his legs now willing to move despite the rest of his body remaining paralyzed. He dragged himself down the bed, his eyes never moving from the leering figure who stood like a mannequin, shrouded by night.

With everything he had, he made a run for it, jumping from his bed with a strenuous grunt. The covers that had before enveloped him so tightly felt like they were stuck to his body. The sheets slid down his legs, tangling his feet and sending Drew into an uncontrollable stumble. He hit the floor hard, the force of his weight sliding him along the boards on impact. Ignoring the mild pain, Drew swung himself around, kicking the covers free from his legs in sheer panic. He stared back at the area around the window. Shock encompassed his moonlit face. The space next to the window was bare and empty.

The window was steamed up. His head snapped back behind him as he thought he heard a sigh. Looking at the window a single word had appeared as if written by a finger in the condensation:

TRUTH

"What... What is it?" he spoke in nothing more than a whisper. "Whatever it is, tell me!" He needed to know.

He turned around to look at the empty walls expecting to see someone, or something, but he was alone. Very alone. He looked back at the window and exhaled loudly. The word was suddenly changing. Its dripping letters squeaked along the pane as Drew leaned forwards to see. It simply read:

HELP

"I will, I will," he almost pleaded, but he had no options. Just the name Benjamin O'Reilly that ran through his mind like a mantra.

As he lay stunned on the floor, Drew's eyes observed every nook and cranny of his room. His mind was predicting that the worst was still to come.

"Na...an?" his voice shook like the earth itself shuddered during an earthquake. Still, nothing stirred. It was then Drew noticed that the once powerful stench had eased. It had dissipated like the shadow by his window, leaving only an unsettling aftermath of bitter coldness behind.

He knew something odd was happening with the house, and he'd seen enough movies to believe that once something spooky began, it rarely disappeared by itself. Instead, it would slowly manifest with increasing energy and power until some sort of action was taken to stop it. Only he didn't know what that action could be. He was no believer after all.

The clock that hung on the kitchen wall sent his heart racing with its sudden chimes. He quivered as the clock again settled into a sinister and wanting silence.

A gust of air spiralled around where he sat. It was like sitting in front of an open fireplace as an icy wind swept down the chimney, spilling out into the room.

He looked up, watching as his genealogy papers piled on his desk began to flap and flutter. It was reassuring to him in one sense, but utterly terrifying in another. The cold. The stench. The shadow. All of this was real. So very real.

The wind grew stronger. One by one, the papers began to lift, twirling into the air and landing with a disorganised rustle, covering the floor in its entirety.

Drew could do nothing but watch as all his work and efforts lay strewn about the bedroom.

All turned quiet after that. And after much self-persuasion, Drew finally gathered enough strength and courage to stand. He felt queasy and off balance, like stepping off a boat and walking onto dryland. He bent forward, taking a long steady breath as both knees shook like reeds in a mighty wind. Drew felt he was about to puke… or pass out. He couldn't quite decide which as his vision blurred into a mush of dark grey and white pigments. The sensation didn't last long. And as Drew's sight slowly returned to normal, the spinning in his stomach also subsided. Standing upright, he observed the clutter of papers on the floor.

Collecting his research with trembling hands, Drew secured it in the drawer of his desk.

He slowly crawled his way back into bed. He fluffed his pillow and tried to rest his head. How could he sleep? Especially at a time like this. Each time he closed his eyes, Drew would startle involuntarily. The feeling of being watched continued.

His bloodshot eyes stuck out through the darkness like a cat in headlights as his hand slipped beneath his pillow. There was something underneath. It was thin and smooth with pointy edges that poked sharply at his fingers. Drew pulled his hand out from beneath, holding the object to his face. A picture of a newlywed couple was grasped in his hand.

A drumming sound abruptly echoed all over the house, sending Drew's heart into overdrive. He jolted up in bed, his fists clenched at the ready despite never having been in a fight. It was then he noticed the slapping of heavy rain drops against the window. A summer storm had finally arrived.

Something wanted him to find out the truth, and although he had no idea what would happen if he failed, he was terrified to find out.

Bloodline

For another night, Drew didn't manage much sleep. Not so much as a wink could he manage. It had continued to rain throughout the remainder of the night. The relentless downpour fell on his ears like gunfire on a battlefield as it hammered down on the rooftop.

Drew looked out of his window to catch the very beginnings of the day. A dim morning light roamed over the street; the sleepy sky still thick with a grey blanket of cloud.

Large puddles formed on the roadsides, flooded by obstructed drains and reflecting a bright orange beam from the towering street lamps that shimmered on the surface of murky water. Drew felt his eyelids sluggishly drop. The time had just turned six thirty and the world was still at rest.

He snatched on some clothes, suddenly no longer feeling comfortable in his own house, and made his way down the stairs to the kitchen.

Soon the rain began to ease to a faint patter. And with it, a sharp ray of light momentarily peaked through the clouds and onto the kitchen drapes. Drew knocked back the last of his coffee, accidently slamming the cup down on the table. He slapped his lips in disgust in a failed attempt to disguise the taste.

Stepping outside that morning, the street felt different. The rain had stopped now, leaving a strange but earthy smell as he walked along his garden path. He crossed the road to Becca's, skipping over the now settled puddles as drops sprayed off the soles of his shoes. He raised his hand to knock, but in that instant the door swung open and Becca stood there looking as amazing as ever. She didn't look like she'd had any trouble sleeping. Not that he could tell, anyway.

"I saw you leave your house!" she grinned, and surprised him by leaning in for a hug. The affection between them had been subtle but noticeably more frequent. There were many lines between a friend and a girlfriend, and it felt – at least to Drew – that each day they moved just a bit further from platonic to something a little more.

"You were spying on me!"

"Perhaps a little," she admitted, and he felt himself blush. She looked him over from head to toe, and a perplexed look adorned her face as she said, "Don't take this the wrong way, Drew, but did you have a hard night?"

Self-consciously he combed his fingers through his hair and attempted to smooth out his shirt. "I had trouble sleeping," he admitted.

"The excitement of seeing me?" she quipped. She was just what his tired eyes required.

"Oh, definitely." He paused a beat or two as she joined him, then added, "There is just so much going around in my head. I think I'm just finding it all a little hard to process." He wanted to tell her about the feelings he had in the house. How he was sure he could see figures looming in shadows, and how he'd felt pressure on top of him. It wasn't just an over-active imagination, nor was it a tired mind horsing around with his mental state.

"You look troubled," she said as they walked onto the street.

Drew played it over and over in his mind until it seemed ridiculous not to speak out loud about what happened.

"There's something wrong with my house, Bec. I mean *really* wrong."

"Other than that God-awful smell and your nan who thinks it's freezing in a heatwave?" It was said in a good-humoured way. *Many a true word spoken in jest*, he thought.

"Yeah, aside from that... Look, I can feel something," he began, wrestling with the words as they spun around his mind. He wanted to choose them carefully. "In the house. I feel like I'm being watched. There are movements in my peripheral vision... Shadows. But, that's not all. I wake up feeling something on me. A weight pushing on me..." He stopped and used his hands to emphasise what he was saying. "It feels like a person."

"A person?"

He nodded. "And they're trying to hurt me."

Drew turned away but soon felt the warm tickle of her fingers finding his hand. He didn't pull away. It was becoming a completely normal part of their friendship.

"Maybe you're more susceptible to spirits than you realise, Drew." She squeezed his hand.

135

Drew went to argue, to verbally wave it off dismissively, but found he couldn't. Had Paul or one of his other mates come out with this he'd instantly be telling them to piss off. But it was her, and she knew what it felt like. It was bloody frightening.

"Don't overthink these things, Drew. I can see that's what you're doing. Relax and let the spirits talk to you. Hear what they have to say."

Cars sped down the street, the occupants with places to go. Even on a Saturday morning the world was in a rush. One by one more people joined the growing crowd at the bus stop queue, located across the street. Both men and women, all dressed in smart attire and ready for what Drew could only guess was a routine day at work. All carried the same joyless face, displaying a look of misery. Nobody really wanted to work at the weekend, did they?

Scrags, a dingy bus company, rocked up at the side of the road, the vehicle's handbrake cracking through the damp morning air as the people waited for the shutter door to fold. Each paid their fare before falling to a seat, looking like lambs being taken to slaughter. Drew watched as the bus drove away, leaving the sound of birds chirping from high in the trees. The sun, piercing through the clouds, was all too bright to locate them.

"Life is changing for us," Becca observed in a whimsical fashion. "Remember when we'd go to the woods and make dens? That seemed to be our world."

"You'd sneak out Bakewell tarts," Drew mused. It wasn't that many years ago and yet it felt like a lifetime.

"It was so simple then."

"It was, Becca. It really was."

He felt her squeeze his hand again and was pleased it was still there. Both of them acknowledged silently that this was the next step.

"Should we get moving?" she asked. "It's a fair slog to.... Where is it again?"

"Saint Mary's Church," replied Drew.

"Right. God knows what we'll find up there. Dad said the place is a complete dive these days. Said he attended there a few times in his choir boy years."

"Your dad was a choir boy?" Drew couldn't help but bite his lip.

Becca shook her head, embarrassed. "Can we not get into that now?"

They carried on to the edge of the town, soon making a right onto Stanley Road and leaving them only a short walk away from the school's iron gates. Becca remained speechless, determined to lead the way and leaving Drew to keep up like a tired toddler on a long family stroll.

Soon they came to a fence along the roadside. Becca pulled her hand free, and one foot at a time she began to climb its rusty old bars. She threw her leg over and jumped from the highest part, her feet landing softly on the overgrown grass.

"Come on," Becca instructed as Drew eyed the task.

Drew sized up the fence and began to climb unconfidently. The bars were still wet with hanging droplets, the soles of his shoes flat, causing his feet to slip. Drew cautiously climbed over the fence, trying to balance his weight as he clumsily toppled over the gate. He fell to the ground with a *thud*, hoping that no one had seen them.

Beyond the gate there was nothing. Nothing but an endless field. Its luscious green grass stretching out into the distance and dropping off the face of the earth. Confusion masked his face.

"Can we go this way?" St Mary's church was on the other side of the land. It bordered the town with a village offshoot. Had they continued to follow the road it would've added a further ten minutes to the journey.

"Less chance of being noticed."

"Noticed?" Drew looked around again. There was not a soul in sight. "Noticed by whom?"

"It's private land, Drew. Last thing you want is some pissed off farmer on a tractor chasing us off."

"You think that could happen?"

"Not if you hurry up and stick to the border like I told you. The tree line should cover us well enough. Now, stop being such a pussy and come on! Besides, we don't know who wants to meet us. I'm not going to walk down the middle of the road waving at everyone like we're in some bloody parade!"

"But meeting in an isolated church is safer?"

"That's why we are going with stealth. Like I was taught in the Girl Guides."

"You were never in the Girl Guides, and besides if you were, SAS training was not part of it. I'm pretty sure of that. You built fires and baked cakes…"

Becca smirked. "Fires and cake, huh?" She walked on.

"What?"

"Just stick to the hedges."

Drew followed after her, sticking to the edge of the field as instructed. The long, wet grass slapped at his shins like seaweed, soaking through the bottom of his trousers and weighing them down. A gust of wind spilled over the field, causing the grass to wave like a shaggy dog's coat.

Without Drew noticing, Becca disappeared in front of him, pushing her way through bushes that grew thick at the field's edge. Drew crouched down, his knees touching his chest as he walked. He pushed his way through the bushes and branches that seemed so intent to prevent his passage. Becca stood waiting as Drew emerged from nature with leaves in his hair. At least something brought a smile to her face.

"Look at the state of you," she said in an attempt to conceal her laughter.

"Well, what did you expect?" replied Drew, hawking out a cobweb that somehow found its way to his lips. "There must be an easier way!"

"Sure. But where's the fun in that?"

A long dirt path trailed before them. It was so narrow and overgrown that it was hardly visible. The trees and shrubs surrounding it had taken their toll, claiming back what would soon no longer be a path at all. With little choice, they continued on in single file. Becca led the way, naturally, pushing back branches that blocked her route and allowing them to fling back into place with a *whoosh*.

"Ouch!" cried Drew while wrestling with a sapling and removing a twig from his hair.

The path wound on, at some points seeming to vanish all together. Drew looked up to the gap in the treetops. It showered down a flurry of dewdrops with each blast of wind that wrapped its way around the trees. It was quiet out here. So tranquil. Yet little less than a mile or so behind them stood the disorganised chaos of daily life. It was nice to indulge in the natural beauty that was on his doorstep. Lately Drew would often baulk at the chance of a long adventurous walk. He missed life as it used to be. Just him and Becca, escaping out into nature. Without so much as a worry in the world. Yes, times had certainly changed.

As the path sloped upward, his feet began to slip on the draining mud.

"See!" Becca said, ducking her head through the brambles. "Better than a day at the library, ain't it?"

"Oh yeah!" replied Drew sarcastically, the ground moving from under him and throwing him back on his ass.

Becca turned back, holding her hand out and gripping Drew's wrist while she pulled him up.

"Bloody fantastic!" Drew scowled, checking out the back of his trousers.

"It's only a bit of mud, you wuss."

"Just a bit of mud, Becca? I look like I've shat myself!" he moaned, trying his best to smear off the dirt.

"You'll be fine, no one will see," mumbled Becca, patting Drew on the shoulder as she turned to continue the climb.

"How much farther, anyway? Feels like we've been walking for miles," joked Drew looking ahead to where the church stood proud upon the hill.

"It's only been an hour. Besides, maybe you need some extra fitness sessions with Mr Rogers!"

"Ha-*bloody*-ha!"

Drew pushed forward, taking extra care with his footing. He was soaked to the bone, his shirt draping over his shoulders as though it were five sizes too big. He thought of a film his grandmother liked. Some musical, where a guy walked down the street, pointlessly threw away his umbrella, and started dancing spontaneously in the rain. He looked down at his appearance, and the thought occurred to him that he'd suit the part quite well. Only he wouldn't be prancing about like that. He was cold, wet, and miserable. And to make things worse, his underwear now stuck to his ass like a second layer of skin.

The ground eventually levelled and finally provided a break in the trees, giving space for the path to widen. After rounding a final bend in the trail, Drew caught sight of a small stone wall, its towered rocks crumbling to the ever-growing vine roots which climbed across its surface. They approached it quietly; not a word was uttered from either of them.

The jovial banter now ceased. Above them loomed a towering spire. While the neo-gothic architecture was impressive, there was something else: a feeling in Drew's gut that made him question whether or not this was really such a good idea at all.

Becca approached the wall, effortlessly kicking one leg over. The rocks beneath her feet shifted and gave way under her dainty frame as she beckoned for Drew to climb over. He scrambled up the rocky wall, his soaking wet clothes weighing him down as the vine roots that clung to his shoes twisted around him like a ravenous snake. He toppled over to the other side, tearing the roots up from the ground and dragging them across the wall with him. A large stone sticking out of the grass broke his fall, ripping the seam of his shirt and grazing his flesh underneath.

"For fuck sake!" Drew grimaced, whacking his elbow to the stone out of anger, its moss-covered surface cushioning the blow like a sponge. "Why is it always me who ends up looking like they've been dragged through a hedge backwards?"

Becca smirked, opening her mouth to speak.

"Shut your face, Becca!"

It was then Drew looked at the space around him. There appeared to be many stones like the one that broke his fall scattered across the ground. Hundreds in fact. Each one covered in a rich green moss. Some displayed as though in a peaceful sleep, shaded under the shadow of leaning trees. He shuffled back, turning to the rock on which he fell. With one hand he sunk his fingers into the damp surface and shredded away clumps of moss. To Drew's surprise, there appeared to be faded writing chiselled into the rockface. The words eerily spelled *Rest in Peace.*

There was something quite sad and permanent about a graveyard. Drew had never found them to be particularly sinister places but rather a sad reminder of mortality. He looked around the graveyard, surveying the disparity in the sizes of stones. He had heard that death is the great equaliser, but obviously some hadn't taken that to heart. The rich and powerful still flaunted their wealth by constructing large monuments to their family members who had passed from this earth. The common and the poor had merely buried their dead in plots that now were not maintained and maybe even forgotten. Some however, even though the stones were small, continued to honour their ancestors by caring for the final resting place of those they loved. There were flowers on the graves, and the ground was kept presentable and as beautiful as possible. Was that not better than being locked away in a mausoleum where nobody ever visited?

They waded through the hanging tree limbs, the scent of damp earth lingering in the air. It was no wonder that moss spread like a plague here. It was easy to assume that not a speck of light had touched the grounds in years. Becca forced a barricade of shrubs aside, stepping out into an open area beyond the boneyard's creepy setting. Drew stretched up tall, eagerly looking over her shoulder.

"What do you think?" asked Becca, her voice expressing a tone of warm fuzziness. "Where should we go?"

Drew stepped out into the small clearing, catching sight of a small stone mausoleum huddled amongst the crisscrossing arms of willow trees. Its coloured glass was shattered, its doors rotting with age. The importance of those inside no longer mattered to the disrespectful members of today's society.

Drew hobbled closer, his eyes never once straying from the tiny structure.

"Well?" Becca pressed. "We can't sit in there. We need a better view. Somewhere we can see everything." She turned towards the church. "We need to head inside."

Drew took a moment to look all around. His eyes darted over the gravestones and then into the shadows cast by the sun on the trees, vines, and bushes that hugged tightly to the stone walls. Then he looked up at the building and wondered whether the person was already there, quietly sitting and watching them.

"Okay, lead on, my fair lady."

They wanted to stay away from the main doors, and a simple glance at the entrance suggested it had not been opened in years.

Drew was no expert in the habits of the local congregation, or anything else remotely ecclesiastical, local or not. Religion had fallen out of fashion in recent years, and this magnificent building looked to be a ghost of its former self.

As they tentatively stepped around the side of the building towards a car park edged with trees, they saw no vehicle. That wasn't to say that someone hadn't done exactly the same as they had done and come on

145

foot or hidden away a bicycle or motorbike, but it made them feel as though they could safely enter the church without fear of being shot.

And then it hit him.

This was the church where his grandparents had been married. The very same. The same shaped steeple and worn, stone bosses. He felt as if that old photo was coming to life as he placed his hand on the door and it opened with a slight creak and a louder scuff of the warped wood on the stone floor.

As daylight spilled into the church's gloomy space, resting birds were awakened in a panic, soon to fly through the smashed glass windows or to the safety of the upper beams. Inside was filthy; the most dirt infested grime hole Drew had ever laid sight on. Still, he said nothing as he dragged his feet along the dust-covered floor.

A number of pews stood in rows, one behind the other. Prayer cushions were either sitting correctly on hooks or had been thrown blasphemously around without care. Pages of pamphlets were strewn throughout the church, and prayer books were scattered around like an afterthought.

It was almost like the abandonment had been a recent thing. Did that have anything to do with them being summoned there? Drew felt a heavy weight in his heart that the place that brought his grandparents together in front of God was now unloved and forgotten. It was the ending of a tradition.

Becca made her way up the steps to the altar. The red carpet was torn in sections, stained with the foulness of pigeon waste, but it enticed her in nevertheless. Drew followed, and there they stood, momentarily lost in a place so important to so many.

"I can hear them," Becca said softly. "Whispers of people passed."

"Sounds scary."

"It's comforting," she said, her gaze now far off and accepting.

"Let's move from here," Drew said, nodding out to the large space behind them. He grabbed her hand. Her skin was cool against the warmth of his. This time their fingers interlocked, and he led the way.

A broken curtain rail was still attached at one end but bent down over the top of a doorway. The deep-red velvet with a golden fringe only partially covered what appeared to be a spiral stone staircase.

With careful movement they held onto the railing and slowly took the small, steep steps.

At the top they found themselves in a gallery that overlooked both the altar and out over the pews for the congregation. It was perfect.

"I'm scared," Drew then admitted quite openly. "Not about this, but the future."

"What do you mean?" They sat down close together on a hard wooden bench.

"I'm meant to go and join my parents' business. Their '*great plan*'." he added his own quotation marks to emphasise the point.

"Let me guess," she said, turning to him, her thumb moving in small circles over his hand with added affection. "You're not sure you want to do it."

"Exactly. Bec, I don't even fully understand what it is they do, and yet I'm meant to drop everything and move abroad... it just doesn't make sense."

Her face dropped as the realisation of the situation hit home. "You'd be leaving."

"But that's just it, Becs! I don't want to! It's not my dream, is it? *It's theirs.* Where were they when I was ill? On my birthdays? Christmas?" He stopped abruptly, needing to take a minute.

"I guess I'd never really thought about that before. About what your parents are up to and what that meant for you."

"It's not your problem, Bec," he said. "It's just... I have my own hopes and dreams, you know?"

Becca's hand supportively brushed his arm as her head rested down against his. And just as Becca was about to speak, through the sudden downpour, they heard the sound of an approaching badly tuned car.

The sound of an engine roared and sputtered as the grinding of tyres crushed firmly against the pebbled road. It was without doubt getting closer. The innocent noise had never felt so frightening. Even though they expected to meet someone, they now realised how naïve they were being. They were following scribbled notes stuffed in school bags; bits of paper slipped into library books. And then, like this was some shit episode of Scooby-Doo, they had gullibly followed the clues.

This wasn't about huge Great Danes; buff blond guys with an aptitude for designing traps; hot redheads who got caught easily by monsters; hungry stoners munching on hot dogs; nor nerdy girls who lose their glasses but piece together the puzzle and solve mysteries. This was a potentially dangerous scenario. Nobody knew they were at the church, and who was to

149

say this wasn't the infamous Child Snatcher starting all over again? Three girls had already been victims. They could very well be the next.

Despite their position, the two youngsters felt exposed.

Becca was quick to make her feelings known. "I don't like this," she said, standing up and whisking them off to the staircase.

"Hurry! We need to go! They'll be walking in through the main door any minute."

Drew felt a tug of his arm as he noticed Becca pointing at the rug in front of the altar. It sat there so innocently but she seemed obsessed with it.

"Come here. Help me," Becca demanded, pulling up a section of loose carpet at the altar's centre.

"We don't have time for this!" pleaded Drew in desperation as he watched Becca's continuing struggle.

"Just shut your face and help me!"

Drew did as he was told. Striding over he knelt down beside Becca. Together, they rolled away the dusty carpet. Beneath lay a wooden hatch minus a handle, its hinges bolted into solid stone. Opening it was no easy task. Becca squirmed, digging her fingers around the edges. The wooden planks withered under her grip and splinters embedded deep beneath her fingernails. With one final strain, she pulled, letting out a desperate grunt, and the hatch began to give. As the gap widened, the hinges creaked and groaned. The opened cover revealed an indefinite tunnel of darkness. Drew gawped inside.

"Quick, get in!" Becca hastily instructed, still leveraging the door with her shoulder.

"What, in there?" Drew gawked.

"Did I pissin' stutter?"

Drew took a second glance into the throat of the unknown. "You can't even see the floor," he fretted. "I could break my legs!"

"You won't," hissed Becca.

"How do you know?"

"You really want to talk about this now? Get in!"

"You get in!"

Both heads spun to the church's outdoors as the sound of steps increased across the gravel.

"Fine!" snapped Becca, dangling one leg over the edge. "You really are such a pussy!" She lowered herself down, her body submerging into blackness as though she were being dipped into a pool of tar. Both hands hung on to the edge while her feet scraped wildly for an invisible wall below. She let go with a gasp of breath, waiting with uncertainty for the ground to break her fall.

"Bec?" Drew called into the hole. "Bec?"

"It's OK," Becca's voice tunnelled up with an echo as if she had fallen down a well. "It's not so far. Hurry up, jump down!"

Without further consideration, Drew followed Becca's every move. He closed his eyes, sensing the cold, musty air drift up and swirl about his face.

With one hand he grabbed the hatch door as he loosened his fingertips and fell. For a few brief moments, Drew felt weightless.

The ground was cold and slimy to the touch. Drew blew out a puff of air, his eyes roaming drearily as he pushed himself up off the ground, welcoming the quietness. It at least gave him a moment to think. He stretched up tall like a stargazing hare, sending a sharp *crack* up his neck. The cellar came as no surprise to him. It was a dank and grimy place. And even though the suffocating darkness camouflaged the room in an endless canvas of black, Drew's opinion would not be swayed. He didn't need proof. The smell of timeless damp alone was plenty.

From somewhere hidden amongst the darkness, Becca's low whisper found him. "Drew?" she called, fumbling her hands along the nearest wall to guide her. Its stone was rough and wet. "Drew?"

"I'm... I'm here," he almost gagged, unable to stop himself from coughing. Breathing had never been so hard. The wind had been knocked clear out of him. Drew wafted his hands like a blind man in a feeble attempt to snatch Becca and drag her close.

"Where? I can't see anything," voiced Becca, never one to favour the dark, no matter how many horror books she'd read nor movies she'd watched.

Dipping his hand into his pocket, Drew pulled out his phone. "Wait a sec," he mumbled.

"What?"

"I said, wait a sec!"

A beam of white light burst out from the back of Drew's phone. He waved it about him, finally locating Becca who by now had wandered to the other side of the cellar.

"Why didn't I think of that!" she moaned as she attempted to wipe the smelly, wet gunk from her palms.

"Hey, there's more to me than just looks, you know," said Drew, surveying the room in a single sweep.

"You trying to blind me? Get the damn light out of my face!" moaned Becca, carefully moving towards him with both hands shielding her eyes.

From the floor above an abrupt *thud* trembled the building's foundations. By the guide of torchlight both Becca and Drew peered up.

"What was that?" questioned Drew, masking his mouth to hold back his persistent cough. The beam stayed steady, directed at the closed hatch.

"The church doors," replied Becca.

"You mean…"

"Shhh," urged Becca, planting a finger to her lips. "Someone's up there," she said, her face masked in shadow.

Drew lowered the light. "We've got to find another way out."

The footsteps walking the floor above echoed in the cellar. The steps were slow and cautious. Almost as though the visitor was looking for something. Or someone.

"Listen," said Becca, tugging at the rim of Drew's shirt. "We'll just stay low until they go. I mean, how long can they really stick around? Once they've gone, we'll climb back up and get outta here, alright?"

Unconvinced, Drew determined the length of his fall. It was far too high up for them to climb. Even if they managed it, who was to say that the person wouldn't be waiting for them. No, there was nothing else for it. They would have to find another way, and fast.

"Look, stop panicking! We're safe down here," continued Becca.

"Safe? You call this safe?"

Becca groaned an irritated groan. "No one knows we're down here, Drew. Stop stressing! You rolled the carpet back before you jumped down, right? We're practically invisible."

Frozen on the spot, Drew's mind went blank. It all happened so fast. How was he to recall any actions he performed in the blur of a moment.

"Well, did you?" insisted Becca, her voice falling heavily on his ear.

"Of course!"

She gave him a long, hard stare.

"You didn't do it, did you?"

"No… no, I did not."

"Seriously!"

"Exactly how was I meant to do that when I was possibly jumping to my death!" His hissed reply had more bite to it than he was expecting.

Slamming her palm to her temple in frustration, Becca grabbed the phone from Drew's grip. "You idiot! They'll see the hatch!" She spun off balance, the slime layered floor trying its best to remove traction from under her feet.

The heavy footsteps above grew louder, climbing their way up to the altar and nearer to the hidden hatch. And for the shortest time, even the atmosphere of the dismal cellar felt to be alive with electricity as Becca and Drew both took a large gulp of musty, cellar air.

Bloodline

They hurriedly made their way through the underground chamber, rushing past rows of stacked chairs and countless piles of neglected Bibles which looked like they would disintegrate at a touch. A small, low arch was visible in the corner, dividing the cellar into a jumble of different rooms. How many rooms exactly, Drew couldn't be sure, his attention was engaged elsewhere, following Becca as her light jumped from wall to wall. The small passage was narrow and exceedingly low, forcing them to duck down and scurry their way through the tunnel-like passage.

"See anything ahead?" Drew asked desperately, his vision blocked by Becca's backside as they came to a bend in the passage.

"Yes… Yes! I see light! Drew, I see light!" she breathed, ecstatically pointing in that direction, if only for herself. She quickly barged forward, her shoulders bashing off either wall before she came to an abrupt halt. Becca screamed in terror, her voice piercing down the passage.

"What? What is it?"

Becca whimpered under her breath.

"What do you see, Bec?" said Drew who was blindly following. "Tell me!".

"There's rats down here, Drew!"

"Rats?"

"A big furry one just climbed over my foot!" She quivered uncontrollably.

"Of course, there are rats! It's a bloody abandoned cellar. Just step over them, kick them if you must. But we need to keep moving, now!" Drew pushed, nudging Becca softly by her rump.

A sharp nip embedded into Drew's shin, quickly followed by another, then another. He looked down catching a scampering movement around his feet. "They're everywhere!" he yelled as tiny teeth sunk relentlessly into his shins. He kicked out frantically. "Sod off!" he uttered, stamping down hard as a rodent shrieked from under his foot.

All the while Becca stood frozen. She felt a paralysing fear circulate through her, accompanied by the patter of tiny feet scratching and climbing up her leg.

"Oh, Drew, they're huge!"

"Move, Becca. Now!" demanded Drew, forcing her forward, eager to finally see the light upfront for himself.

Overcoming her terrified state, Becca lunged onwards with a sickening whimper, her feet striking any pest who dared to cross her path.

Drew could see it now; a hint of daylight peeking out over Becca's shoulder in the distance and stretching its grandeur against the passage walls. It was like a window to paradise. He never thought he'd be so happy to lay eyes on the dark grey clouds again.

They didn't have far to go. Just a few more yards. Heavy breathing filled the passage as rats continued to squeak fiercely as they passed. Becca stumbled, stubbing her toe on what she could only imagine to be a small set of steps leading them out of the tunnel and into the open air. She gathered herself, brushing off the pain with the clench of her fists. "Shit!" remarked Becca, clambering nearer to the light before exclaiming, "There's a gate!"

Drew's heart sank immediately, his stomach wrenching as he began to hammer his way up the narrow, stone steps. He envisioned the worst: that on today of all days the gate would be locked, bound by chain and secured with the use of a giant, rusted lock. He could imagine their faces squeezing against the iron bars as they cried, pleading for anyone nearby to set them free. His mouth felt dry as he swallowed, watching Becca as her hands reached out for the bars and pushed.

To Drew's relief, the gate swung open without so much as a sound. He staggered out, his heart rate pounding into overdrive as they fell to the long, wet grass. Never again would he take for granted the remarkable colours around him. Tilting his head up to the chalky sky, he sniffed deeply, exhaling the finest air. He had never felt so satisfied.

The passage led them out onto the south side of the hill, a closed off area hidden away by a small mound, covered by bowing trees that rustled their song in the wind. The rain had stopped for now, yet the clouds appeared thick with thunder. A clear observation that the worst was yet to come.

Becca lay on her back, the rise and fall of her belly slowing over time.

"Hey, how are you? You good?" asked Drew, reaching out and pulling her close for comfort.

"Uh-huh," she hummed; her eyes still closed as stray hairs flapped about her forehead in the light breeze. "I'm sorry, I kinda freaked out a little down there, huh?"

"Only a tad," replied Drew, offering Becca a reassuring smile. "Good to see those horror books of yours came in handy though."

"Oh, shut ya' face!" she joked, cuddling herself deeper into Drew's chest. "I've never read anything about rats, have I!"

"Ah, that explains it then," said Drew with a roll of his eyes.

They sat quietly, watching and listening. The wind slithered through the treetops, softly hissing as it turned the leaves belly up in preparation for the storm.

"You reckon we should head back up there. You know, just to check out who it was?"

"You want to go back through the tunnel and wrestle rats again?"

"No chance!" snapped Drew. "We could walk around the side and take a peek. Maybe look at the car or something?"

It wasn't long, of course, before the dry spell ended. Slowly but surely, a light mizzle began to float down from the heavens, evolving into a torrential cloudburst. Still, they sat contently, the covering of treetops barricading them from the vicious downpour.

"Bit of odd luck really, wasn't it?" said Drew as he looked back at the arch sticking out from the earth.

"Uh?" replied Becca rather drowsily.

"The gate. It's funny, really," Drew continued, rising to his feet and walking towards the dark hole. "I half expected it to be locked." He grabbed the iron bars, swinging it closed with a rattling *clang*.

"Yeah, me, too!" said Becca, lifting herself from the earth.

Drew glanced back inside the passage. A shiver ran up his spine. He hoped to God he would never see the sight of it again. It was then he turned around, kicking something hard that hid beneath the cluster of weeds.

"You found something?" asked Becca curiously, tilting her head to one side.

Drew fell to one knee, pushing away the weeds and nettles that stung at his hands like a hive full of bees. He gathered his posture, lifting in his grasp a solid chain. Its two ends clinked together as they dangled barely off the ground. Hidden beneath was a bulky padlock, its catch unlocked and the key still firmly in place.

"You're not thinking what I'm thinking?" said Becca, jogging over and snatching the chain from his hands. "The chain for the gate?"

"I… I think so," he mumbled. "I mean, it's possible, isn't it?" replied Drew, observing the lock nestled on the ground. He picked it up, studying it with interest.

"You think someone's been here recently?" asked Becca, still holding onto the chain and watching it wriggle. She couldn't quite understand why anyone would want to venture down there. Not if they knew what was good for them.

"You reckon someone else could be wandering around out here?" asked Becca, dropping the chain to the earth.

"I guess… I mean it's possible."

"Best to check it out though. I'll go this way," she pointed. "We'll meet around the other side of the mound," instructed Becca, suddenly taking off. Drew found her wild side alluring and annoying in equal parts.

"Becca? Becca, wait!" Drew called, allowing the lock to roll off his palm and submerge itself amongst the feathered grass.

"When you're quite finished faffing about, I'd appreciate it if you'd lock that." A voice travelled from a nearby dip in the hill.

Alarmed by the distant voice, Drew sprang to attention, hesitant on whether to stay or make a run for it. His head spun frantically to the nearby woodland, his eyes resting on a person who stood shrouded by the hanging limbs of a weeping tree. Someone was watching him.

A few years before

The shiny red balloon broke free from her grasp as the wind snatched it away without a care. The young girl panicked. She couldn't lose it. Not now. Not after all this time. To anyone else it may have seemed like such a small, insignificant thing. But to Billie it was so much more than that. Much more. It was what the balloon represented.

She wanted a kitten. More than anything in the world. A fluffy little thing that she could hold and kiss and cuddle. A little companion. A friend that she could name and call her own. She deemed herself too old for dolls these days. No one really played with toys anymore. But a kitten was, to her, the next level. It was something to play with and to care for. It wasn't cheap plastic. It would purr, lick its paws to clean behind its ears, and nuzzle into you at night. It wanted love, desired attention. Not to mention squeak and meow the way small felines do. It was their way of speaking. She'd learnt that on a YouTube video about cats that stated they never meowed in the wild. The sound was meant for human ears only. She loved the thought of that. The cute little things wanting to communicate. If only she were allowed to adopt one!

But now that dream was almost dashed. She ran after the balloon. Her ten-year-old legs pumped as fast as they could away from the fete. Her parents were in their own little world as usual, drinking overpriced coffee and gossiping with other adults, hidden in the shade from the scorching sun. She, on the other hand, was encouraged to stay with her friends. Well, other kids to be precise. But they didn't want to play with her. They never did. Kids at her school could be so crap.

She had walked to the edge of the playground daydreaming, distracted by the sound of the ice-cream van that grinded against a curb nearby. In her excitement, she'd unknowingly loosened her grip and the long plastic-ribbon had been set free from her fingers.

"Don't lose the balloon!" her father had ordered earlier that day. *"If you can't look after something as simple as a balloon, then how on earth can you be trustworthy enough to take care of a kitten!"*

There was no choice. She had to get it back. Fast.

With sweaty palms the young girl followed, watching as it floated around the side of a large gymnasium. It looked like it was descending before a sudden gust lifted it high off the ground. She prayed out loud, forcing her feet to keep up, watching as it dropped towards a huge bush with bright red petals. The large branches reached out towards it with claw-like fingers, threatening to attack the balloon with its thorns.

"No!" she gasped breathlessly.

At first it bounced, just slightly, before surprisingly resting softly on the ground. Relieved, she ran harder, ignoring the tiredness of her feet. She was almost there, too. Just a few more paces as she stretched out her arms to grab it. But it was no use. Another gust of wind pushed the balloon against the thorny branches, and after it wiggled slightly, it burst with a loud, displeasing *Pop!*

She stopped dead, inhaling dramatically before whispering her thoughts to herself.

"No, no, no!" Tears flooded in her eyes as her vision became glassy and distorted.

And so, that was that. In an instant her dreams had been dashed. The chances of her getting a kitten had been ruined.

It just wasn't fair. Her father would never trust her again.

"Oh, deary me," a calm, but friendly voice called from behind her. "Please, my dear. Don't cry," he said, reaching out to lay a hand on her shoulder. "Come now, wipe those tears."

Billie-Jo Hooper turned her head and saw a tall, friendly man leaning over a fancy-looking walking stick. She looked past him. He appeared to be alone.

Billie-Jo sniffed up loudly, pointing towards the saggy red debris left hanging in the bush: the remains of her once beloved balloon.

"I know, I know," he hushed. "I saw it… I saw it all. But please, don't cry." He lifted his stick with a wave, aiming it in the direction of a nearby carpark. "My daughter, she has a spare balloon should you want it." He smiled kindly. "It's really no bother."

Billie-Jo wiped her nose. She couldn't believe what she was hearing. Maybe, just maybe all was not lost after all. She saw a flash of a tabby kitten with a giant pink bow around its neck. "Really? Is it red?"

The man leaned down, resting his chin upon the stick. "The reddest red you've ever seen, my dear." His grin widened as a chuckle flew out through his teeth.

She giggled in amusement. "Can you get it... please?"

The man nodded swiftly "I could, but my leg... is hurt, you see." He tapped the side of his foot using the tip of his stick. "It really is quite painful. Especially for me to walk all that way." He looked somewhat disappointed as he spoke. But as quickly as it vanished, a smile returned to his handsome face and he clicked his fingers in the air.

"Say...Why don't you come with me, then I can give it to you, and you can run back here to the fete. No one would ever know you were gone. What d'you say?" His brow narrowed. "Save the pain of an old man like me?"

Billie-Jo turned around, glancing back towards the gym from where she came. Her parents were just the other side of it. She probably wouldn't be too long, would she? The last thing she wanted was for them to be worried or cross. Her father was mean when he was mad. She couldn't bear it when he was like that.

"I... I should probably get back," she spoke the words emotionally.

"Pity," the man said. "Such a shame that, to not have a balloon. Wouldn't you say, my dear?"

She nodded slowly. Her eyes, although no longer full of tears, remained blotchy and tender to the touch.

"You know, I reckon we'd only be a couple minutes! That's not long, is it?"

She pulled a face that looked like she was thinking hard. The kind of face she'd put on when trying to figure out her dad's crossword puzzles during breakfast. The man was right though, it wouldn't take too long.

"Okay then," she said.

"Okay?"

"Yes!"

"My car, it's parked just this way," he said, throwing her a sideways wink and holding his hand out to guide her.

Billie-Jo studied the man's hand. She didn't want to hold it. It didn't seem right. But she did want the balloon. No, want was too small a word. She needed it. And without any further hesitation she slowly slipped her hand into his.

"There we are," he smiled. His palm engulfed Billie's hand. "Not so hard, was it?"

She shook her head as she walked.

Carefully, they began to stroll along the isolated path, listening to the sound of adults nattering close by and the excitement of children shouting. The man stumbled on the broken path. He would have fallen. That is if it weren't for Billie. They walked on to the busy car park, passing a couple of cars before stopping. Then the man's hand squeezed tightly. An old black van with dents and scratches on the panels was parked in front of them. Its bumper was hanging loose at one side.

"Hold on a second, love," the man asked kindly, reaching into his rear pocket.

Billie-Jo waited uneasily, looking behind her at the path. There was nobody around. And now, not even the sound of gossiping adults or screeching children could be heard.

Just then, a hand smothered her face. A handkerchief was forced over her nose and mouth causing her eyes to sting.

She tried to breathe. She couldn't. She squirmed and kicked, scrummaging for freedom against the heavy hand as she opened her mouth to scream. But something didn't feel right. Something felt so very wrong. She felt... sleepy. Exhausted. Billie's eyes began to droop. And with them so did her body as her whole world drained out of sight.

It was only a few minutes later when Billie's name was heard by her parents as they searched the grounds.

No one saw Billie-Jo Hooper after that. She would forever be associated with the mysterious disappearance of Layla Jones and the awful and sinister legend of the Burntwood Child Snatcher.

Two innocent young girls abducted in broad daylight. Never to be seen again.

The stranger appeared from the shadows, half camouflaged by the ancient woodland. She was an elegantly dressed older woman, her hair pulled back. Large pearl earrings dangled down against her jawline. She was wrapped up in an expensive looking overcoat and wore brightly multi-coloured wellington boots, mostly concealed by the knee-high grass. Her face was still attractive enough, enhanced by the skill of subtle make-up.

"Well, somethin' wrong with your ears?" asked the woman, parting the hanging branches as she stepped out into the clearing.

For an awkward moment, no one dared speak. And the woman, to Drew's abiding discomfort, stood still, observing him with great interest as heavy dewdrops slapped down against the lines of her forehead. She looked somewhat out of place as she stood there, like she'd been teleported from some designer outlet store.

The woman bent over slightly, bearing herself on a rotting tree trunk, relieving the aches in her feet and the relentless strain on her knees. She rubbed them tenderly. "This may come as a surprise to you," said the woman, keeping a watchful eye on Drew, "but the use of basic manners is still appreciated in most circles." Her glance returned to her knees. "It is rather rude to not answer when spoken to."

Drew glanced over his shoulder looking for Becca, but she had gone. *Oh, nice* he thought. He couldn't believe that she'd just darted off like that, leaving him alone to deal with this stranger.

His attention drifted back to the woman as she now began to step forward. Despite the fact that he no longer felt to be in any real danger, Drew couldn't help but feel wary, even though the woman wasn't any great threat. Her main attack would more than likely be her harsh tongue as she dressed him down for being young, as most old folk often did.

"No. I mean… Yes," answered Drew rather bluntly.

"Yes?" the old woman repeated, with one brow raised. "Yes, what?"

"Yes… to your question," gulped Drew.

"Yes, it comes as a surprise to you? Or yes, you understand it to be considered ill-mannered? *Which is it?*"

He took his time in answering, his brain unable to function as words clung like glue to his tongue. "Yes… the second one."

"Ah," the woman rejoiced while smacking one hand to her thigh. "Now we're getting somewhere." She smiled, showing off the yellow tinted shine of her teeth. "So, there may just be a gentleman somewhere inside that shell of yours after all."

Drew nodded then shrugged, not knowing if it was appropriate to do either.

"Your manners are nothing like your grandfather's," she said, knowing the effect the words would have on him.

"Grandfather?" spouted Drew. "You mean... My grandfather? Arthur Hall?"

"The very same. I can see a little of him in you." She stared long and hard. "Now, let's not hang around out here exposed to the elements, we'll catch our deaths." She looked up, scowling at the sky. "Looks like the worst is yet to come," she muttered. "Come, let's go inside. At least it'll be dry. Not that you wouldn't know that already."

"I've not...," Drew began, unsure of what to say. "I mean this is..."

"Spit it out, lad. Has the cat got your tongue? Goodness me. Now chain that gate back up. Anyone would have thought you were born in a barn."

Drew did as he was told, quickly wrapping the long, stubborn chain around the bars, curling it tightly and crossing the links before locking. The padlock clicked as the wind blew fierce, howling down into the dark, dismal passage.

She nodded when satisfied. "I apologise, Andrew. I know who you are, but you haven't the foggiest about me. Why, you don't know me from Adam?"

"Who's Adam?"

The old woman frowned, "It's just a saying, for Pete's sake," she chuckled light heartedly. "My name is Gentry Atkinson, my dear. But please, call me Gentry." She paused momentarily, surveying the angry clouds. "Now, if you're quite finished, I suggest you put your best foot forward. These hills are tricky enough to trek at the best of times," she said, turning her back and wandering into the conifers. Within seconds she was gone.

Drew spun around. "Bec!" he whispered, following the side of the collapsing stone wall, only to find it dominated by climbing vines and dense nettles. "Bec! Where the frig are you?"

"Young man?" called Gentry from afar, her voice drifting out from the woodland. "Come now, keep up."

He expected the pace to be slow, especially since the climb up and around the hillside was so challenging. Drew thought hard through the silence, thinking back to the old photographs of his grandparents' wedding. The woman in the picture, the lady who looked so glamorous, so out of place... Could it actually have been this woman? Could it have been Gentry? There was certainly more than a passing resemblance.

"You wrote the notes?" Drew managed, puffing in between words as the front of the church came into view.

"Notes? What notes?"

"The notes in the library books. Was it you?"

The old woman pondered. "Oh, those notes. Yes, I dare say I did," she finally agreed, although her tone was far from convincing. "I was actually beginning to think you'd never get them! What were you messing about with in the library? Are you a simpleton? Unable to follow simple instructions? You certainly took your time..."

"No, I... I was looking at old records about my grandfather."

"Ah, yes, *Arthur*," she nodded knowingly. "What did you learn? Come on, do tell." The way she spoke his name was with something more than simple recognition. There was a hint of genuine fondness.

"Tara!" shouted Gentry suddenly, changing her course of direction. She looked concerned as she wandered, her tall boots sinking into the moss as she trudged. "Tara!"

Confused, Drew tried to see where the old woman was gazing as she searched the nearest treeline. Was it a relative? A granddaughter or a niece, perhaps?

"*Tara!* Come –"

"I'm sorry," Drew began, stopping the old woman mid-flow. "Who exactly is Tara?"

"Oh," huffed Gentry, somewhat delighted by the question. "She's my dog, of course! Little rascal, so she is. Loves the woods, too. Who am I to deny her the simple pleasures?" She gasped back another long, deep breath, puffing out her chest as she did so. "TARA!"

Drew's face soured in objection, listening to the mad woman's shriek. *No wonder the bloody dog won't come back,* he thought as he shot a displeasing scowl.

"Maybe she's lost?" Drew suggested, observing the forest floor. "Do you often walk her this way?"

Stopping to rest, Gentry clapped her palms to her hips. "Daily, my dear. Daily," she panted, and for the first time Drew noticed that she was older than first appeared. A good ten to fifteen years older. Her makeup had done a wonderful job of smoothing out the rough ridges of time and invigorated her complexion. He would wager she used a host of fancy creams that over the years had most likely cost her the same as a brand-new car.

"Well, when will she likely come back?"

Gentry's gleaming smile swiftly transformed into a depressing frown as both eyes stared blankly into space. A recognition came over her. "Oh," she uttered, a hand rubbing roughly to her chest.

"We can go look for her, if you like?" offered Drew, albeit slightly unenthusiastically.

"We'll have a hard job of it," sniffled Gentry all of a sudden. "Poor girl's dead." Her soft-spoken words were no more than a whisper, filled with a tremble of emotion.

"Dead?" said Drew. "But... But you've just been calling her."

"I'd forgotten."

"Forgotten?"

"Yes," replied Gentry with an edge of annoyance. She visualised her canine friend jumping up at her side and scampering through the wood, her tongue flapping freely out the side of her jaws.

"You'd... forgotten?" repeated Drew. "Are you absolutely sure?"

The old woman cocked her head. "Yes, quite sure. My habits on the other hand are not."

There was a sadness in her eyes as she pursed her thin but bright-red covered lips.

She looked back at Drew sharply, finding her feet once more as a grumble prowled the colliding clouds above.

"You unlocked the gate then?" asked Drew, pointing back to where they'd recently circled, after seeking out a dog that didn't exist.

"Me?" questioned the elderly woman with a tilt of her chin. "What on earth would give you such a wild notion?" But for all of her gracious manners, her lies were obvious.

"You just said so, back there," stated Drew.

"I... I did?"

This was beginning to be hard work. The fear Drew once had was now replaced by frustration as Gentry finally agreed, "Ah, yes, so I did." She grabbed an old grey hanky from her coat. "Chain plays holy hell on my wrists, you know?"

A thunderous clash bellowed over the land, sending with it a torrential rain like they hadn't seen in years.

"We should get moving," said Gentry, and without panic continued to scan the sombre sky. "Come, follow me."

Eventually they reached the grassy peak and were soon standing at the church's main entrance. Drew half expected to see Becca standing there and grinning like the local loon, but no matter where he glanced she was nowhere in sight.

High above them the sound of roaring thunder beat down its rhythmless tune, forcing Drew to think of his nan as she sat alone in the house. It was selfish of him to leave her most days the way he did. And today, he was more aware of it than ever. She was never fond of the clash of thunder. He was sure now that Gentry was of a similar age to his nan but looked to have led an affluent life.

"How did you know my granddad?" Drew ventured, as the gravel cracked underfoot.

"I'm sure it will not surprise you to hear that I was a model once." She bothered her hair a touch and wiggled her body slightly as she laughed.

Drew didn't know where to look. The etiquette of answering that question escaped him.

"I'm well past it now, of course," she continued, "But at one stage I was a real looker. I was on magazine covers, don't you know?"

Drew smiled, and nodded. "That's... Nice." What the hell was he meant to say to that?

They followed the path, listening to the wind as it whistled around the church. Gentry continued to list her impressive resumé as if she needed his validation to continue.

"We'll head inside for now," Gentry called back, spitting out water that rolled down into the creases of her lips. "At one stage, I couldn't move for suitors wishing to take me out and show me off!" She giggled a little, but it all seemed contrived and heavily bogged down with regrets.

"I can imagine," Drew said, mainly because it was what she wished to hear.

They made it through the large doors of the church as a breathless Gentry unbuttoned her coat and left it to dry on a bench.

It appeared to Drew that when the old woman thought about her younger years it seemed to transport her back in time. They slipped into the last line of pews and dusted the grime from the seat.

"Your grandfather, I feel, was a little besotted by me. I asked him to take my agent headshots, and he single-handedly helped build my portfolio..." She touched her left ear lobe and gazed off into the eaves of the church as a smile played dreamily on her face. "There were a couple of quite racy shots, I'll have you know!" She suddenly exclaimed, perhaps trying to shock but almost certainly bragging. It was clear the old gal loved to talk about herself.

"Your grandfather was a true gentleman. He didn't get embarrassed at me draped over a bed wearing little more than lace and a smile. Often men couldn't control the temptation when faced with it. I'll have you know others have ravished me for much less!"

"I'm sure," Drew said, unable to remove the disturbing picture in his mind. Instead, he tried to focus on the large granite pillars that stood like the legs of God holding up the roof.

"You know, one time in Paris a photographer couldn't get me out of my clothes quick enough!" Her face glowed with the memory. "I have never orgasmed so hard, I can tell you that much! I've never had it that good since... Shame really."

Drew wasn't used to a woman of age speaking out so freely. Or a woman of any age speaking of such things. She really was self-absorbed.

He coughed into his fist. "So... about the notes."

"The notes?" Her smile dropped as she realised her reverie was cut short and was instantly tugged back to the present.

"The ones you wrote and slipped into the library books?"

"Ah, the notes." Her expression again became quite serious as she conceded to answer his questions. "Yes, your grandfather found something... I fear that is the reason why he disappeared."

"What did he find?" Drew sat up and took notice.

"He was in his darkroom looking at his last shoot..." She stopped and made a playful face. "He was probably looking at scantily clad women he'd shot, or some of my old shoots... when he realised that in the background of a photograph, he'd accidentally caught something else. Or indeed someone I should say."

"Doing what?"

"Taking one of the missing girls."

She had Drew's attention now. Was she right? Was that really the reason why his granddad had disappeared without so much as a trace?

"Taking one of the missing girls?" repeated Drew. "Who was it?" he mumbled the words, trying at best to remain calm. This was it. The big question.

She shrugged, casually lounging back into the hard, wooden pew. "I only wish I knew. Truly, I do. He was getting all excited about something, I can tell you that much. To be honest I was a little offended. He never harped on about my photographs the way he did about that snapshot! It had him mesmerised. Enslaved!"

"Why?" Pushed Drew. "What did he tell you?"

Gentry sighed a mighty sigh. "He was a polite man. A little withdrawn perhaps. But I knew he wanted to say more. He'd tell me I was pleasant looking and that the camera-"

"No, not about you! The picture!"

She turned quickly, giving Drew a funny glance as she clenched her jaws to speak, "Well... There's no need to use that tone, is there? Nor to become so rude. I can see you take after him in that respect."

Drew held back his tongue. "Forgive me, Gentry. I know you were probably one of the most beautiful women in Britain-"

"In the whole world, some have said!"

"*In the world.* Of course, of course," he exhaled. "But with all due respect, you didn't come all the way here to tell me about your modelling career, did you?"

With her jaw set, the old woman mulled this over. She stood up without warning, glancing around the building before finding herself on all fours, searching beneath the long row of pews.

"You OK?" questioned Drew.

"Where has that dog got to?" she snapped angrily. "Tara! *Tara!*"

This whole ordeal was becoming more frustrating than Drew could have ever anticipated. He pictured Becca laughing at him from high up above in the gantry. He'd have to get her back for this. If, of course, this woman hadn't bored him to death before nightfall. He was half surprised she'd not whipped out photographs of her glory days by now.

"Uh, your dog," he began. "She's no longer alive." He tried to be tactful but his patience was wearing thin. That and his lack of sleep were gradually catching up with him. By now he was desperate to get to the point.

Again, Drew watched her eyes drop as she slowly climbed up to her seat. "Oh, yes. That's right."

For a time they sat there in complete silence, listening to the wind as it howled above the damaged rooftop. Drew thought back to the strange events at his house over the previous few nights. Here, in a place where you'd expect spirits and energies to reside, he felt nothing. He wondered whether Becca did. That could explain why she'd made herself scarce. Perhaps she was overwhelmed by the presence of lost souls and couldn't cope. Perhaps it was all too much. Guilt washed over him for thinking she'd deliberately left him here alone.

"Gentry, can I ask you why you saw fit to contact me now?" Drew asked. "I mean it's been years since the abductions, not to mention the day my granddad walked out."

"Disappeared, my boy. Disappeared. And yes, I can see how that question would be of relevance to you." She looked away with troubled eyes that were now red and spilling with sadness.

"I've been away, you see."

"Away?" He was chipping at the stone, doing his best to squeeze out some blood.

"Allow me tell you a story, Drew," she flashed a smile that was instantly replaced with trembling lips. Drew couldn't help but sink back into the uncomfortable seat and prepare himself for the journey.

"I dated Roger Moore for a spell. You know, James Bond?"

Drew nodded. "*Shaken not stirred*." The actor was well before his time but he knew of him.

"Precisely. Well, we had a fling, if you like... Michael Caine? He bought me a drink and we ended up spending a memorable night together in the Dorchester Hotel." She paused, swallowed back some sadness, and sniffed loudly. "I've met rock stars and TV stars. But, despite them all... your grandfather was the first man who treated me like a real lady, but... he was so distracted."

"Distracted? With photography?"

"With his wife. Your nan." She cleared the dryness of her throat. "Drew, I know you don't want to hear all

179

of this, and maybe you find it irrelevant, but I was living out my dreams. I was being flown all around the world. I was drinking expensive champagne and dining out at gourmet, five star restaurants that would accommodate me at the drop of a hat. I was living the best life I could ever imagine! There was just one thing I was missing. Something no amount of money could ever buy."

"What?"

"I didn't have love. True love."

"You were never married?" Drew thought that hard to believe.

She scoffed at that. "Oh, I've been married. Of course, I have." It appeared to be a stupid question. "I was married to a Texas billionaire for a while. He made his money through oil."

"So… What happened?"

She allowed herself a half-smile. "I hated oil. He was in his seventies and as fun as a girl with no arms on a swing. He suffered a heart-attack. Nasty business really. So I was back here as soon as the probate was awarded." She moved on quickly, tapping Drew firmly on the wrist. "Don't judge me," she scolded him. "He fell in love with me like all the others. You ever had sex with an old man?"

Drew looked stunned

"No, no, of course you haven't. Well, I can tell you now, son, it's no pleasant experience. Firstly, it's like looking at a man who's been deflated. All saggy skin and droopy wrinkles. And then there's the matter of his-"

"I'm sorry, Gentry, but what has this got to do with anything?"

"I'm getting to that! Just do me the courtesy of keeping it zipped and allow me to speak!" she barked. "Anyway, the point is, I've had other men, but your grandfather was something special. Very special. The problem was I was nothing compared to your nan." She huffed like it was unbelievable. Even to this day she still didn't understand.

"What makes you think the photo is what made my granddad disappear?

"Your grandfather became a rather serious man when he had either a deadline or a project. The only time he let his hair down – *so to speak* – was when he was out with his friend. Those two were thick as thieves, so they were. Then he began to talk about the missing girls. At first, I thought he just wanted to support the police. But then he said he'd been looking into it more and more. I asked him what it was all about but he clammed up."

"And that was after he discovered the picture?"

"I don't know exactly. It was around that time. He didn't say much to me about it, in fact he was going to begin another photoshoot of me but without warning cancelled. I was furious. Outraged. That would've been the day he went missing."

"And his friend?" Drew pressed.

"Ben. Ben O'Reilly." The name rang a bell. Drew remembered the guy in the wedding photos and again in the newspaper clippings.

"You don't happen to know where he lives these days, do you?"

She nodded knowingly. "He's at Sunny Meadows," she said quickly before mocking the place. "There's no meadows there as far as I can tell." It's a retirement home surrounded by new builds. It was made up of a number of apartments where residents could still live independently of each other or, if they chose, could join in with activities, food, and socialising in a communal area and shared gardens.

"Forgive me again," Drew began. "But, I still don't understand the lengths you went to contact me and bring me here? It feels a little pointless if you don't mind me saying."

"Pointless? Is that right? Well, why don't you ask your grandfather, Drew? Speak to him and see what he says."

"Huh?" Drew scowled. "I'm not sure I'm with you?" The old girl was proving to be as nuts as a box of frogs.

"My point is, he knew things, and now he's no longer here. I may not have my looks anymore, but I'm not ready to die." It was a bold statement.

"You think my grandad's dead?"

"*Don't you?*"

He did. He often thought about his granddad off in another part of the country, or perhaps he'd secretly joined Drew's parents in Spain.

"I guess I've never said it out loud. But my nan said he'd walked out on her and was probably living it up with another woman."

Gentry shook her head disappointedly. "He would never have done that, Drew. Heed my words. That man would've died for that woman. And I, of all people, would know."

"I know my grandparents were married here, at this church," said Drew, imagining how the church would have looked that day. "Weren't you there, too? I think I've seen you in a picture?"

"Just one?" She looked disappointed by that. What did she expect? Pictures of her in her birthday suit framed and lined up the staircase?

Gentry cast her arms wide and sighed in consolation. "Believe me, this old building didn't always look this way. When I was a girl, this was my local parish. It was a lovely place once. A clean and cared for building with the most beautiful churchyard you had ever seen. My family and I lived only a short walk away, in a cottage that has for a long time been wiped clean from this earth. My father and I would regularly attend here for the services after the sudden death of my mother. That and the small community events that took place. It was the best thing for me, for the both of us, in fact. We spoke very little at home. Being amongst other people just seemed to help us deal with the burden of grief.

"I made friends here, you know? Good friends, too, or so I thought. An outspoken young lass by the name of Aggie. She was quite the fire cracker, always getting us into mischief. It was harmless mischief, but mischief nonetheless. We spent our days traipsing through the woodland together, eating sandwiches in the church yard as our fathers spoke of things we had no desire to hear. Yes, we had become the closest of friends. Such good friends that we'd often finish off each other's sentences. At one stage some of the locals would even struggle to tell us apart." She laughed silently to herself. "Yes, I would tell Aggie everything. All a young girl's thoughts and feelings. Basically, everything I would never have dreamt to tell my father. In return, she simply listened. She was just what I needed. And in a way, she filled the gap of what I dearly lost."

Gentry rested her neck back against the pew, reliving everything. "What am I thinking, you don't want to listen to this," she muttered, laughing off her story with the shake of her head.

Drew felt the pang of guilt. This woman clearly had no one and appeared to live a life of eternal regrets. "No, please continue, I'm listening," he insisted.

"You're sure?" asked Gentry, happy to speak her memories out loud. It seemed to be all she had nowadays.

"Well, alright then." She inclined gracefully. "It was during a dry summer's day in August when a new family attended the Sunday service. A woman with a face of stone, accompanied by her young son. Oh, he was a handsome young man. His slick jet-black hair seemed to compliment the roundness of his sea blue eyes. And as Aggie and I sat together with one hand knitted in the other, giggling like two immature schoolgirls, I remember the boy's gaze drifting from his mother as he threw me a charming smile."

"Look at you," Drew grinned, noticing how pleased she seemed by it.

"I was a looker, remember," said Gentry. "I wrote him a note asking him to meet me at the steeple."

"And he turned up?" asked Drew.

"He did. Though I was never alone, of course. Aggie never failed to be by my side. From that first meeting the three of us became the dearest of friends. So dear, in fact, it was hard to believe how Aggie and I ever got along without him. The three of us spent the rest of the summer together, skipping stones at the nearby river or lazing in the fields once our chores permitted. We were inseparable. All the while my fondness for his charm and wit grew stronger. He was a caring sort of creature. A real gentleman towards me. There was no doubt about it, I was falling for him. And even to this day, I believe he had fallen for me, too. Yes, it was the perfect first love. Almost like a fairy tale in many ways. But I suppose all things special are never meant to last. A feeling you will come to discover, I'm sure.

"As the winter months rolled in, our relationship grew and blossomed, our affection far more than childish scribbles on paper. We were meant to be together. There was only one problem. Aggie was always there. She became unkind and spiteful, a completely opposite reflection of the sister I thought I had found. And as the time sped by her manner grew bitter with jealousy for the love I carried.

"It was on the first Sunday of December when whispers swept through the town, and my father, a stern and private man, discovered the affection I had shown for another. He confined me to the house, forbidding me to follow my heart, determined that no daughter of his would ever drag his, or her, name through the mud. I spent weeks confined to the house. Months perhaps. It was impossible to tell. Time as I knew it seemed to stop, drifting into an endless space of night and day.

"It was on a cold and frosty night when a rapping struck my bedroom window. I opened it, wishfully longing to gaze upon my love once more. Though it was not him but Aggie standing frozen at my window. She embraced me. And in that very moment the friendship we once held burnt brighter than the clearest stars. *'You must come with me,'* she urged, beckoning me to follow her into the night. To say I hesitated would be far from truthful. The hour was late, and my father, as strict as he was, slept soundly. I grabbed my coat, my heart racing with excitement, and followed the frosty trodden tracks.

"We reached the doors of the church just before midnight. And as we entered, the hall was dimly lit with beams of scattered candlelight. *'Come,'* she demanded. *'This way.'* I followed Aggie up to the altar, laying my eyes upon a small hatch carved into the surface of the stone floor. She opened it. From down below a single orange flame flickered as I peeked my head down into the hole. *'He's down there.'* Her voice trembled from behind me. *'He's waiting for you.'* A smile broke my lips as my neck stretched farther into the gap. I was desperate, you see. In many ways blinded by what my heart truly wanted. Little did I expect that as I was about to thank Aggie, to express my appreciation for all she had risked, the sole of her boot should be solidly thrust against my backside, sending me plummeting into the darkness.

"By the time I awoke, Aggie was gone, the hatch closed, and the candle was dying before me."

"Did you get out?" asked Drew, leaning forward with anticipation.

"Well, I'm here, aren't I?" replied Gentry with the rise of her chin.

"You know what I mean, that night. Did someone find you?"

Gentry shook her heavy head. "No, not until the next evening. I spent the whole night and following day in that hole, screaming at the top of my lungs, pleading for anyone to hear me. I got so desperate, I ventured blindly through the passage, weaving my way through the endless rooms. When I finally found the iron gate it was locked. Having no choice, I backtracked to where I had fallen, curled myself up into a ball, and cried myself to sleep under the closed hatch.

"It was the priest who found me, his silhouette shining in the light like an angel. He took me home to my father, who placed me into bed. I remained there for several days afterwards, refusing to switch off the lights."

"And what happened to your friend?" asked Drew. "I hope she got what she had coming to her."

"Ah, well. By the time my father permitted me to again wander the grounds of the town, believe you me, I had a mouthful to dish out to that girl. I could never understand why she left me the way she did. The sheer cruelty. The heartlessness of it all I wouldn't have wished on my own worst enemy. I stomped my way on foot, past workers' cottages and over the village stream that would lead me back to the church. That's when it all became clear."

"Clear?" asked Drew

"Yes, son. As clear as the look on your face. You see, as I grew nearer to the graveyard walls, who should I see but Aggie and my summer love passionately embracing. Her hands rested firmly on his. Needless to say, my heart sank as I watched them from afar. But nothing hurt as much as when Aggie's eyes found mine. She grinned devilishly, leaning into him and planting a kiss on his lips."

"Wow! What a bitch!" commented Drew. Gentry's brows lifted as she waved her hand to calm him. "Hush now, there is no need for that. It was an awfully long time ago."

"Oh, I'm sorry," said Drew sympathetically.

"No need, my dear," replied Gentry. "To be honest... she was a bitch."

"So, what did you do?" asked Drew.

"I did the only thing I thought appropriate. Nothing."

"Nothing?" barked Drew.

"That's right, nothing," repeated Gentry with a stubborn fold of her arms. "What else was there to do? She had already made me a fool in front of the entire village. The last thing I was prepared to do was give her the satisfaction of thinking she'd broken me, too."

"But..."

"There are no buts in life. You cannot control what you can't control. This place showed me the truth in the end. It's a place I believe in. It is packed with memories and despite what it looks like now, it is a wonderfully calming place. That's why I chose to bring you here. No matter what happens, you will remember this place and it will become a story for you, too." Like most things Gentry said there was an element of truth, a dash of logic, and a whole heap of insanity wrapped around it, but the woman appeared harmless. Perhaps the disappearance of her first and last true love was what brought her back to the church.

The old woman stood, collected her bag and said, "Drew, this is with you now. Look through your grandfather's things. I'm sure someday soon you will find what you're seeking."

"How can you be so sure?" Drew grunted.

"How can I not be sure?"

"But-"

"You have so many questions," she smiled, gazing deep into his eyes. "I know you've had visitors. Whispers in your ears, have you not? Stop pushing them aside, there is no need to be scared. Place your trust in your ancestors; they are the ones who will guide you. Help you. You must let them, okay?"

"Okay," he agreed, although he wasn't entirely sure what he was agreeing to.

"Good," Gentry nodded pleasingly. "Now where is that dog? Tara! *Tara!*"

The light had already begun to dim as they both walked out into the church yard, listening to the rustle of shaking leaves from nearby branches. The pair had not realised the clouds had already parted their ways, cleansing the sky with sheets of pink and orange. The rain had finally ended.

Gentry briefly staggered on her feet. Her kneecaps cracked as she studied the young man's face for the final time.

"You have his eyes, you know?"

Drew offered a thankful smile. It was nice to think he had at least inherited something from his grandfather.

"His worst quality, of course. I always said so."

The strange woman cut a desolate figure as she faded into the branches, muttering her late dog's name under her shallow breath.

Bloodline

With the turn of a key the engine sputtered an array of knocks and rattles in the distance. Drew stood by watching, draped in the shadows of the old, abandoned church as the car made a spectacle of reversing. The gears crunched before the old car crept out of sight behind the trees. A cacophony of engine noise and carbon pollution disappeared down the lane leaving a residual plume of thick dark smoke.

"Wow!" came a familiar voice from behind him as Becca stepped out of her hiding place.

"Where the fuck have you been?"

"Sorry," replied Becca, linking both hands innocently behind her back. "I just… I dunno. She was weird."

"Weird is right," agreed Drew, watching as the thick smoke lifted.

"Why was she shouting out that girl's name? Tanya?"

"Tara. It was her dog."

"Her dog? I didn't see no dog?"

"That's because the dog's dead."

Becca stared blankly. "Then why the hell was she shouting at it?"

"Because she kept bloody forgetting, that's why! I don't think she's alright, you know... upstairs?"

"Oh."

Drew studied Becca intently. She looked drained, the colour had all but gone from her cheeks, leaving her weak and shaken.

"Hey, everything alright? You look a little under the weather."

She flashed a reassuring smile. "I'm fine. It's this place, I think. It's full of energy. Remember what I said?"

"About you seeing dead people walking around like the kid from that movie? Yeah, I remember."

"That's not exactly what I said," she replied unamused. "But yeah, I hear, like, whispers sometimes. Well, muffled voices really. Kind of like they're speaking to me over the static of a radio. It's all fuzzy. Not a single voice either, but like a room full of people. It's just..."

"Just what?" interrupted Drew.

"Well... I just can't make out the words. Not all of them, anyway."

"That sounds... awful?" Drew hesitated.

"No, it's not so bad. I don't feel scared or anything. I just... I feel drained. Like trying to understand is completely draining all of my energy."

"You think that's bad? That guy out of the movie Sixth Sense was dead the entire time and still going to work!"

She shook her head unimpressed. "So, what did you find out?"

Drew wasn't even sure how to answer at first. "It was hard work. The old girl talked a lot. Rambled would be more accurate. She seemed like a bit of a narcissist. Not in a bad way, I guess. Just that she did her best to pull the conversation back to her each time. You know, I learnt more about who she'd opened her legs for than anything else."

"She told you nothing?"

"Well, that depends if you class who gave her the best drumming of her lifetime as nothing."

"She said that?" He nodded. "That's it? So, all this was for nothing?"

"No," Drew huffed. "It wasn't that bad. She actually knew my granddad. I mean really knew him. Dated him for a little while when they were younger, too. And then some years later he apparently photographed her."

"What? Like porn?"

Drew slapped his forehead with the palm of his hand. "No, Becca, not porn. Nor anything remotely *arty*. It was mostly headshots for her modelling days." He waved that away. "Anyway, she said that my granddad was developing pictures when he came across one where he'd accidentally caught a girl being abducted."

"What! No. Way!"

Drew nodded. He was feeling very overwhelmed by the events of the afternoon.

"And where's this photo now?" persisted Becca. "Who did it?"

"That's just the thing, Bec. She doesn't know, either, but she thinks his disappearance is connected to that photograph and his research into the abductions."

"Is that it?" Becca looked deflated. "I was hunkered down for all that time for that?"

"There was one more thing, although I don't think it's very important. Maybe just a coincid..."

"Go on..."

"She mentioned a man I've seen before. Ben O'Reilly."

"Who?" Becca's expression looked puzzled.

"He was my granddad's mate. I saw him in the wedding photos and in another stack of photographs my nan reluctantly gave me. Gentry says he might've known something."

"Thinks or knows?"

"It's just a hunch," shrugged Drew.

"O'Reilly?" Becca muttered under her breath. "Old Ben O'Reilly? My dad knows of him." She stopped almost for dramatic effect.

Drew leaned in closer. "Really, go on..."

"That's it."

"Oh..."

"He sounds shady, or was. I think he's just some sad, old man now. He used to fix lawnmowers for a living, so my dad said."

"Well, I'm going to speak to him. It's worth a shot, at least. Apparently he's at somewhere called Sunny Meadows, which if I'm correct is just over the road from the short-cut we took to get here, right?"

"Yeah... but Drew," hesitated Becca. "You're going to have to go solo on this one. I don't know what's up, but I'm shattered. I mean really. I don't feel great. I need to go home. Sleep it off, I think. Plus, my mum's got some private tutor visiting the house tonight, cow!

She's desperate to improve my grades. You'll come see me when you're done though, yeah?"

"Oh, really?" Drew didn't know why but he felt like his world was falling apart. Part of the excitement was experiencing it with Becca. Maybe all of this had got too much for her. Maybe this was more than she could handle. After all, they weren't just some kids playing detective anymore. This was real life. In many ways it had become far more real than Drew had ever imagined it could be.

"I'm sorry, Drew. Honestly, I am."

"It's okay, Bec," he said, trying his best to hide the disappointment.

She grabbed his hand, and like getting a jolt of energy he began to feel better. They headed out around the wall and carefully made their way down the embankment and out towards the wooded sides of the field.

"Drew, I've enjoyed this," Becca said, adding an extra swing to their joined hands. "I know we always hang out, but – *God, this sounds so dorky* – it feels so different, doesn't it?" Drew got it. He liked it. No, he *loved* it, too.

"Like we're doing adult stuff now and not being kids."

"Exactly."

Their pace increased after that as stupid grins smeared across their faces, though neither would admit why to the other.

The sun had now bullied its way from behind the clouds, and the grass alongside them was beginning to dry out.

"You know," Becca said, as they got to the fence leading towards the main road. "You don't have to continue with this." Drew went to speak but she quickly held up a finger to stop him. "It's a lot of pressure. I know you want to find out what happened to your granddad, and… I get it. Really, I do. But your nan is home alone, and you're out here chasing ghosts from events that happened years ago."

Drew turned to face her. He gently pulled his hand free from her grasp and held her by the shoulders. "Look, Bec, I hear you, but I've come this far. I just feel like I want to continue. I need to. I'll be back to see my nan before she goes out tonight for her bridge club. And if this Ben character knows nothing, or if I can't find him, then I still don't have much to go on…" He paused momentarily, a light bulb illuminating his brain. "The cellar. Oh my God, Bec. This is perfect!" He looked at her with wide eyes as she read his mind. She looked worried.

"You're going into the cellar." It was said as a statement more than a question.

He nodded, "Nan's out. She always stays at home, but tonight is her monthly outing. She'll be gone for almost two hours! We can be in there, search it from top to bottom, and be out well before she shuffles back through the door!"

"We?"

"Don't tell me you don't want to be part of this?"

"I don't want to be part of this," she said flatly and dripping with sarcasm.

"Really?" Drew looked a little hurt.

"No, you moron. I'll come around, and if I die…" She was now putting on an act.

"Don't be so dramatic."

"I've seen enough horror movies to know you should always stay clear of cellars. Literally nothing good ever comes from entering a locked basement. But, for you, you pleb, I guess I'll embrace the experience!"

Drew smiled excitedly. And despite the tiredness he felt growing within him, the adrenaline continued to pump around his body. He knew eventually his body would crash, but at the moment he was trying his best to fight it.

They climbed over the fence, and then at the bottom of the hill they embraced before heading their separate ways.

"Be careful, Drew," Becca said, her arms now snaking around his neck.

"I will," he replied automatically. He, too, was caught up in the moment, eagerly sensing the moment he'd been waiting for.

That first kiss.

He swallowed, feeling the pressure. Their eyes locked in place as they began to move in closer.

"Come find me later, yeah?" whispered Becca, as she swiftly turned away.

Disappointed and alone, Drew raised a hand. He waved. "I will," he muttered under his breath. "I will..."

Bloodline

Drew walked through the old estate which had seen better days. Front lawns were decorated with cars on bricks, sofas, broken bikes, swings with missing seats, and plenty of scattered litter.

There was an obvious lack of community pride in the forgotten cluster of streets, mostly due to snitches and the nefarious acts committed by most of the residents. Those who were law-abiding citizens double-locked their doors, spoke to no one, and counted down the days until they could move out. Nobody chose to live there. You were either born there, forced to live there by the Housing Association, or offered it as part of your parole to integrate-inmates-back-into-society program.

Normally, Drew wouldn't have even dreamt to walk around the outside of the estate. Not if he knew what was good for him. But mid-afternoon on a weekend wasn't the worst time. Had it been in the evening, or at night, then there would be no way in hell he'd ever step foot around here. Not even with the police regularly patrolling the streets.

As he walked through the avenue, Drew made a right, cutting through an alleyway that fed onto the back of some old abandoned stores and leading on to a new estate that had popped up just that year. Originally this had been a meadow, and beyond it were fields leading towards a huge, ancient woodland and lake. But of course, green fields and beauty didn't make as much money as houses squashed together.

On the outskirts of the new development was a large and sprawling building. Built in the 1960s, its ugly concrete structure remained depressing and characterless. Sporadic flower baskets hung lifelessly on its walls, splashing a bit of colour to a place that was little more than drab. There was no getting away from it, this was one step away from a nursing home, and everything about it only reinforced that fact.

Drew wasn't sure how to approach this place, and for the first time realised he didn't have much of a plan. In fact, he had none whatsoever. He vaguely knew what the guy looked like, give or take some years. But he had no idea the whereabouts of his flat. He saw a sign for the security office but decided that wasn't an option. He would look like he was scouting out the place if he approached them. A trouble maker up to no good. That being said, Drew did question how good the personnel might be who ran security in a place like this. He assumed their vocational aspirations to be on sloping decline rather than bursting with ambition.

By now Drew was lagging a bit. It had been morning since he'd last eaten. And now it was late afternoon.

When he walked through the main entrance, he caught sight of a lady standing by the lifts trying to pick up her shopping bag. The plastic handle had broken, resulting in a couple of oranges trying to escape across the floor to freedom.

Drew stopped them from rolling, scooping them up in a quick and single movement. The lady turned and smiled in defeat. She was small and round with a crop of white hair in the style of the late Queen Elizabeth's.

"My daughter told me I need to get help, but whilst I'm still able, I think I should continue, don't you?" she said forcefully. She didn't know him at all and yet was happy to strike up a conversation.

"Yes, of course. But I think your daughter might just be a little worried about you."

The woman stood up straight but scoffed at the response. "Too caught up with her good-for-nothing husband is what she is!"

"Here, let me help with that," Drew offered, noticing the sack with a broken handle.

"If you don't mind," she said, but was quick to add, "I'm sure I can struggle."

"Whilst I'm here, you should put me to good use."

"Such a gentleman," she observed. "Very well, then."

Drew hefted the bag and wondered what the hell was inside, and more to the point how the woman had carried the bags as far as she must've.

There was a rumble of pulleys, wheels, and other mechanisms of the lift as it clunked behind the closed doors.

"Don't just stand there, then," she demanded as the doors rumbled open and she stepped out into the well-lit hall. "Who are you here to see?"

"Ben O'Reilly. Do you know him?"

She pulled a face as though she'd chewed on a sour grape. "I do. Same floor as me, I'm afraid. Man walks like he's got rocks in his pockets! Stomping along all the time. You seem too polite to be a relative."

Drew thought for a second. He had to be careful about what he claimed, and as this woman had not come down in the last shower, he was sure that honesty was the best policy.

"No, Ben was my granddad's best friend. I've not seen him for a while and wanted to look him up."

"Where's your granddad?" she said before adding, "Not that it's any of my business, of course."

"Well, that's what I wanted to speak to him about." Drew followed down the lengthy hall, gesturing for her to lead on.

"This way," she commanded as she started to slow, stopping in front of a fancy white door with a golden number ten at its centre. "Just leave them here, if you wish." She nodded towards the bags as she fumbled in every pocket before producing a set of keys.

"That's fine. I'm not going to do half a job."

"Of course, young man."

It took a moment of trying a number of keys before her shaky hand finally slid the correct one into the keyhole. The lock clicked as she gave it a nudge with her shoulder. Inside, a bird began to squawk.

"Behave, Arnold!" she shouted as the bird let out another high-pitched screech. It flapped its wings hysterically, its talons clanging hard against the cage.

"You have a pet?" Drew observed, placing the bags onto the kitchen floor and looking at the parrot through the serve hatch.

"Yes, yes," she confirmed, placing her purse on the sideboard. "He's called Arnold. After my ex-husband, you know."

"Really?"

"Yes, he never shut up either. I wish I'd caged him, too. Would've stopped him chasing round after all those other women!" She laughed, coughing between each deep hack.

"Well, it's been nice to meet you," Drew began, doing his best to excuse himself. " I best be on my way though."

"You can stay for a cup of tea, you know?" she offered. Her harsh exterior suddenly softened towards him. "Perhaps some ginger cake? All growing boys love their ginger cake now, don't they?"

"I'd love to, but I really need to meet Mr O'Reilly, and plus my nan will wonder where I am if I'm gone too long."

"Oh, I... see. Well, she's a lucky lady! You take good care of her."

Drew flashed a polite smile her way. "Thanks..."

"It's Higgins. Mrs actually. But please, you can call me Ma'am."

"Oh...." replied Drew, slightly taken back. "This may seem like a strange request, but I don't actually know the flat number where Ben lives."

"Oh, my, that is a pickle. Well, take a left out of here and keep going. His is the last door on the right. He's probably blasting out that heavy guitar music! One should not listen to music such as that. It is quite bad for the soul."

"Do you know the number?"

"Number fourteen is his."

Drew bid her goodbye and saw himself out.

The corridor was darker now, decorated in a 70s cappuccino paint. The old place was overdue for a refresh, with the odd cracks and peeling having begun probably twenty years ago. The white ceiling was smudged with a brown water stain that had slowly worked its way from one side to the other.

For a second Drew's mind went blank as he stood at number 14 contemplating what he was going to say. He knocked a couple of times, although the first was slightly too soft to be heard at all.

After a few seconds of silence, Drew knocked again, this time making sure his knuckles struck harder as the door jolted open a crack.

"Whatever you're selling, I ain't interested! Try the old goat at number ten!" snapped a voice as the door slammed shut with a rattle.

"Ben?" Drew called through the panel. "Benjamin O'Reilly?"

With the door once more unlocked, the gap creeped open slowly. An eye and a long, bent nose peeked out through the crack.

"You're too young to be my son, so what is it you want? If it's money, you can go plait fog. I have none."

"You knew my grandfather."

"Who?"

"My grandfather. Arthur. Arthur Hall?"

The man paused, studying Drew with interest. He 'ummed' and 'ahhed', tripping over his words before he finally said, "You're Art's grandson, eh? Don't see the resemblance myself. Art was broad and, in most ways, a charming sort of fella. Women loved him. Adored him. Without fail the man always got what he wanted. An impressive knack of knowing how to get their knickers wet, if you like. You on the other hand are..." He paused, chewing on his tongue. "You'd better come in."

"Thank you," Drew said as he entered the old man's flat.

Drew took in the stark white interior, surprised at how neat and tidy the place was. He wasn't expecting that.

The door slammed closed behind him. The catch snapping loudly in place.

"I've been expecting you," he said.

To be truthful, Drew wasn't altogether comfortable with those words or the way he said it.

"You have?"

The old man nodded as a grin plastered over his face. "I have."

Bloodline

There was an awkward moment between them as Ben's shadow cast over Drew. "You've not heard anything at all, have you?" he mumbled quietly.

"About my grandfather?"

Ben slowly nodded. "Arthur, yes."

"No," Drew admitted. "But he's the reason I'm here. You were friends, right?"

Ben stood rigid. Had his arms been outstretched to his sides he wouldn't have looked out of place in a cornfield. He'd certainly have more than just crows shitting themselves, that's for sure.

Like the flick of a switch, the old man relaxed, pointing down towards the leather couch for his guest to take a seat.

"Please sit..." insisted Ben. "And tell me, what was your name again?"

"Drew."

"Well, Lou, I'm sorry. I don't get many visitors nowadays, and when I do, they nearly always want something from me. Money, usually."

"It's Drew."

The old man grumbled in his seat. "Apologies."

Drew obliged the offer, sitting down as he once again marvelled at just how tidy the place was.

"I just want answers, that's all. Information, or anything, really."

"How's your nan keeping?" Ben questioned, almost dismissing the request.

"She's... good. Well, for her age, you know?"

The old man carefully manoeuvred in his chair, and with that very action showed that he was also well past his prime.

"She knows you're here then, your nan?"

Drew shook his head. "No, I never mentioned it."

Half a smile reappeared on Ben's wrinkled face. "Probably best keep it that way, I'd wager."

"You didn't get along?" asked Drew.

Ben had large hands. They looked like they could wrap around a person's neck with little to no effort. They'd been huge useful tools at one stage. Now, despite their size, they brushed carefully against his chin as he calmly said, "Oh, at one stage we got on like a house on fire. Time does things to people... well, people do things to people, and eventually you forget about those good times." He was speaking in riddles. And like much of what had been said that day, Drew was struggling to keep up. It was typical, whenever he broached the subject of his grandfather, the person would always become vague and answer in Mensa-style statements. His nan, Gentry, and now O'Reilly. Why couldn't they just answer the question with a straight fucking answer! Why did everything have to be in a roundabout way, floundering around in irrelevance.

"What happened?" Drew was beginning to think he was a shrink for old timers. A helping hand to get over the past. "If you were all such good friends then what changed that?"

"What changes anything pleasant? A woman, of course," the old man chuckled. "Isn't that always the way? She was trouble. A tarted up bit of skirt who thought she was more important than all of us. You know, like we were all small town and she was so much more sophisticated.

"I was married once. Well, twice to be exact. Three times if you count the trip to Dover. None was much fun..." He looked over at Drew. "I'm digressing. My story is no different from millions of others. My point was I didn't need a wife. I'd been with a few women, not that I'm trying to boast. In fact a lot weren't much to write home about, but then neither am I. I know that. But when this woman came on the scene..." The words trailed off like he was back there reliving it. "She knew your grandfather from way back. They were an item when they were young..." Drew knew he was talking about Gentry. It fit so obviously.

"This woman... Are you talking about Gentry?"

The man's head whipped towards Drew in surprise. "How in God's blazes do you know of that name?"

"I didn't. Well, not before this morning."

"This morning? You've met her?"

Drew nodded. "I have."

Ben's expression remained blank as he ran a hand through his hair. It was like subconsciously he was wanting to look his best for her. If only for her memory.

"So, you know then that she's different. Even her name suggests she is above everyone, a nod towards her perceived aristocracy. Though to be honest, she was a corker. I think that only gave her ideas of grandeur. Being constantly told how great she was inflated her ego to the point she believed the hype. Men loved her. Christ, even I would have given her one back in the day." Ben removed his glasses, polishing the lenses on his shirt. "Look, Lou, you're still young, but these women can be hypnotising. You get caught up in the moment. She was dating these big-time Charlies and taking yachts out in Cannes and St Moritz... but then she was back. Nobody really knows why, but she appeared back on the scene and..." The big man now looked slightly uneasy. Something now troubled him. "...she brought something dark with her. I don't know whether she'd been so badly hurt out there that she was looking to hurt others before they got to her first, or... I don't know. All I do know is she came back demanding your grandfather's time and his attention, going on about her portfolio updates, but you must understand she was in her fifties then. I don't mean to be disrespectful, but her boat had sailed long before that. Shit, she'd been on it when it had left, but now that boat had long since docked, or sunk, or whatever bloody analogy you want. She was no longer wanted. The modelling industry is fickle and no place for growing old. Nobody wants to be reminded of their mortality. She was bitter about that and held almost every person she met accountable.

"She came back single, saw your grandfather and how happy he was in his marriage, and she set out to do the only thing she could. Sabotage it. And my God how she tried. She did everything she could to get between them."

Drew was taken aback. He didn't want to think about his grandparents that way. He thought they had been as solid as his parents. "Did my grandfather... Did he cheat?"

Ben looked at him troubled. "I don't know. Your grandfather was a good man, and his morals were strong but...".

"But what?"

"Gentry knew how to flirt with men. Look, Lou, I was taken by her the same as everyone else. I'm not proud of it and she made me look a fool more than once, but there was something about her. She used her... I hate to say this, but her 'womanly charms'. Or maybe it was that we were weak. *I* was weak..."

"But how does all this tie in with my grandfather disappearing?" Drew was more confused now than ever. It was just more information being added to the mix. More stories crammed into the puzzle. He just wasn't sure how it all fit together. If nothing else it seemed to relate less and less to the answers he was looking for.

"What about this photograph I keep hearing about?" That got Ben's attention.

"The photo? You know about that?"

"I'm not sure I know about anything anymore." Drew rested his elbow on the armrest of the sofa.

"Well, the photograph changed everything," continued Ben. "Gentry had been doing her best to pull your grandfather away from your nan for some time. He just wasn't interested. I'll be honest, I'm not saying that absolutely nothing happened between them. I had my suspicions, but if it did, it happened once. Maybe twice... And he knew it was a mistake. Your nan disliked her since they were kids. She was cordial at first, of course, but later on they couldn't so much as be together in the same room.

"If I were a betting man... Which I am, then my money would be behind Gentry having something to do with your grandfather's disappearance."

"You think he ran off with her? Or..."

"Or something else, is my bet. Gentry is a woman who knows what she wants and goes after it. She had endless amounts of money but never appeared completely happy with her life. When her claws could not pull your grandfather towards her.... She changed. She went from this sultry mistress to something dark. She began to drink by herself. Not through choice but because all her bridges had finally been burned. Her tongue was forked and she grew spiteful... I think she did something. She made him disappear."

Drew found all of this hard to take in. The woman he'd met this morning didn't appear capable of anything so bad, but then did anyone? She did have a way about her. And her charisma and self-confidence allowed her to speak with anyone.

"Are you saying you think Gentry murdered my grandfather?"

Ben stood up, his knees cracking under his weight. His large stature loomed over Drew as the old man slowly nodded.

"Yes, Lou. I honestly do. If not by her own hands, then by someone she knew who could."

en walked over to a cupboard. A flat-packed monstrosity bought for practicality rather than aesthetics. He opened it up, his hands rooting around the disorganised chaos of papers inside. "Here," he grunted, holding out a piece of parchment to Drew. "Take it."

"What is it?"

"This, my lad, is the photography award your grandfather won. The winner was announced the very next day after his disappearance. He had worked a long time for this award. Most of his life, in fact. It was all he ever wanted. That's why I knew he wouldn't have just left."

Drew took the parchment in his hands, swelling with pride as he read the name out loud. *"Arthur Hall."* Beneath the name read the words *International Winner* .

"How did you come by this? Why doesn't my nan have it?" Drew asked, his sight flicking away from the paper.

"Your nan was beside herself. With her old man missing, she no longer wanted to interact with anyone. Became a sort of recluse, if you like. Closed herself off to me and anyone else who showed concern. Except for you... The poor cow blamed Gentry for what happened. I guess who could blame her for thinking that? I certainly couldn't."

"But what about-"

"The photograph? I'm getting to that, Lou."

"It's Drew!"

"Drew, you must understand it's all as jumbled to me as it is to you. I've not spoken about this to anybody. Really, not a soul. It's been years. Art came to me harping on about something he'd caught in the background of a photograph. The old chap was panicked. I could see it in his eyes. Something troublesome consumed him... But he wouldn't tell me why. If you remember your grandfather, he didn't like the limelight, nor did he ever indulge in confrontation. He knew there was no getting away from it. If he decided to release the picture, his name would be all over the media. The questions would probably never cease."

"So... How many people actually knew about the photo?" asked Drew, by now sitting on the edge of his seat. He felt like after all this time he might actually be getting somewhere.

"I have no way of knowing," replied Ben with the curl of his lip. "All I know is he confided in Gentry, and I assume he told your nan, too..."

"That's all?" asked Drew.

"I can't imagine he'd have told anyone else. Like I say, he was quite reserved those last few days. And if I knew Arthur as well as I think I did, he would have kept the whole thing close to his chest until he was ready to share it."

"And you? You have no idea who was in the photograph?"

Ben unsatisfyingly shook his head. "I wish he had said something. Truly, I do. The pressure of only him knowing was telling. To carry a burden such as that is… Well, unhealthy."

"And I guess you don't know where this so-called photo is now?" Drew knew all too well it would be a long shot. The photograph had more than likely been destroyed around the time of his grandfather's vanishing.

Ben shook his head and grumbled, picking at the fabric of the sofa. "Gone, I presume. It never turned up. Not under my nose I can assure you. I wonder whether your nan knows, but then again, why would she keep it to herself?"

Drew shrugged his shoulders at the thought.

"We can't judge, young man. Your parents left her and then your grandfather disappeared shortly after. It would've been a difficult time for anyone. Especially for someone as kind hearted and giving as her."

Drew sat back trying to take everything in. He remembered when he was small, listening to his parents as they broached the topic of leaving. It was all whispers behind closed doors. A sentence here and there. He'd naturally assumed he'd be packing his bags and accompanying them to the airport. Even at such a young age he was shocked to find out that wasn't the case. The house had seemed undeniably small with the four adults. Especially when the arguments started. On many nights Drew had shut himself away in his room. He hated the shouting and harsh raised voices.

And then, just like that, his parents were gone. A few short weeks later his granddad followed.

"When was the last time you spoke to my nan, Mr O'Reilly?" Drew ventured, noticing the tension as he said it.

"Not for years," he paused. "I'm sorry for that. Your nan was hurting, but she blamed me for Gentry being present. Probably still does. I get that." The old man screwed up his face, finding the strength to continue. "I admit I began to drink a bit too heavily. When I was fond of the bottle, I had fanciful ideas of Gentry and me getting together. I made a complete arse out of myself on more than one occasion. I'm not proud of it. The posh tart was a permanent hangover for me. I drank to build courage and in return it never did get me what I wanted."

"And you think Gentry got rid of him?"

"Who?"

"My grandfather!"

"Oh, yes," he nodded. "I have no proof, of course. Just a theory. But I think Arthur paid a visit to Gentry, and whether it was jealousy of your nan that got her livid or the photograph you speak of... I believe she flipped."

"But you don't know that for sure, right?"

He shook his head. "No... I don't. Like I said, it's a theory. But call me old fashioned, I have a feeling."

"A feeling?" scowled Drew.

"Aye, you see, Gentry isn't the glamorous old bird she likes to portray. I'd be surprised if any of her ex-husbands or boyfriends are still walking amongst us."

"Like Roger Moore?" It was said with jest.

Ben O'Reilly chuckled heartily. "She told you about that, huh?" he said as his attention shifted to the window.

Drew nodded. His entire investigation appeared to revolve around the triangle of his grandparents, Gentry, and Ben. Then there was the mysterious photograph. However, was it enough motivation to warrant somebody's disappearance?

"Where are my manners," muttered Ben, sluggishly finding his feet. "Can I get you a drink?" he asked, picking up a bottle from the table.

Drew looked up at the man in front of him, watching as the bottle trembled in his hands.

"No, I'm fine," said Drew, shuffling forwards off his seat. He had heard enough for one day.

"Really? It's no problem. A brandy or a port, perhaps?"

"I'm sixteen..."

"Oh, I don't get many visitors," said O'Reilly once again, flicking the light on in his kitchen. "Only my nephew."

Drew massaged the ridge of his nose. "No, that's quite alright, Mr O'Reilly. I really must get going." He stood up fast. His attention zoning in on an object placed upon the bookcase. A picture. Drew didn't know how but he somehow missed it earlier.

"That's him," Ben pointed to the silver-streaked frame. "My nephew."

Drew felt his body quake. He knew this person in the photograph. There was no mistake about that. His stomach sank. His heartbeat raced as his legs grew weak and flimsy. Drew couldn't believe his eyes. Staring back at him, football in hand, was the smiling face of Mr Rogers.

Bloodline

The fresh air hit Drew's lungs as he struggled to regain his breath. He couldn't believe it. Mr Rogers, of all people. Was it coincidence? Possibly.

Anybody who indulged in true crime cases always understood two things:

1: You could not convict somebody without proof beyond a reasonable doubt;

2: Coincidences may not convict but could reveal some circumstantial evidence to indicate a suspect. It would be only a matter of time before an incriminating piece of evidence surfaced that would lead to probable cause and allow for a warrant to be issued for an arrest.

Drew took the long way back. Needless to say, he had enough on his mind to warrant the extra few minutes' walk. And the very idea that his prime suspect could have been sitting under his nose the whole time blew Drew's mind. The thought crossed his mind that Rogers could be watching him right now.

Drew kept to the main road. It was the safest thing to do. But periodically he couldn't help but glance behind him. He felt as though he were a walking target; like an arrow was strung at the ready, aiming for his back as danger lurked on every street. The worst thing was, he didn't know who the assailant might be. He had to be smart. And whoever this was, he had to be ready. Was that what happened to his granddad? He wondered. Could he have gone to Gentry that day to share what he discovered, only to end up butchered? Or perhaps he went to Ben? His oldest and most trusted friend, someone he could rely on and confide in. Drew suspected everyone. Whoever it was, did they not like what they saw? Did they react in the only way they saw fit; by silencing the old man forever? At this stage anything, and everything, was possible.

Drew thought long and hard about his nan. How she'd been rapidly going downhill of late. That was his biggest worry. What if by continuing this search, he was causing her too much emotional strain? Too much stress? He would never forgive himself if his dogged determination to solve all of this would take her to the point of a serious illness. Or worse.

But then he'd always wonder. He'd always seek the truth. He couldn't just drop it. He owed his grandfather that much, didn't he?

As Drew passed the old bus station, his mind flashed back to the past few nights at home. He'd have been lying if he said he wasn't uneasy about turning his lights off tonight. And after several days without sleep or rest, tiredness was really starting to cloud his anxious mind. His head felt thick and foggy. And yet, he was sure when the time came, he wouldn't be able to relax.

Without answers it was hopeless. Sleep would not come easy.

The roads were now bone dry. It hadn't taken long for the sun to peek out from behind a cluster of thick, woolly clouds. And thanks to the rain earlier that day, the insufferable heat had eased.

Drew thought about home. More precisely the door located in his nan's kitchen. The one that led down to the cellar. It was strange to think he'd never been allowed to go down there. What was much stranger was the fact that he didn't even know what it looked like. When his granddad was around, he knew the door was to remain closed to protect his film from being over-exposed. At the time Drew never considered disobeying. It was a simple instruction, and one that Drew never thought twice to disobey. He wasn't even sure he knew where the key was kept. Or even if there was a key anymore. For all he knew, the place could be empty, completely gutted of his granddad's possessions and memories. However, Drew knew there was more of a chance that it hadn't changed from the day his granddad lived there. A time-capsule his nan didn't want to disturb, nor did she want to be reminded of it, either. Who could blame her? She was more than happy to pretend that the room below the house never actually existed. That it had filled in just like many of the other houses in the area. They were cold and damp places after all: an unnecessary requirement for any home currently. People just didn't want them anymore.

It wasn't long before Drew crossed the road and wandered up his deserted street. And although he was desperate to start banging on Becca's front door, for once he ignored his heart. It was high time he started to follow his head. His nan deserved better of him. Drew understood that all too well. He needed to step up and look after her the way she had done for him. He'd accepted that it was now his responsibility not to neglect her. Not even for Becca. Not even for, *dare he say*, true love.

That said, it didn't stop him from thinking about Becca as his steps grew nearer the house. He gazed over at the Bradshaw's windows in the hope of one quick glimpse before making the walk up his driveway.

On the doorstep, packages stood piled on the porch, his nan's name printed on each label. He scooped them under his arm, juggling the parcels as he struggled to open the door. The heat rushed out as he stepped inside, the odours hitting him like a wall as he entered. But to Drew's surprise, the dominating smell was not of something he'd come to expect, but of deliciously cooked food. His mouth watered as a noise called out from his stomach.

Drew peeked his head into the kitchen, witnessing a sight he had not seen in years. The room was full of light. On the stove, four jet hobs burnt brightly as pots and pans bubbled away above, wafting up a thick misty steam across the window's grimy surface. The oven light flickered in the corner just as it had done for years, giving light to a large roasted chicken, glistening as it sat in its own juices.

The table was set for two, exactly how Drew recalled seeing it as a child. Fancy plates with gold plated patterning were spread across its surface. The hanging light caused the expensive silver cutlery to sparkle. And tall wine glasses that usually never saw the light of day were placed by the familiar settings.

"Well, good afternoon," said a frail voice, followed by a blatant chuckle. "What perfect timing, Drew." The old timer straightened up from her hunched posture and walked around the table, her stick shaking under her bone-like wrists as she began to shuffle the plates. She was smiling and appeared slightly sprightlier than normal. It was usually the case when she was going out to meet up with friends. Again, he wished she'd do it more often.

"Nan, what's all this?" asked Drew.

"Well," she said, her back towards him as she faced the gurgling saucepans. "I figured it was time we had a home cooked meal for a change. It's become something of a rarity these days, don't you think?" She tipped the water from the pan, setting the vegetables aside to drain, and swung herself around with the aid of the counter. "Besides," she added, "it gives us that extra quality time that I still believe we've been missing."

"I should really be doing this for you," Drew smiled.

"Nonsense! You've been out all day." She hobbled over to the oven and pulled the door down as the sound of crackling fat spat out from the tray. "Ah, nearly done," she mumbled. "You know, it's been years since I've cooked a roast dinner. I'd actually forgotten how much I loved to cook." She gave out a humorous laugh and caught a view of the packages huddled under Drew's arms. "Oh, excellent. They've arrived then. I've been waiting all day!"

"Hmm?" hummed Drew, forgetful of the parcels he was carrying.

"My medications," his grandmother replied, motioning at the brown paper packages. "Be a dear and unwrap them for me, will you? My fingers just aren't cooperating today."

Drew tore open the brown paper wrapping, each containing transparent tubes, full to the brim with a mixture of multicoloured capsules. He glanced at the tubes' labels, unable to pronounce the names of the different medications let alone identify their purpose.

"That's an awful lot of tablets, Nan. Are you sure you're not selling them to the local hoodlums to top up your pension?" Drew grinned. "You really have to take *all* these?"

"Only if I wish to stay alive," she smirked while observing her hoard on the counter. "My, there certainly is a lot this time. Seems like I gain more pills every month. That's doctors for you, I suppose. Rather than identifying the problem they'd rather mask it. They're all the same."

Drew collected the tubes, extending his arms out with a rattle as his grandmother stood them upright on the counter. "Quite the candy shop I have going here, isn't it?" she chuckled, and for the first-time stared Drew up and down. "Good grief," she gasped. "What in the name of God's green earth have you been up to? You're completely filthy! And you've torn your shirt."

Drew looked down; his clothes were still covered with dark patches of mud as his mind drifted to the fields, the hillside, and eerie church cellar. He had to admit he looked a bit of a state.

"Oh," hesitated Drew. "Sorry…"

The old woman shook her head and tutted. "You look like you've been pulled through a hedge backwards, young man." She pulled out a glass jug from the cupboard, threw in a couple of Oxo cubes, and poured in boiling water. "What in the Devil have you been up to?"

"We just walked up to St Mary's," Drew said, not wanting to say too much.

"St Mary's…" she threw a frown his way. "Whatever for? That's quite a hike. Who have you been with? *That girl?*"

Drew didn't understand it, but his nan appeared to blow hot and cold whenever she spoke of Becca. One minute she was being invited over for shits and giggles, and the next her name was said in the same way as Jimmy Saville's!

Drew scrambled for a half-truth. "It was after your beautiful wedding photos, Nan. I realised that I'd never been. I wanted to visit, take in the history, you know? It would seem such a shame not to. It's a wonderful place."

His nan added another couple of dishes filled with steaming vegetables onto the table and nodded. "It is, or at least was, a lovely place. Now wash your hands and we'll sit down." He wondered why she didn't wish to engage further but was quick to change the subject to his cleanliness instead.

After pouring drinks, Drew's nan dished up and eventually sat down whilst attempting to mask the effort she'd made.

"Thank you for this, Nan," said Drew as he hungrily licked his lips. "It all looks and smells great!"

"I hope you've worked up an appetite." She placed a napkin into her collar in the strange fashion she saw fit when eating formally.

"Are you kidding, I'm starved!"

She sighed tiredly, taking in the spread in front of her. "We've both grabbed small bites these past few months, and I apologise for that, Andrew. It's really not a suitable way for me to conduct myself."

As Drew went to speak, his nan threw him one of her stern, *'don't interrupt me looks'*, holding an old and frail hand in the air. "Please, let me finish. I'm off gallivanting tonight, so the least I could do was make sure my grandson ate well."

"Really, you didn't have to," Drew took a bite of a crispy roast potato, "but, wow! Nan, this is delicious."

"Come now, Andrew." The old woman brimmed with pride "It's not that special. You make a fool out of an old lady!"

They ate on, and for the first time in weeks, Drew was pleased to see his nan expressing her fondness for food. There was never anything wrong with her appetite when food was placed in front of her. But all too often, she'd forget to prepare meals for herself.

"Have you found out anything more in regards to your fool's errand?" She spoke up with a wave of her knife as if to emphasise the point.

Drew paused as his fork clinked loudly on the plate. He knew he didn't want to say anything. It wasn't worth getting caught between lies. Instead, he slowly shook his head. "No," he said whilst swallowing. "I guess all crossroads can lead to dead ends, too, right?"

His nan nodded, glass in hand, and took a sip of ice cold juice. "Unfortunately, my love, in life that is often the case."

They continued to talk as they ate. And as subtly as Drew could, he tried to broach the subject of her health. It was no good, however. As usual, his nan was a closed book, unwilling to indulge the conversation further.

"You must understand, Drew. I'm an old lady. I have an expiry date. We all do. And I'm pretty sure mine is fast approaching." She didn't mean it to sound as comical as it did.

"You will outlive everyone, Nan."

"Oh, I don't know about that," she shrugged, rising up from her seat and hobbling towards the sink.

"No, no, Nan," Drew insisted. "You go and rest before you go out tonight. I got this. You cooked so it's only fair that I should tidy up. Let the man of the house do it."

"You're a good boy," she smiled proudly, carefully walking out towards the lounge to reunite with the comfort of her chair.

Drew submerged the dishes into a sink of hot, soapy water as his eyes drifted over to a small door in the corner, camouflaged by coats.

He was now more determined than ever to open it. Just to see. Just one quick peek to discover what hidden gems were concealed in the bowels of his old nan's house. What secrets it waited to divulge.

He could only imagine.

It was an hour or so after dinner when his nan had finished fussing. She'd been second guessing everything from her hair to makeup to what colour cardigan she'd wear. She always built her bridge night into something more important than it actually was. That said, Drew knew all too well it was nothing more than a bunch of old farts, huddled in the corner of Burntwood's community centre, gossiping about their unseen families and the weather. Old age was an unpleasant affair.

Every month, without fail, his nan hobbled out the doorway just as a horn blasted and the taxi's wheel grained to the curb outside. She'd used the same firm for as long as Drew could remember.

She grabbed her tartan-designed flask that, as usual, she'd filled with two cups of Earl Grey's finest. She refused to entertain the idea of drinking the refreshments at the club, citing it to be some cheap brew and outrageously overpriced. Piss water, she called it one Christmas, though Drew expected it was the cherry talking.

"Are you sure you'll be alright?" she fussed again, tucking the flask in the crook of her elbow. "I'll only be a couple of hours. And there's an extra plate of food in the microwave should you get hungry."

"I'll be fine, Nan, really."

She smiled lovingly in return, stepping out in the humid twilight. "See you soon then!" She turned back to wave as if she'd be gone for weeks. Nevertheless, he waved right back as she carefully trod down the driveway. As usual the cab driver was already out of the car and striding towards her, throwing Drew a man-to-man nod and linking his nan by the arm. They walked steadily down to the roadside, avoiding the pavement dips and cracks.

"Off for another night on the town, are we then, love?"

His nan laughed out loud, playfully wafting her wrist over his gentlemanly charm. "Oh, give over," she sniggered.

"I'll take good care of her," he called up reassuringly, hiking up his jogging bottoms with his spare hand. "She'll get there safe and sound." He held her tightly. "That is... if I can fight all the strapping young men away." He grinned jokingly offering a sideways wink. The man looked slightly unkempt, but Drew was familiar enough with him. And he knew that despite all this he was a kind and caring fella to his nan. She was quite fond of him, too, in her own personal way. She always had a soft spot for a person in need.

There was a flourish of hand waves before, eventually, the ten-year old, silver Mercedes C-Class pulled out and disappeared down the street.

Drew cast his eyes over to the Bradshaw's house. He was about to make a move when he saw the front door across the road swing open and Becca come dashing out like a child on Christmas morning. "Hey, you!"

"Hey! How was the nap? You feeling any better?" Drew asked as she crossed the street without looking.

"I slept like a log," she winked. "Well, that was until that damn tutor showed up. Seriously, I don't know what my parents want from me. There's only a few terms left of school. If I've done shit with my grades up to now, I'll doubt they'll drastically improve by next summer," she huffed loudly. "Anyway, how did you get on?"

They turned towards Drew's house; the front door swayed sleepily on its hinges. It was Becca whose hand searched out his first.

"You're not going to believe what I found," he began like he had a tidbit of juicy gossip, but as he mulled it over, he wondered whether it was actually as exciting as he first thought. Perhaps it was nothing.

"Well... Go on. Do tell!"

"That Mr O'Reilly. He's only got himself a nephew-"

Becca stopped in her steps, placing both hands on her heart. "The revelation! Does this man know no boundaries to his shock tactics!"

"I've not finished yet, have I!" He paused for dramatic effect. "His nephew is none other than bloody Rogers!"

"What? The school teacher?"

"The very one."

"The same bloke who wants to give you extra-curricular activities after class?"

"Exactly!"

"The man who wants nothing more than to have his way with-"

"Alright, alright," Drew nudged her. "That'll do."

"Still... Shit, Drew. I'm not being funny. But that's a big fuckin' red flag right there."

They stepped inside, slamming the door behind them. And for once, the smell of drains was slightly hidden, overpowered by the floral mist perfume his nan had hosed herself down with before being chauffeured off to the ball. She seemed to never run out of the stuff.

"Jesus! I can still smell it! sniffed Becca. "You'd have thought it eased with the rain."

Drew shrugged. He didn't want to talk about the smell. There were much more important things to discuss. Like cracking on and finding a way of opening up the cellar door. There had to be a key around there somewhere.

"It'll pass," he said, though he knew she'd never buy that. Not when he wasn't convinced of it himself.

They both squeezed through the doorway of the kitchen. The tension between them was growing evident. It was a train-crash of emotions waiting to happen, Drew could feel it building. All he had to do was wait for the collision. It was bound to happen sooner or later. It was, like most things, just a matter of timing.

"What else did you learn?" Becca asked. "There must have been something."

"That Ben thinks Gentry has something to do with my granddad's disappearance."

"Gentry?"

"Indeed. The old nutter who takes her dead dog for a walk."

"What? Like she killed him or something?"

Drew shrugged, turning away to look through a kitchen drawer filled with junk. It was a catch-all for everything: spare screws, odd single batteries, receipts for irrelevant items, a book of stamps, discarded coins, and an assortment of random paperwork which included flyers, takeaway menus, and old MOT certificates. They didn't even own a car!

"Or whisked him off someplace."

"So basically, you still don't know?"

"Not exactly, no." He was now bent over and gazing deeper into the back of the drawer. "Ben talked about him, my nan, and granddad doing loads together back in the day, but then Gentry came back on the scene and apparently it all changed."

"Changed how?" asked Becca leaning herself on the counter."

"It all went pear shaped."

"Everything?"

"So he tells me."

"How so? He must have said something."

Drew placed a handful of paperwork from the drawer onto the counter. "Jealousy, I reckon. It was kind of hard to tell. Ben seemed to have a thing for Gentry, but the old girl had some kind soft spot for my gramps. The whole thing seemed a tad messy."

"Hmmm," said Becca as she tapped her nails on the chopping board.

Drew stopped and looked up at her. "What does that mean?"

"Maybe Ben did it."

"And what makes you say that?"

"You said it yourself. Gentry liked your granddad, and Ben liked Gentry. No, I'm not a mathematician, but you do the maths. If your granddad was out of the scene... bingo!"

"You don't go and kill someone in cold blood though. Not your best friend. And certainly not for that."

"Who said anything about cold blood?" question Becca. "All I'm saying is love makes people do crazy things, Drew." She gently brushed his arm. "Besides, people have done evil things for a whole lot less." She leaned into him in a joking way and lovingly combed her fingers through his hair. "You poor, innocent and naïve child. If everyone was like you then there would be no murder in this world."

"I dunno," Drew muttered. "He was a big tough guy in appearance, but he spoke about my granddad like he really missed him. I actually felt a little bad for him."

"Well, maybe he did. Maybe he didn't. Guilt can make you act in strange ways, you know?"

"I guess..."

"And what about the infamous photograph? Did he even know who was caught in it?"

Drew puffed out his cheeks and began to stuff the contents back into the drawer. "Don't be daft. It's the great unknown. An urban legend that I'm beginning to think never really existed."

"Why would they make it up?" She took a step towards the cellar door, leaning her weight on its panel.

"Maybe it's a coverup. Maybe they both pretended he'd found something and created a motive for his disappearance, ever thought of that?"

"Yeah... it's a possibility," said Becca, resting her hand on the doorknob. "Now, you finding the key to get down here or-" The door clicked as she pressed down on the handle.

Drew's neck snapped around as the door opened freely with nary a squeak. With it, the malodourous smell intensified, spilling out into the kitchen as they peeked their heads through the gap, following the steps that tunnelled down into a dark, endless abyss.

D rew searched the side of the wall for the light switch. It *clicked*. A soft red glow illuminated the shadowy room below, flooding the eerie light up the wooden steps. It gave off just enough light to see but not so much for over-exposure of photographic film.

"Wait. How did you...?" Drew looked hard at the empty keyhole.

"It just opened. I swear!"

The wooden steps cracked and groaned beneath their weight. And despite the lack of light, Becca was close behind, not wanting to miss out on whatever answers they might find.

Drew paused, sensing Becca's breath as it hit the nape of his neck.

"You ready?" she whispered.

He nodded in return.

Below, the room opened up to a place lost in time. A large oak table with a couple of stools was placed in the middle like a centrepiece. There were rows of shelving and a line of faded photographs hanging on a clothesline, secured with small, black clips. Drew couldn't help but imagine his granddad standing next to the large ceramic sink. The large plastic tray was still there with the plastic tongs hung just above. Underneath the counter were half a dozen large plastic bottles of various chemicals used to develop, rinse, and fix the images before hanging them up to dry.

The lack of light made the corners of the room dark and somewhat spooky. Everything down here appeared red and black. It was as though all other colours had been drained from his life.

Drew walked up to the scattered row of photographs still hanging on the line. It seemed odd to think they'd been dangling here all this time, eagerly awaiting for his granddad to casually walk back down those steps and admire his work.

For the entire time, Becca was strangely silent. She hadn't uttered a peep. Drew glanced around the cellar, squinting his eyes to the darkened corners.

"Hey, you alright there?" he asked, spotting Becca far back amongst the shadows. He could hardly see her under the lamp. However, one thing was for sure. She didn't look right. "Cat got your tongue or somethin'?"

Her hand slowly lifted up out of the darkness, pointing high towards a wall adjacent to where he'd previously been browsing. He'd been too drawn to the familiarity of the darkroom set up to properly study its display, and now that he did, he struggled to take it all in. The wall was an overwhelming rogue's gallery of pictures.

Pictures of people.

The angelic and now overly familiar faces of Layla Jones and Billie-Jo Hooper were smack bang in the centre.

"Oh, no..." he mumbled to himself in desperation, stumbling forward and knocking over an almost empty bottle of hydroquinone. He bent down and quickly set it upright, afraid of what might happen if the chemical spilt and spread.

Drew's attention reverted to the wall of photos. Other faces were familiar, too. Very familiar, in fact. Their pictures were plastered high and low like this was some kind of private eye investigation. Even string was pinned from each picture. The lines crisscrossed in a disorganised manner, in most cases spanning from wall to wall. But it was the individuals that caught Drew's interest. He narrowed his eyes and concentrated.

Gentry

Ben O'Reilly

Mr Rogers

A guy with large soft features he'd never seen before

A woman with long stringy hair

His nan

His parents

Becca

Becca's parents

And himself.

Drew couldn't believe his own eyes. They were all here. Everyone! *But why?* he thought, unable to comprehend its meaning. What did it all mean?

"What... What is this, Drew?" uttered Becca. Her voice quivered. She sounded kind of scared. That, or she just didn't know what to make of it all. Then again, neither did he. But there was something else. Something odd about the way she acted. He'd never known her to be like this before. Not ever.

"My grandad... He must've seen something. I mean actually seen something," said Drew as his attention returned to the collage of photos. "D'you think he was trying to solve it? Crack the case for himself?"

"Drew... I..."

"Becca?" He scowled through the darkness. "What's wrong with you?" Once again, the poor light made it exceedingly difficult to locate her. "You sick?"

"I... I just don't feel too good," she grumbled. "My head... It hurts."

"Must be the safelight, Bec," reassured Drew, lifting his head to the bulb. He pointed to a stool behind her, tucked away beneath a counter cluttered with tools. "Grab yourself a seat. Rest a minute... It's all..." but his words slipped away into the shadows. He didn't quite know what to say. He wasn't sure about anything. Was his granddad trying to solve the mystery here? Had the theory that had played on Drew's mind been true?

"Are we suspects?" Becca managed as her eyes peered out through the darkness.

Drew struggled to answer that. How could they honestly be suspected of such sinister events? They were little more than ten when the first two girls went missing. The very fact that their pictures adorned the wall brought into question the whole integrity of his granddad's investigation. And his sanity for that matter. If this was true it really showed just how amateur his grandfather was. Maybe the infamous photograph was misread by him and it spun the old chap off into some world of his own where he desired to be somebody he wasn't. A fantasy world where he was Columbo, or Poirot. Perhaps he dropped hints and accusations which ultimately caused his demise.

Drew felt a familiar wave of disappointment, something he knew all too well. Though this was completely different. For a second he was confused and an element of pride had crept in, like his granddad was the likeable hero he almost imagined him to be. The great, award-winning Albert Hall. The old guy who solved the case of the Burntwood Child Snatcher!

But now Drew wasn't so sure. Bloody clueless to be honest.

From above, a loud noise invaded the cellar, followed by shuffling steps along the upstairs hallway.

"She's back?" Becca said, a worried look smeared across her face.

"Shit!" Drew cursed, knowing there was no way in hell of getting out of there without being caught and questioned.

"I thought she'd be gone for hours!" Becca rubbed her head with a pained and faraway expression as Drew peered anxiously up the staircase. The footfalls grew louder.

"Drew…" Becca said, resigned and through the pain. "The door... It's open. I didn't close it! The red light will shine right out!" Drew heard her gulp through the silence. "There is no way she doesn't know you're here now. You... have to face her… *We* have to face her."

Drew edged backwards, still wondering whether he could hide and ride it out as the scuffing steps drew closer.

"Andrew?" His nan sounded worried. "Andrew, are you down there?"

Drew froze on the bottom step. His hand clenched tightly to the rail.

"I thought I made myself perfectly clear, you're not supposed to come down here!" There was a tremble in her voice as her tiny ankles slowly appeared through the bleak, red light, shortly followed by the rest of her, her flask still in hand.

"Nan? You're home." He sounded guilty.

"Well, I'd have thought that to be clearly obvious!" she scowled. The lines on her face were so much deeper under the angry glow. It was a perfect look, like she wanted to take her belt to him. "So, you waited for me to leave just so you could go sneaking around down here, I see?"

Despite the old woman's small stature, Drew still found himself taking a couple of steps backwards and clumsily bumping into the table.

"No, it's not like that, Nan," he lied. "Becca and I were just-"

"*Becca and I. Becca and I!*" Even whilst holding the flask she managed to emphasise her displeasure by putting her hands on her hips. "Is she here, too?" She scanned about the room.

Drew nodded over to Becca who now sat slumped on the stool, resting her head on the table. "She's... She's over there."

The old woman lurched her neck and shaded her eyes from the burning glow. "I can't see a thing in this infernal light!" she complained.

Slowly but surely his nan reached the bottom step. She took a long, deep breath and suddenly appeared to mellow. "Andrew," she sighed. "What exactly is it you're looking for down here? Really?" She paused and waited. "You can tell your old nan, can't you?"

Drew was struggling to find the words. The sleep he had the last few nights had been patchy at best. He'd walked far more today than he had done in some years, not to mention the emotionally taxing effort of trying to take in all of the information he'd heard throughout that day. He'd done his best to process it all, but it was all too much. It was damn right draining.

All he could do was glance up at the board of pictures. His nan's glare followed.

"Oh, I see," she said, suddenly understanding, and lifted a hand to her forehead. "Oh, dear. Oh, dear. What a complicated mess this all is."

Drew couldn't help it. He suddenly felt the urge to cry. He just didn't know why.

His nan placed the flask on the table with a *clunk*, unscrewed the plastic lid that doubled as the cup, and began to carefully pour. "You look like you need this more than me, son," she said matriarchically. She slid it across the tabletop. The steam from the beverage rose from the surface. It looked somewhat beautiful under the warm, theatrical light.

Drew took it. "Thanks, Nan," he said. He really was grateful. Even now, after all this, it was her taking care of him.

"So..." she said aloud. Her bony fingers drummed on the table's surface. "Where do we start…"

Drew took a sip and slapped his lips, realising just how good it tasted. He blew into the cup before taking another larger gulp. "How about all of these pictures?" He pointed to the wall. "I… I don't understand, Nan. Why am I there? Why are any of us here?"

The old woman nodded briefly. "Yes, yes," she began. "The pictures…. You see your granddad was a good man…" she paused with that.

"Nan, that's all I've been hearing. That's all I've ever been told. '*Your granddad was a good man!*' But what? What happened? Why did he leave? Why did he leave you? And why…" He took a moment to compose himself. "Why are there pictures of Layla and Billie-Jo here?"

His nan snapped a look his way. "Who?" She demanded, blatantly bypassing his questions. "Who said those things? Who exactly have you been speaking with?"

Drew took another sip to moisten his tongue. His throat felt dry; his mouth parched. He stood up, slowly making his way towards the wall and tapped at the photo of Gentry.

"It was her. I spoke to her today at St Mary's…"

His nan's face pinched together in contempt. "That whore tells nothing but lies!" She got quite animated and flailed her arms in the air. "Godforsaken lies, I tell you!"

Drew flinched back with surprise. "Nan, please. Calm down. I know. I know." He didn't know. And to make matters worse, he didn't know what to say or do. But one thing was for sure, he hated seeing her get over excited like this. With her heart the way it was, she was liable to keel over if she wasn't careful. Her medication could do only so much. The doctors had always said so.

"Then…" Drew looked at the wall and hesitated. "Then I saw him." His finger slid across the photos before finally stopping at Ben.

"Mr O'Reilly?" His nan questioned. The anger drained from her face. "He was a good man once. That was until that bitter hag turned back up on the scene." She clenched her fists at the thought. "That woman always resented me. Not only that, she worked her magic on him and your grandfather many years before. Ben on the other hand would do anything she asked of him! He'd probably jump off a cliff if she so much as asked."

"But what happened?"

"What happened…" she repeated to herself. "Everything, Drew. Everything happened."

Drew placed the cup down, almost missing the tabletop. "I'm listening."

"It started with him down here. Your grandfather, I mean. Scurrying himself away night after night just like he always did. Locked away and faffing around with that bloody camera. Not to mention his potions back there-" Her voice lowered as she thumbed a twisted digit towards the sink. "He found something, you see. Or so he claimed. A picture. Everything went wrong from there."

Drew felt like he was finally getting somewhere. The information he'd been seeking was about to be revealed.

"What was in it? The picture, I mean?" he tried to keep his feelings buried. His speech had risen half an octave, and the pace quickened with each and every word.

"It was more than just one picture. He was out and about one morning when something piqued his interest. Said he just had to capture it."

"The missing girls?"

"No... he was inspired by some floating balloon. A bloody balloon! Can you believe it? The fool!" she tutted annoyingly. "It had popped after floating into some thorns, I think. I know, you don't have to ask. Your grandfather could look at the most mundane things and see something nobody else could. This was a classic example. He became obsessed with it, and naturally, as he so often did, wanted to take a few shots. It was some weeks later when he was down here with his chemicals and developing his snap that he noticed something oddly suspicious in the background..." she sighed heavily. "Young Billie-Jo."

"And... Who else?" By now Drew was literally dying to know.

His nan tilted her head and looked at him carefully. She poured him some more tea and handed it over. He took it. "Sometimes..." She gave herself a moment. "Sometimes it's best to let sleeping dogs lie, Drew. It would do no good to anyone digging up the past like this."

The cup came away from his lips as he annoyingly shook his head. "But Nan, don't you see?"

"See what, Andrew?"

"That there are two sets of parents out there, wondering what happened to their children. If you know who did it, or have your suspicions, then it is your duty to say so. They need to know. Can't you understand that?" He couldn't help raising his voice. The sound of their voices. Their faces. It all had been haunting him.

"What do you wish me to say, Drew?"

"The truth, Nan! The truth!" he pleaded. "Please... Think of those girls." He sniffed up. "Those poor, innocent girls."

She gritted her teeth in the stubborn manner he'd become accustomed to. "Take a look at the board then, Mr Smarty-Pants! They all have a string coming from them, right?"

He nodded briefly.

"If you look closer, you'll also notice many of his once potential suspects have crosses. The innocent."

Drew felt relieved as a bead of sweat ran down his temple. But his nan wasn't finished there.

"All except for one photo," she added.

Drew studied the pictures intently, his eyes sharp as they pierced through the darkness. He saw it. The only picture without string. The only photo left unmarked.

His parents.

"But... the only one left is Mum and Dad?" He spun back around to his nan. "What...? What does this mean? What are you trying to say?"

The old woman held no expression as she guiltily cocked her brow.

"No..." muttered Drew. "No, it can't be..." he mumbled.

She reached up high to a shelf, pulling down a wallet of photos and quickly began to shuffle the pile.

"Here," she insisted. "See for yourself!" and fanned out a handful of enlargements."

The first showed Billie-Jo talking to none other than Drew's father. The second saw her holding his hand, and farther ahead in the distance his mother could be seen leaning against a tree, smiling.

"No... there must be some sort of mistake... This can't be true... And Dad... he never used a walking stick. Not like the man in these pictures."

"Come now, Drew. Why do you think your parents rushed off without you as quickly as they did?"

"Their business... they were travelling..." He was still in denial. Feeding back the lies that had been spun for him for years. His breathing became quick as his chest tightened, causing his mouth to parch. More so than before. He took another gulp.

"Come now, don't you see? There was never a business, Andrew. It was nothing but lies. All of it."

"Lies?" Drew's mouth hung wide. It was all too much to process.

"Yes, although looking back now it feels more like a dream. Or a nightmare. The lie has become my reality. Just as it has yours."

Drew sat quietly. The sound of his heartbeat thudded in his ears. For a moment, the thought of passing out occurred to him.

"They weren't allowed to see you once your grandfather found out," she continued. "Your grandfather was a tough man in his own right. Wanted me to turn them in, so he did. Me! Turn in my own flesh and blood!" her voice raised as she desperately grabbed her chest. When she spoke again, her words appeared to soften. "Your father made a simple mistake. He was a lost man, Drew. A misunderstood soul on the wrong path, you might say. He walked daily through the woodlands to clear his mind. A desperate attempt to ease his mind from temptation. But when he saw that little girl out walking her stupid mutt on the common... He just couldn't help himself... Something triggered. Like the flick of a switch in his brain. The man was sick, Drew. Upstairs, you know?" She tapped a finger to her head. "He tried to get people to listen. As God is my witness, he did. But no matter who he spoke to, no matter how he pleaded, the man was passed from pillar to post. He needed help. And the world turned their back on him."

"But Mum?"

"Your mother!" she snorted. "She was the instigator." Her frown narrowed. "She was everything your father didn't need to get well. She drove him deeper into the darkness. She made him *Do. Those. Things*... Your mother fed his weakness. There was no hope for him after that."

"But I don't understand. Why... Why would she do that?"

"That home she was brought up in as a child." The woman grumbled. "They did all sorts to her, apparently. Messed with her head. There was no saving her. Not after all she endured. The sickening things she told me... You were too young to know all this. But your mum... She was never right, Andrew. She was beyond help. A lost cause." She took in a steady breath, closing her eyes as she talked. "Whatever was going on in their heads, I can't say. Nor can I bring myself to think of what happened to those poor girls. The thought still keeps me awake at night."

"And what about Granddad, Nan? What happened to him?" said Drew as he felt his eyes spill sadness. The glow of the red around him was so surreal he wished it were a dream. That he would wake up at any moment, finding himself lying in the comfort of his bed, the sun shining brightly through the curtains.

"He kept raving on about the photographs, threatening to turn them in."

"So, what happened?"

She paused. "He slipped... Hit his head down here." She spoke sharply. "An accident... There on that step."

"How do you know it was an..." Drew coughed suddenly. He felt wheezy and his head felt dizzy. "Accident.... How do you know?"

"I was there..." she looked away to the floor.

"Nan? It wasn't.... you, *was it?* Did you hit him*?*"

"No!" she barked, lifting her stare to meet his. "It was something he drank. Probably some of these chemicals down here found their way into his drink. I couldn't help him," she said, now becoming hysterical. "He couldn't breathe! I was terrified!"

Drew's mind flashed to his bedroom. The feeling on his chest. The tightness and the nausea in his stomach. Was that it? Was this what his granddad had felt?

"He was poisoned," a quiet voice whispered from the corner.

Drew looked over at Becca. Under the circumstances he'd almost forgotten she was there.

She sat still, slowly blinking as her head drooped down, and removed her hand from her head. It was red. Red and blotchy. Not just because of the light. The colour was much different. Darker. And dripping down her skin to her jawline.

"Becca!" he shouted, looking back into her pale, sunken eyes.

"Nan?" he said, tugging his grandmother's sleeve. "What's happening to her?"

"Who?"

"Becca!"

"Becca?" she pondered, focusing her gaze to the corner. "Well, Andrew. That, I'm afraid, was quite unfortunate. Quite unfortunate, indeed."

Bloodline

A year ago

The school bell continued to ring as Becca stepped foot outside the gates. It was an overcast day, grey and gloomy, but that didn't matter. Not to her. Today was the beginning of half-term, and she more than anyone was glad to see the back of that hell hole. She wished once again that she hadn't been so rebellious in her earlier years. That she had just stuck to the guidelines which would have seen her integrated into the local school alongside the normal kids.

Though despite everything, deep down she knew it wasn't meant to be. She knew she could never do it.

For the most part of school life, the slagging off and on-site bullying didn't bother her. Not really. All girls could be complete bitches at times. And being surrounded by nothing but the same sex day after day only encouraged the matter. Boredom can be a funny thing. It wasn't like you could drop the mic and leave whenever the hell you wanted. Just give them all the finger and wander off down the street. You were imprisoned. You lived and breathed their air, every little thing was done together, every moment shared. There was no way to escape it.

Drew Hall was her best friend. It seemed an odd thing to say now, being fifteen and all. She had changed over the last few years. *He* had changed. But that said, the only thing that had changed in their relationship was sex. Not the actual act, of course, but the topic of conversation itself. The gossip at school. The movies. The music. It was all anyone ever spoke of now. But like most things in life, it was the pressure to act that made sex bigger than it really was.

When she and Drew were together, they referenced it only in terms of what others said. Though to be truthful, both were rather skilful at steering the conversation away from themselves if needed. It was always hard to judge how the other felt, and neither wished to show their cards. Instead, they wanted to hold onto their innocence as long as possible.

Becca did like him. Really liked him. And she openly admitted (if only to herself) that she kinda always had. She was pretty sure he felt the same way, too. She knew all too well about people who'd stepped over the friendship line and their relationship had ended in disaster. It was no big secret. Like it or not, that seemed to be the consequence. And this, she thought, was what kept them both in limbo.

As usual, the drive home was long and predictable. The town was always heaving at that time of year with parents collecting their kids on the last day of term.

Families' cars were all packed up and raring to go for that short break away, only too eager to avoid the evening traffic. It was always the same.

"This is ridiculous," complained Becca's dad as he planted his palm to the horn. "Gridlocked. Again!" He slammed his foot on the brake, stopping the car with a jolt. "They bloody need to pull their finger out and do something about these roads. Make them wider or something..." He gave Becca a nudge of his elbow. "Hey, you think I should complain to the council?"

Becca gazed out of her window dreamily. "You do that, Dad," she sighed. She really couldn't give a toss.

It was funny how things had changed between them. Once upon a time Becca considered her dad to be her knight in shining armour. Someone she depended on and confided in. He was her person. She'd even go so far as to say a shoulder to cry on. Yes, he was nothing less than her childhood hero. A man with a gleam in his eye and a heart of gold. These days, however, Becca couldn't so much as tolerate being in the car with him, especially when he began one of his fatherly rants over stuff like this. She couldn't stand it. There were plenty of times she even offered to catch the bus. Persisted would be more like it. Though no matter how much she begged, the walk home was never an option, at least not where her father was concerned. Not after the vanishing of those two young girls some years back. The parents of Burntwood had never been the same after that. Same could be said for her dad.

The car pulled onto the driveway, and she was home at last. Becca unpacked her suitcase by means of chucking most of the contents into piles of clean and dirty laundry. There was little time for her parents that day. A single peck on the cheek would have to do. She changed quickly, smearing on a red shade of lipstick which she'd stolen from her mother's dresser drawer and hidden behind her bookcase for safekeeping. It had been there for months. *Stuck up cow wouldn't notice* she thought. Afterall, her mum owned hundreds of them.

Becca scraped back her hair, tying it up before quickly sliding down the stair rail for the door. Excitedly, she dashed down the garden path and crossed the road. It was still early in the day, but she was hopeful that Drew would be home. If that didn't tell them both exactly how much she cared for him then she didn't know what else would.

She sighed and pondered the thought of whether this weekend might be the first time he kissed her. Not some quick pucker on the lips either, but one of those movie kisses where the world seemed to stop, and she'd do something cringy like go up on tiptoes and kick back her leg.

About to knock, Becca caught movement around the side of the house and instantly assumed it was Drew. She smiled to herself. A tickling sensation swirled in her stomach. Maybe this was it. Maybe he was just teasing her, enticing her with his trail of breadcrumbs as she followed around the side of the house?

She jogged past the large oak tree that to this day still bore a sad looking swing as she pushed herself through the gap of the gate, its bars lost to ivy. There was a lawn with a shed at the bottom and rose bushes and plants bordering either side. Beyond the garden were the woods where they spent endless summers and warm evenings exploring nature's beauty together.

She looked around, confused, and found that Drew was nowhere to be seen.

Becca glanced back at the house and up at the tallest windows. Her gaze was drawn downwards to a steep set of steps and a large open window located at the bottom. The narrow stairway was dug into the brickwork of the house like a tunnel, presenting a deep red glow on approach. She edged closer. Without doubt it was the door to the cellar. She'd never been down there herself, although it was certainly the sort of place where Drew might've hid, believing it amusing to jump out and scare her.

The steps were well worn and covered in moss. Clumps of grass and weeds had broken through the brickwork, trying their best to return it to nature. It was clear that this was a forgotten part of the house.

At the bottom, she tried the door. It was not only locked but looked like it had been sealed shut with hammer and nails. She considered the window. A large rectangular pane opened at the latch. She'd be able to squeeze through with no trouble.

She threw a glance behind her, just in case Drew happened to be standing by with a mischievous grin on his face. He wasn't. So, without hesitation, Becca decided to go for it.

First, she stuck her head inside as her eyes adjusted to the light. It appeared to be some kind of dark room. Not that it was in any way surprising. She had always known Drew's granddad had been a professional photographer, but the thought never occurred to her that he'd have his very own setup down here, too.

She pulled up the latch, easily squeezing herself inside before slipping down onto the floor below.

Her blood ran cold as she turned to face the far side wall, observing the pictures of two small girls staring back at her. The missing girls. Yes, she was sure of it. And if that wasn't bad enough, surrounding them were photographs of people she knew herself – her and Drew included.

"Becca?" a confused voice called out from behind her. She hadn't noticed the figure standing motionless in the corner. The darkness and dim light made it so much harder to see her surroundings.

"The front door no longer good enough for you? Is that it?"

"No, no, Mrs Hall." Becca held up her hands and waved that off. "That's not it, really. I…"

"Yes…?"

"I just thought Drew was… in here. I thought…"

"Well, Drew's out." The old woman looked dramatically around the cellar. "As you can see, he's not around here, is he?"

"No… I guess not. I'm sorry…" she turned back slowly to the wall. "Mrs Hall, what is-"

The old woman was staring daggers. "It's quite frankly none of your business," she remarked, walking closer to see her.

Just then, Becca noticed a photograph. It stuck out to her as unlike all the others. It was Drew's father! Holding hands with one of those girls from the newspapers. A missing girl. She couldn't quite place the name.

"What!" She handled the print. "What is this?"

"Put that down!"

"That's that girl…. You know, the one that vanished. I remember her face from the news."

"Put that down, you little whore!" snarled the old woman. "You're just like them all! You know that?"

"Sorry?" asked Becca, her body edging back to the wall.

"You! You harlots come around our men, trying to take what you want. And then, when you don't get your way, it's them who get into trouble!"

Becca's heart was really pounding. For a second she thought she was going to throw up.

"I'm… I'm sorry… Look, I'm just going to go… alright?" she turned and headed for the stairs. Like a flash, her sweaty palm gripped the rail as her foot pushed up from the step.

254

Whack! Something rapid struck clean across her head. It felt blunt and cold, accompanied by a blinding light that flashed like gunfire before her eyes. Becca passively slumped down to the dust covered floor.

Whack! Another strike came plunging down, finding its mark below her temple. Only this time, Becca felt no pain. There was simply nothing. Nothing but the sudden urge to sleep.

The stomach cramps began like someone flicked a switch, leaving Drew doubled over in agony. He stared long and hard at Becca. Despite the ruddy hew, her skin looked almost translucent. Ghostlike. Tears rolled down the groove of her smooth, rosy cheek, trailing past her red glossy lipstick. She reached out, pleading for Drew to hold her. It was a sound he'd never heard before. Static flowed out of Becca's open mouth, garbling her words as she stretched out hard to reach him.

"Becca!" he cried, clenching at his stomach as he tried so desperately to touch her. To be with her. To feel her hand once more knitted in his.

The red light flickered with madness, throwing shadows about the space before painting the room in blackness. When the light returned, Becca was gone.

Drew's head twisted from left to right, his mind working ten to the dozen as he peered through the haze to find her. She could not be seen. The thought of her swirled around his head. The image was so vivid. So powerful. His childhood friend. His first true love. Vanished.

"No..." he mumbled softly. "No!" Drew looked up at his nan. His face filled with hatred as the spasms took hold of his body. "What. Did. You. Do!"

"Me?" His nan placed a hand to her chest. "*She... She* was the one who broke into the house," the delicate figure shrieked. "*She* was the one who came down here. Poking that big nose of hers where it wasn't wanted."

"When?" Drew tried to stand but couldn't. The knots in his stomach tightened. "When did she..."

"Oh, that day, you know?" she huffed. "When you started to do that after school training with your teacher."

"But that was..." It all came flooding back. One day in the cloak room Mr Rogers had told him that he had good potential. The kind of frame a young man could build up. Maybe even make a career from. Drew had never been the most impressive athlete at school. Not by any means. Yet the young lad's determination was always strong in his favour. Besides, he always wanted to look his best for Becca. That, in truth, was his real goal. He was finally going to ask her out for a date. Not as friends either, but an *actual* date. A real-life boyfriend and girlfriend type thing. But staying behind after school had meant he hadn't been around to see Becca as soon as she arrived back for the holidays. He'd missed her. However, it was a chance he was selfishly willing to take.

Drew remembered that weekend like it was yesterday. He sat on the porch steps and wondered where in God's blazes she was. It was never like Becca to not visit him as soon as she stepped foot back in Burntwood. Some would even say, completely unlike her. Then the moment finally came.

Becca's parents had pounded on the door, disturbing his nan's peaceful slumber and delivering the news that she had not returned home. Drew was beside himself. Sick with worry. He'd even gone so far to say he felt part of him had been stolen away. He felt selfish as he stared out of his bedroom window night after night, watching as Becca's parents came and went with such grief. He slept restlessly those next few nights. Those few nights soon rolled into weeks. He waited, wishing that someone, *anyone,* would bring news to the neighbourhood. But no matter how much he wanted it, no matter how hard he prayed, still, no news came. He repeatedly consoled himself by the mantra of no-news-is-good-news, but deep down, suppressed by his fragile mind, he knew it was all false hope.

After a few months the neighbourhood returned to a semblance of normal. The police patrols seemed less frequent. And despite the ongoing precautions, the parents of Burntwood allowed their children to venture back onto the streets unsupervised. Drew however, could not forget so easily. How could he? After everything they'd been through together. He was torn apart. Totally distraught.

It wasn't long after that his nan had decided to arrange an appointment to see a local doctor who prescribed Drew some small yellow tablets to ease his mind and body. Drew knew what they were. He'd heard so much about antidepressants growing up. And now, everyone who was anyone was taking them. It was nothing special. *He* was nothing special. Still, Drew swallowed them down all the same. There was truly no fight left in him.

At some stage the tablets did what they were supposed to, burying the fact that Becca was gone and locking away his feelings of the events deep within the catacombs of his mind. He began to eat again. Even began to smile. The restless nights he had once endured flickered away like a dying candle. There came a time where Drew had never felt so healthy. He felt like a new young man. An enthusiastic man with his whole life ahead of him. More importantly, he felt kind of happy. He'd almost forgotten what that felt like.

It came as no surprise that Becca's family moved away, leaving the house to remain abandoned. Many said it was to be expected. People guessed they couldn't live with the torment anymore.

From the kitchen window Drew's nan would often watch him as he wandered up the street alone, stopping in front of the old Bradshaw residence before sneaking himself through a broken window. He never returned home until dark. The old woman said nothing at first. She always thought it was best not to pry. After all, he'd been through the wars those last few months. But as the visits became frequent and the night stretched longer, the old woman finally took it upon herself to ask.

"What happened, Nan?"
"Drew, it doesn't matter now."

"Doesn't matter?" he croaked. "You killed her! My one true friend. Why? Nan, why?" he snapped."

"Andrew," his nan said evenly. "She saw the board."

"So?"

"So.... The lass had already seen too much. Even started asking me questions... If I hadn't played my cards right the old bill would've been swarming this place within the hour. I couldn't let that happen. I wouldn't. Why... You would've been taken away from me, Drew. Placed into care. They'd have found him..."

Silence pierced the air.

"Found... Who?" The words formed a lump in his throat as he spoke. "Where. Is. He?" He growled, both hands still pressed hard to his gut. His fists clenching tighter. "Where's your husband?"

The old woman fidgeted with her wedding band before her stare travelled off to the wall. "Arthur's... in there," she added plainly. "Behind the partition thingy." She momentarily looked guilty. "He may be gone from this world, but he is still very much with us." She closed her eyes and breathed calmly. "Don't you feel him?"

"Feel... what?"

"Why, his presence, Andrew. That bitter chill that seeps into your bones at night. The restless shadows that wander the house, gone in the blink of an eye. Not to mention the stench. For a time, I thought it was only I who sensed him. Only me, and me alone who suffered the man's unfinished business. My punishment for what I did. A torture I shall never escape."

"Unfinished business?" Drew groaned cluelessly. "What unfinished business?"

"To warn you..."

"Me?"

"One can only think so. At least, I see no other reason for him to hang around in limbo. Certainly not for me, that's damn sure. Not after what I did."

Drew curled himself up into a ball, fighting the urge to scream as the breath hissed through his teeth. "And Becca?" he barely managed to ask.

"Becca..." his nan paused again. "She's over in the corner." The woman stretched out her arm and pointed one crooked finger through the darkness. "Back there. Behind the old boiler. I had little place left to put her. The lass is..." She slid her tongue across her lips.

"What? She's What?"

"Tucked away in a sack."

Drew heaved violently. If he didn't feel like he was going to vomit before, he sure as hell did now. "A sack?" He retched again. "You... left her *in a sack!*"

"I had no choice!" barked his nan. "The body began to decompose. The smell... that wretched stench was getting worse. You tell me, what else was I meant to do with her? I don't have the strength to carry her nor the constitution to cut her up and throw her into bin bags. There was no other option, Andrew. Don't you see?"

"But..." Drew coughed again, hacking up phlegm as he retched. His lungs burned like fire that spread throughout his chest. "Nan? What's... what's happening? Why am I...?"

The frail woman bent down with the crack of her knees, offering him the cup to his mouth as she slowly began to tip. "Drink up now."

Drew jerked his neck, smacking the cup clean out of her hand.

"You... you've put something in it." He coughed again, sensing the taste of metal that slathered over his tongue.

"Andrew, you must understand I never wanted it to be like this. You are everything to me. Things... just got out of my control. I thought... I thought I could fix things. I thought I could protect you. I did for a time..."

He coughed once more, igniting the invisible flames inside of him. He gasped mightily, struggling to catch his breath.

"You put something... in the... tea?" he managed as his focus blurred out of view.

"I did," his nan admitted as she walked towards the wall replete with photos. Her fingertips grazed the prints, carefully unpinning each one and collecting them into a messy pile. Drew watched her from the floor in a daze, his stomach spasming, sending waves of pain washing through his body.

He wasn't aware of the fire until he smelt the smoke. With all his might, Drew mustered the strength to turn, twisting his body only to see his nan bent over the draining board. Flames escaped the sink beside her. All the evidence. The whole truth gone up in smoke. Drew tried to speak, his mouth gasping like a fish stolen from the water, knowing what was next to come.

"Please, Drew. Don't worry." She shuffled, picking up the cup before walking to the half side table. "That sensation you're feeling. I assure you... it's quite normal. There's no need to be afraid." She poured another plastic cup of the tea. "It didn't have to be this way, you know?" she grumbled quietly to herself. "I didn't want to hurt any of them. I'm not a killer..." She sobbed. "I wasn't.... once."

Drew tried to speak, emitting a helpless gurgle.

"Your parents are what caused this, not me..." his nan continued. "I was left to mop up their wrongdoing! The mess! I was only trying to look out for you..."

Drew felt his body give way as his limbs spread lifelessly across the hard, wooden boards. Her meaningless words sounded like he was deep underwater. It was as if he were drowning. Drowning in pure air.

Drew screamed desperately from within. And as everything began to blur, the air around him turned undeniably thin. Sweat poured in streams from the crease of his brow as the small red space pushed him tighter and tighter to the floor. His eyes rolled involuntarily, unable to gain the focus they once had. And just as his mind turned blank and his body fell limp, the dark veil of unconsciousness gripped him as his nan lifted the cup to her lips. After that, only her soft voice managed to reach him through the darkness. A gentle whisper. "Sleep well, dear heart."

Epilogue

It was strange to think the house smelt somewhat new, though it was not obvious judging by the outside appearance. The old building sat perched slightly higher than the others in the street. A sort of heritage landmark, symbolizing how the great traditional British home used to be.

Bryn squinted into the setting sun. His expression painted with satisfaction and accomplishment as the last of the day's heat washed clean over his face. It went without saying that Bryn was proud of what he'd achieved for his new family. Overjoyed, would be more precise. And why the hell not? God only knew he'd earned it, working seven days a week and any hours he could scrounge. Days. Nights. You name it, the poor sod did it. And after years of hard work and graft, building up his own carpentry businesses from scratch, he'd finally managed to get back onto the property ladder, to squiggle his signature down on that dotted line. He had waited years for this. Yes, the time had finally come for Bryn to reap his reward. A new home. A fresh start for his newly formed clan: his partner Kim and stepdaughter, Josie. And as the last of the removal vans rolled away from the pebbled driveway and disappeared off down the narrow winding street, Bryn leaned back against the rotting garden gate, placing both hands on his hips. He sighed aloud, taking in the view before him.

Bryn was always fond of the crooked looking place. Even as a young child, he'd obsess over its long wooden porch and period style windows, sure that in time it would be a place to call his own. All he had to do was be patient. The old Victorian structure had certainly seen its fair share of better days. As did the surrounding grounds. There was certainly no doubt about that. Despite it all, the general upkeep of broken guttering, fallen shingles, and damp wasn't enough to sway him from this once in a lifetime purchase. After all, there was nothing he'd noticed that a little spit shine wouldn't fix. And if adding a little extra elbow grease was what it took to finally see their rental days behind them, then God damn it, he'd do everything within his power to make it happen. No matter the cost. Besides, he was a professional carpenter.

As the sunset mellowed in the distance, a tiredness ran through his body. The man felt content, tired but content. From way up high a crow peeked its beak from the highest chimney and cried to a blood thirsty sun.

"Perfect!" Bryn muttered irritably to himself. "If it isn't one thing it's an..." With the cuff of his unbuttoned sleeve, Bryn smeared the sweat off his temple. He didn't need this. Not only were there another one hundred and one things to do before the day was through, but now he had to somehow find a way to gut out the chimney and remove any evidence of the nest before Kim found out. Especially if he knew what was good for him. Time was not on his side.

"You just going to stand there admiring the house, or are you actually going to give me a hand with dinner?" His partner, Kim, frowned from the doorway. Somehow, she managed to look just as exhausted as he felt, which was difficult to believe considering she hadn't so much as lifted a flippin' finger that day.

"Yes, dear. Be there in a tick." He gestured a nod to the house. "Just taking in the sensational view," he replied whilst throwing her a 'shut the fuck up' sort of smile.

For the last few days, they'd been all hyped up on adrenaline and the pure joy of having something grand to call home. And why the hell not? That was, however, before the realisation of their monthly outgoings stepped in, not to mention the outstanding solicitors' fees, property surveys, and insurances that would soon be overdue. At this rate, they'd be eating dry rice crispies for a year. But that didn't matter. Not to Bryn. His dream house was finally his own. A debt finally paid to himself. He embraced the thought, drinking back the sight before him.

Bryn grabbed another box from around his feet and steadily walked up the driveway.

"Upstairs!" Kim instructed, directing Bryn with a single point. "It's Josie's!" Everything she said was done with a playful giggle recently. He loved to see her like this, almost punch-drunk on life itself. Kim's old job had brought her down dramatically over the past few years, stressing her out with tedious hours and endless deadlines that were near impossible to meet. Bryn never said a word. Being a relatively new member of the Dobson clan, he knew it was not his place. But he'd known all too well what was really going on. He'd seen it countless times before. If the boss didn't like you, they'd inevitably break you. It wasn't rocket science, just simple management tactics. And poor unfortunate Kim could take only so much.

After years of mental torture, she eventually convinced herself to pack it all in. And in good time, too. As luck would have it, a new opportunity opened up just around the corner from their new home. And Kim, as keen as she was, snapped up the job in a heartbeat. She became some sort of project manager for a local restoration scheme, funded by the Burntwood

Council. She'd only been there a week and already she'd got stuck into restoring some run-down church just on the outskirts of town. The money wasn't all that great. But to be truthful, it didn't matter. Not to him anyway. Kim was a whole new person now – not that Bryn didn't love her before. But now she was different. Young and excited again. There was a twinkle in her eyes as she spoke. A playfulness about her smile. Not to mention her keen enthusiasm in the bedroom.

"Where d'you want this, Josie?" said Bryn, entering his stepdaughter's room.

"Don't you knock?" snapped Josie.

"Sorry, I just –."

"You can't just walk in like that, Bryn. It's an invasion of my privacy. I have rights, you know?"

"Rights?" questioned Bryn with a confused stare on his face.

"Yeah, rights. It ain't difficult. My room. My space. At least have the decency to respect it. Aren't you meant to be some kind of lawyer or something?"

Bryn shuffled the box in her arms. "I'm a carpentry safety inspector, Josie."

"Whatever," she shrugged whilst continuing to scroll through her phone. Despite all the endless hype, Josie wasn't so keen on the move. And who could blame her? Her best friends were all on the other side of town; not exactly a stone's throw away. And worse still, the superfast wi-fi her newly acquired dad promised was yet to be set up. Her teenage angst and mood swings were heavily kicking in. Bryn expected as much. It was bound to happen. After all, he was the new man in her life now. The father figure that Josie would eventually wonder how she ever did without. Time was all Bryn needed. Time and patience. That's all. And in due course, Josie's hardened shell would soften and the father-daughter relationship that Bryn had dreamed of would blossom. He smiled inside. Truth be told, it hadn't been the easiest year since the passing of his first wife. Bryn had all but decided he'd never experience love again. Not in this life. He had neither the strength or desire to seek it. And as each month slowly passed by, each night alone with his thoughts, the noticeable absence of his childhood sweetheart only grew stronger, sinking Bryn into a dark and dismal abyss. A lonely place, where he was destined to stay. Who'd have thought that only one year later, he'd be standing where he was now. That after one car service, five business trips, fifty-three visits at his local pub, twenty-one boxes of cornflakes, twelve new pairs of socks and a routine prostate exam at his local quack's, he'd have a new woman by his side. A caring soul. Someone who understood what he'd been through. The pain he still felt inside, eating at him like ravenous illness. Someone who not only required his love, but more importantly for Bryn to know his worth. He was thankful to be part of something special, a real family again. And furthermore, a daughter waiting for him to prove himself. He was sure in time he would succeed. Bryn had been given a second shot at happiness. An opportunity to be the father he wanted to be. It was a chance to make amends and leave his sorrows behind him. A chance to do things right.

"I can't live like this!" Josie grumbled, tossing her phone at her feet.

"I'm... I'm sorry?" asked Bryn, still with the box in hand. "Live like... what, exactly?"

"Like this!" she hissed. "First you asked me and my mum to move across town away from everyone I know, and now this..." She nudged the phone with her toes. "No network! You promised me, Bryn," she whined. "You said it'd be sorted. So... where is it?"

Bryn shuffled the box in his arms. "Josie... it's a ten-minute ride across town to your friends. Twenty minutes if you wish to take the bus. Hardly halfway around the world now, is it?" She didn't respond to that. "And secondly, I received a text this morning saying that the technician would be here to check the lines first thing tomorrow. It's an old house. Deal with it."

"But you said-"

"I know what I said, Josie."

"So...?" she flared her nostrils.

"So... what?" he replied, cocking his brow as he said it.

"Well, you think that's fair?"

"Frankly, my dear I don't give a damn."

"Bryn!"

"Look, Josie, life isn't all shits and giggles. You can't expect to have every bloody thing your heart desires as and when you want it." He took a deep breath. "As promised, you'll have internet tomorrow. Now, please. Give me a chance. I'm trying here... In the meantime, stop being so dramatic and get your head out of that damn screen."

"And do... what exactly?" she huffed, folding her arms with attitude. "There's nothing to do around this shit hole."

"I don't know..." He looked about the cluttered hall. "Read a book or something. There's a lot of stuff in the garage left by the previous owner. Papers, too. Go scrummage around before they get donated or thrown in the bin. You never know, something might tickle your fancy. Your mum's copy of Twilight is there somewhere and some book about shades of grey. I thought you girls loved that stuff!"

"Nobody reads that shit anymore, Dad."

"No... No, I guess you're right," he sighed, feeling the ache spread up his arms. "Josie?"

"Hmm?"

"The box. Where do you want it?"

She shrugged again. "Don't care."

"I can put it in the cellar, if you prefer?"

"You're not funny, Bryn," she muttered, glancing back down to her phone; the only connection to her past.

"Why don't you go have a look around while it's still light out? You've got a garden now, and there's woods out yonder."

"Great. Bears, too, probably."

"There's no bears in-" He observed the disappointed look plastered across her face. "Not in Burntwood, love. You're more likely to run into a badger with a nasty disposition."

"Don't be such a boomer, Bryn."

"I'm not..." he sighed, dropping the box to the floor. "Tell you what, I'll try to be more, like, groovy, man, shall I?"

She stood up and barged past with the flick of her hair. "Case and point," she muttered as her feet thudded down the stairs

"Hey, Josie! Whatcha up to?" Kim sang out from the kitchen. "Fancy helping me with dinner? It's meatballs and pasta shapes, your favourite?"

Josie's eyes rolled. "I'm not fuckin' five," she muttered as she slipped on her shoes by the door.

"Hey, where are you off to?" asked Kim as she cranked up a song on the radio.

"I'm just gonna... go grab some fresh air real quick."

With a stomp in her step, Josie's boots scuffed along the pebbled path until she soon found herself at the garage. To her surprise, the door was still half open, a clear indication that Bryn's task of carrying in the rest of the boxes was yet to be completed. Maybe she had been a little too hard on him just now? Afterall, the move wasn't entirely his fault. Her mum had been talking for years about the concept of upsizing to a house located on the border of town. Out of the way of the hustle and bustle. It was no real news flash to Josie. She just never expected her mum would actually go through with it. Let alone with some guy who'd she'd been courting for little more than a year. That said, for his faults, Bryn wasn't all that bad. A little straightlaced perhaps. Not to mention the man's constant need to father her. Josie had spent her entire life without so much as a manly figure about the house to depend on. And if she had managed for the last fifteen years, she sure as hell didn't need one shadowing over her now.

Josie looked back onto the street and up to the sky. At least it was still sunny. Well, kind of, she thought as the sunset blossomed upon the evening clouds with a flourish of red and gold. It kind of reminded her of one of those shit abstract paintings. The kind where you had to narrow your eyes to truly appreciate its worth. She'd learnt that one in school. Though truth be told, she never understood how squinting both eyes could improve your outlook on art. In fact, all it did was make bad art look less unsightly. Maybe that was the point? She shrugged, crouched beneath the rolling door, and flicked the light switch on the wall.

Just as her new wannabe stepdad mentioned, in the corner of the garage, huddled away in the one place left untouched by damp, stood a large pile of flimsy boxes. Junk to be more precise. Unwanted belongings left behind by the previous owner. Books, papers, a stack of old television magazines. Kitchen utensils, clothes, a small broken radio, and a set of ornaments wrapped in grey coloured tissue paper.

WANT TO RETURN AN ITEM?

For items purchased online, you can send them back for a full refund within 28 days, provided it has not been used and the original packaging and swing tickets, where applicable, need to still be in place. You can return these items via our online returns portal.

1 Repack your items. No packaging, no problem! Just pop your items in something non see-through, sealable & waterproof.

2 Visit help.usc.co.uk. You will need your order number and email/last 4 digits of your phone number.

3 Select your preferred return option (print returns label at home or in store options). Once you have processed your return in the portal you're ready to post it off.

4 We will keep you up to date on your returned items via email.

For further information regarding returns, please visit help.usc.co.uk

Josie scouted through the clutter of boxes, hopeful of finding something valuable. An old necklace. Or a vintage ring perhaps. She could dream, couldn't she? There had to be something amongst this heap of junk that would momentarily pique her interest. If not, what was all this for?

She browsed through the collection of wrinkly paperback books, tossing those by unknown authors over her shoulder as she delved her hands deeper into the box. Still, there was nothing. Nothing but a scraggy old kitchen cloth and a mouldy old set of doilies.

"Jo. Dinner!" The distant sound of her mother's voice echoed its way to her ears.

She huffed irritably, pushing aside the tired looking box and climbed back up from her knees. "Pile of shite," she uttered, stubbing the box with her foot. She was about to leave, too, but just as she turned to walk away, an object hidden in the messy jumble caught her attention. A small box. At first glance, it appeared to be something of a shoe box, its small, crumpled lid held in place with the use of a single ribbon. Josie didn't hold her breath. Knowing her luck it would mostly likely contain nothing but a pair of stinky old trainers. That, or mishmash collection of water-stained cutlery. Regardless, Josie was willing to take a gander. What did she have to lose?

Carelessly, she barged her way through the disorganised mess, stretching as she scooped up the box with a strenuous grunt. Impatiently her fingers picked at the fabric, loosening the entwined knots before gnawing the ribbon between her teeth. At long last, the fraying sash came free and she snatched it away with a yank. She flicked up the lid, allowing it to fall freely to her feet. Any hope Josie had of discovering something worthwhile was dashed to pieces in an instant. There appeared to be nothing but papers inside. Cut out

273

snippets of old newspapers folded neatly, one on top of the other.

Josie frowned and dug her fingers beneath the rustling papers. She never understood why people found the need to keep such things. Her mum was a prime example. During the nineties some British princess had died. A fatal car collision abroad, apparently. A devastation to the nation. Or so her mum had described. Any newspaper articles featuring the princess, Kim would take it upon herself to save, storing them away within a folder under her bed. Never to be seen again. People could be so odd.

It was then Josie found something that caused her to wonder. There were photographs stored there. Black and white Polaroids. And although slightly damaged due to the storage condition, Josie found herself locked in a daze as she studied the images at hand. They appeared to be some vintage wedding shots, taken back in the day. She shuffled the photos in her hands, each time coming back to the first.

"Hello... Who are you?" Josie whispered to herself as the woman in white stared back through the print. She looked radiant. A picture-perfect example of how every bride should be. Beside her, a tall man stood smiling at the camera, half his face faded from years of water damage. Josie smiled a little. She didn't know why, but there was something warm and comforting about the image of the newlywed couple. A sort of fuzziness inside which spoke out to her. That was how happiness was meant to look.

"Josie! Food! Now!" Her mother's voice returned from the house.

"Just give me a sec, will you! *God!*"

Her eyes returned to the photo, half considering keeping it for herself. It would've been a shame to see it thrown out with the rest of this trash. Without a second thought, she dashed out from the garage, tucking the photo safely into her pocket. It was getting darker now as she walked back up the path, noticing the street lamps come to life with a burning amber glow.

"Hiya!" A soft voice yelled from the curb.

At first, Josie froze on the stoop, noticing the lonesome figure on the footpath. Her stomach dropped. That was all she bloody needed right now, some fuckin' know-it-all adolescent girl wanting to be her new bestie.

Joise gritted her teeth. "Uh… Hey…," she replied, edging closer, surprised to see a teenage girl with long blonde hair and light coloured makeup standing under the dimly cast light .

"Just moved in then, have you?" The girl looked up at the house.

Not looking all too happy about it, Josie nodded in return and shoved her phone down her bra.

"Well…" continued the girl. "I'd love to tell you it's excitement central here, but unfortunately, it's not. Far from it actually. The whole estate has gone downhill over the years… It's a bit of a dive really."

Josie threw a polite chuckle her way, stopping at the border of the lawn. This girl actually seemed alright. Probably about her age, too, if not a little older.

"I'm Josie," she found herself saying on impulse, only to feel a little awkward for doing so. "Nice to know I'm not the only one around here who thinks this place is kinda lame."

"I live back there, just across the street," she pointed a thumb over her shoulder. "You know, my boyfriend used to live in your house."

"Did he?" Josie cocked her head back to the place she was now to call her home.

The girl shrugged sadly as though she were deep in thought. "Yes, but... he's not around anymore."

"Oh..."

A soft breeze tumbled down the open street, catching the naked trees and fluttering the girl's dress as she spoke. "None of them are around anymore…"

"None of them?" Josie asked, puzzled. What was she going on about?

The girl stepped backwards, her heels balancing off the curb. "Sad, isn't it?" she mumbled.

"What is?" Josie nearly barked.

"What happened here…" The girl paused. Her eyes watering as she listened to the howling wind wave over the rooftop. "Those. Poor. Souls."

Josie slammed the door without a care as she entered into the house, allowing it to jitter off the wall and swing on its hinges behind her.

In the kitchen, a large steaming bowl was placed on the table's centre, throwing out the scent of rich tomatoes and herbs as Kim portioned the food onto their plates.

"Shut the door, why don't you," frowned Kim, settling herself down in a chair.

Bryn made his way across the room, opening a cupboard and pulling out the only bottle of dry red wine. "Food's getting cold, kiddo." He winked playfully as he struggled to remove the cork.

Josie stood motionless in the doorway. Her fists trembling as her blood boiled red in her cheeks.

"You alright, hun?" asked Kim, tilting her glass to the bottle.

Josie breathed in deeply. "Why didn't you tell me?"

"Tell you?" mimicked Bryn inquisitively. The bottle *clonked* upon the table's surface. "Tell you... What?"

Her voice grew louder. "Don't play games with me, Bryn!"

"Josie," her mother calmly interrupted. "If you're not going to tell us what's got your knickers in a twist, how on earth are we meant to know what you're blabbering on about?"

"Ask him!" Josie's stare hardened.

With a heavy hand, Kim placed down her fork. "Bryn, what is she implying?" she sighed. All she wanted was a quiet family dinner. Why did every meal have to be ruined by drama?

"I haven't the faintest idea," replied Bryn, knitting his fingers below his chin. "Please, Josie, do enlighten us... Then perhaps we could enjoy the food that your mum has kindly prepared."

"Don't do that!" Josie pointed her brightly painted nail at Bryn.

"Do what?" He held up his hands in surrender. "I'm not doing anything!"

"You know. I know you do!"

"Enough!" yelled Kim. Her hand plummeted down, forcing the plateware to quake. "For heaven's sake, Josie. Whatever you have to say just spit it out, won't you!"

Josie bit hard on her lip. "People died here, Mum!"

"Died?" Kim's expression mellowed. "What do you mean, died?"

"Murdered," Josie continued. "Two old people and some kids. Here. In this house. It was all over the news so she said."

"Wait a second," demanded Bryn, sliding the plate from under his nose. "Who said? Who exactly have you been talking to?"

Josie composed herself, pulling out a chair and pouring a drink of water from the plastic jug. "Some girl who lives across the street. She told me everything that happened here. This place hasn't had an owner since. Explains why you got it so cheap."

"Girl…" Bryn shook his head. "What girl?".

"I just told you, from across the street."

"Josie," Bryn hesitated, catching Kim's glare as he paused. "I met our neighbours opposite this morning. They don't have a daughter. They don't have any children for that matter. Just a frisky dachshund named Dwayne."

"But… I spoke to her. Just now, outside. Said she'd lived there all her life. Wanted to warn me."

Kim grabbed her daughter's hand, clenching it tightly to comfort her. "Jo darling, maybe it was all just a silly prank? A chance to scare the new kid on the block?"

"A cruel joke," added Bryn as he tossed back a gulp of his wine.

Josie flinched her hand away in reflex. "No, Mum. This was different. It wasn't a prank," she strongly insisted. "They found two bodies in the garden. Four in the cellar. All poisoned. She even described the old couple in the photo down to a T. I hadn't even shown her! Didn't even mention I'd found it."

"Photo?" Kim snarled dubiously. "What in blazes are you on about?"

As quick as a flash, Josie dug deep into her pocket, slapping the image on the table before coasting it across to her mother. "Here!"

With a heavy sigh, Kim sucked in her cheeks and held the image toward the light, carefully studying the figures. "Why, this was taken at St Mary's."

"The old church you're restoring?" asked Bryn mid sip, drifting away from the subject.

Kim shot a quick smile in return. "Yes," she pointed. "You can tell by the grey sandstone situated here on the porch entrance." Her attention panned back to the couple. "You say this girl knew these people?"

"Yes!" Josie cried out loud.

"Well God knows, I'm no photographer. But at a guess this looks to have been taken during the mid-forties. Maybe even fifties. It's rather difficult to tell due to the extent of the damage."

"So?"

"So… This young girl must've been acquainted with them during their senior years. Maybe one of them showed her this wedding photo. Old folk tend to enjoy doing such things. A trip down memory lane so to speak."

"What does that have to do with anything!" Josie spat. "They died here."

"People die all the time…" Bryn exhaled. "I guarantee that any old house could count a death or two."

"But not like this!" Josie brushed her hair through her hand, trying to contain her frustration. "Come on! Why am I the only one disturbed by this? Death by poisoning isn't normal. Neither is finding a clump of bodies scattered in your own backyard!"

"Alright, alright," hushed Kim, rubbing her daughter by the shoulder. She looked at the image a final time, admiring the handsome couple before handing it over to Bryn. "Did you know about this?"

Bryn shot Kim a look of confusion.

"About the house, I mean?"

279

He removed the napkin from his collar, dabbing it gently to his lips. "Let me see that." he said, raising the photo to his eyes before letting it drop to the table. His tongue skimmed his teeth, and before he said more, Bryn reached out calmly for the bottle. "Yes." In that moment he felt their eyes burn into him.

"Yes?" Kim repeated. "Yes... What?"

"Yes, I knew," answered Bryn as more wine glugged into his glass. "You must understand. It wasn't the reason why I put down the offer. I'm no murder house adrenaline junkie. Nor did I want it only for its affordable price."

Kim leaned back in her chair, the empty glass twizzling between her fingertips. "What exactly are you trying to say then?"

It was difficult for Bryn to explain, more now than ever. But still he had to try "It's just... Ever since I was a kid, riding my bike through the street, I always dreamt that one day this place would be mine. A place for me to raise a family. A place for happy times and long summer nights on the porch. As I grew older and the years passed by, especially in more recent years, that dream seemed to have become unreachable. Particularly after the passing of..." Bryn croaked as he sensed the touch of Kim's hand lovingly caressing his. "Then you came into my life. Both of you." He gave Josie a heartfelt smile. "At long last, I just wanted to fulfil that dream, you know? Reach for the stars and all that." He squeezed Kim's hand in return. "Yes, I knew about what happened here. To this day I feel disgusted by it. What occurred to those people... Well, I think it's best not to say. The point I'm trying to make is..."

"What, honey. What is it?"

Bryn glanced from one face to the other before staring out into space. "Houses don't kill people, my love. They don't ruin people's lives or destroy families.

Only people can do that. People hurt people." He cleared his throat before continuing. "Yes, I was told what history this house bears. And yes, it was damn right selfish of me not to say anything to you. To the both of you. Truth be told, I thought the subject wouldn't be mentioned. I hoped it wouldn't. Not now of all times anyway. All I wanted was a fresh start. A new chapter with my new family. You and Josie."

Kim ate in every word he uttered with an admiring gleam in her eye. "Oh, Bryn. You needn't have kept this from me," she whispered. "This is all you really want?"

"Truly," he nodded, drinking back Kim's beauty as she reached across the table, planting a peck on his lips. "Thank you," she smiled.

"Mum!" barked Josie, standing quickly and knocking the chair back off its legs.

"Josie... Calm down. I –."

"I won't!" she replied angrily. "How can you be so fine about all this? It doesn't bother you?"

"Well..." Kim stumbled for words. "I'd be lying if I said I wasn't a tad uneasy about living somewhere where something so inhumane took place. But Bryn... he's right. What happened, happened. There's no going back now or denying it. This house can't hurt us. If anything, we'll become stronger as a family. Our happiness will outshine this house's morbid past. Give it a chance, Josie, you'll see."

Without another word, Josie barged out of sight, her feet thudding up the stairs as the door slammed shut to her bedroom.

Bryn sucked in an exasperated breath, chewing his bottom lip as he considered what to say. Given the circumstances, only one thing felt suitable. "I'm sorry, Kim," he uttered. "I'm a fool. An inconsiderate fool."

Removing the half-empty plates from the table, Kim stood over her partner, massaging the back of his shoulders. "You're no fool, Bryn. A little spontaneous, I'll give you that. But I do love you."

"And Josie?"

"I'll talk to her tomorrow. She'll come round. This move has been a difficult change for her. She'll adjust."

"You think?" asked Bryn.

"In time, my sweet, in time."

He looked up over his shoulder as he pulled her in a close embrace. How could he have carried on life without her? The way she looked at him. The touch of her skin against his. She was all he could ask for and more. "Thank you."

She winked in return, kissing him sweetly on the forehead. "Come. It's late. I have an early start tomorrow. I'm due at the chapel at six."

"You head on up," replied Bryn, flicking away the photograph and guiding Kim onto his lap. She giggled like a schoolgirl as he enticed her for one last kiss. "I'll clean up down here. Go get yourself comfy. I'll be right behind you."

By the time Bryn wandered into the bedroom, Kim was already curled up in bed. He changed quietly, slipped back the covers and snuck his way between the sheets.

"There you are," Kim sighed tiredly. "Thought you might have lost your way. What kept you?"

"Nothing. Just my thoughts," he whispered whilst shuffling his body next to hers.

Kim rubbed her eyes in an attempt to remain awake. "Thoughts? Is something troubling you?"

"Far from it," he smiled through the darkness. "I just popped in to see Josie. You know, just to see how she was doing."

Kim let out a short burst of laughter. "And how did that go?"

"OK. She was a little on guard at first, but as we talked, she soon began to mellow. I think... I might actually be getting somewhere with her."

With the rustle of sheets, Kim manoeuvred onto her side, catching the light of a silvery moon. "That's great, hun, really." She breathed out slowly, both knees curled up to her chest. "Hold me," she invited him.

Bryn moved in closer, nestling his body against Kim's. His hand touched her delicately, following the curve of her thigh and coming to rest at her hip.

"Cold, my dear?" he asked, sensing an involuntary quiver.

"Freezing!" she mumbled, wrapping the cover tighter around her neck. "We seem to have a draft in here."

For a moment they lay in silence, listening to the creaks and groans of the old house as it settled. The wind surrounded the grounds, whistling through the nearby trees and rattling the windows with each gust. Bryn rested with his eyes wide open, satisfied and grateful for the luck that had unexpectedly struck his path. Timing had certainly been kind to him. There was no denying that. And once more, Bryn couldn't help but think long and hard, appreciating the favourable fortune he'd received. A devoted partner. The house that was destined to be his. His mind flashed back to the photograph left abandoned on the kitchen table. Of the man and woman on their wedding day. So happy, so full of love that they were destined to share it forever. To remain together forever. It had been so long since he'd looked upon them.

Kim groaned gibberish, uttering words of nonsense as she drifted between dream and reality.

Bryn leaned in closer, catching the fragrance of her short red hair and dropping his head to the pillow.

"Goodnight," she mumbled faintly, embracing his presence with a single squeeze.

And with little more than a whisper, Bryn softly combed the hair from Kim's face, reciting the words that his mother said to him.

"Sleep well, dear heart."

Question Mark Horror

Jim Ody

Jim lives in a dark and fantastical world. He's the author of over twenty published novels and a dozen short stories.

He was last seen in Swindon, Wiltshire.

M.L. RAYNER

Born and bred in the county of Staffordshire. Matt is a keen reader of classical, horror and fantasy literature and enjoys writing in the style of traditional ghost stories. His hobbies include genealogy and hiking, and he enjoys spending time with his wife, Emma, his children, and his family

There's nowhere to run
But plenty of places to hide...

Tall Trees An Idyllic Campsite, situated on a picturesque
lake, and surrounded by woodland.

Three Groups Of Strangers:

All meet for the first time, each one of them with something to
hide. But someone knows all of their dark secrets and now
they want to play a game...

PLAYTIME JUST GOT DEADLY

Ghost Stories Infused with Unsettling Horror

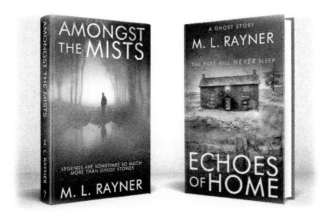

'*As engaging as anything I've read this decade. Rayner is required reading for horror fans.*'

Jonathan Edward Durham, author of Winterset Hollow

Printed in Great Britain
by Amazon

16454979R00171